RETURN OF THE TALL MAN

Ben Allison stood six feet four bowlegged inches above the floorboards. And that was without benefit of his patched Confederate cavalry boots. Yet even if he towered life-size as all West Texas, the idea of merely *looking*, twenty-four years later, for a lost white baby in hostile Indian country, guided only by Joe Meek's map and a cheap gold locket, came out considerably short of sensible. Especially measured against a man's chances of going there and getting back with his hair in one piece.

RETURN OF THE TALL MAN

Clay Fisher

GUNSMOKE

This hardback edition 2003
by BBC Audiobooks Ltd
by arrangement with
Golden West Literary Agency

ISBN 0 7540 8247 4

British Library Cataloguing in Publication Data available.

Printed and bound in Great Britain by
Antony Rowe Ltd., Chippenham, Wiltshire

Contents

1

The Scripture

THE OLD MAN stood peering up through the glittering windrows of ice crystals which even now, hours later, seeded the canyon air. The utter stillness hung like a hoarfrost shroud above the motionless, sprawling body of the avalanche. Behind him a china-eyed pack mule, ageful and mountain wise as the man himself, made no move other than to wall his oddly colored eyes, wigwag the ragged semaphores of his ears. The old man looked back at the mule.

"God help anybody that was up *there* last night," he said.

The mule grunted noncommittally. There was no other answer save the trickle of a small stone dislodged by a slight movement of the old man's feet in the treacherous mass beneath him. He waited, holding his breath, until the stone had found a safe lodging. Then he shivered, looking upward again.

It was the tenth day of December, 1866, sunrise of a bitterly cold Montana morning. The slide had spilled down during the night from the shoulder of Rotten Rock Mountain. It had been a bad one, carrying away a quarter-mile of the Virginia-Salt Lake stage road, depositing it eight hundred feet below and halfway across the ice-choked bore of the Madison River. The old man shook to a second chill, started once more around the dangerous waterside fan of debris, the gray-muzzled mule following free behind him.

It was chancy work. The wrong step could start the slide moving from above, inundating them where they stood, or shake loose the frothy pack below them, spewing them into the freezing blackness of the river. Either way would guarantee certain termination of their earthly travails. Chilkoot Johnston could not speak for his mute companion, but as for himself he felt he still had a few mortal griefs owing him. In consequence, he eased his way along the slide as warily as an old boar grizzly. Yet he was not wary enough. Midway of the fan his reaching foot struck a pocket of powder snow, and he went in to his arm hollows. The mule stood safely ten feet in the rear and stayed there. This time not even his eyes or ears moved.

By grace of a Providence which the old man had tempted many times in his long life, his plunge initiated no new slippage in the poised rubble. After a prayerful wait, he began cautiously digging himself free. Presently his fingers brushed against a substance the peculiar waxen feel of which brought his neck hairs erect. He paused, glancing again toward the great wound on the mountainside. There *had* been someone on the stage road last night. And from the faint warmth of the skin beneath his fingertips that someone was yet alive. With redoubled caution Chilkoot returned to his exhuming of himself and the still-bodied stranger from their near sharing of an avalanche tomb on Madison River, seventeen miles south and east of Montana's fabled Alder Gulch and the sinister vigilante city called Virginia.

It was forty-eight hours before the man from the landslide regained consciousness. When he did, Chilkoot, bending over him, peered into two gray eyes as vacant as the windows of an abandoned house.

"Rest easy, son," he told him. "It will all come back to you."

But it did not come back to the man. Not even when, a week later, Chilkoot watchfully told him his name.

"Ben Allison," he said, "San Saba, Texas. Least that's what's burnt here inside your gun belt."

He unrolled the gun fighter's buscadero rig which held the old model Cap and Ball Colt, showing the stranger the legend branded upon its inner leather. But the latter only shook his head and answered quietly.

"Sorry, old-timer, it don't mean a blessed thing to me."

"Well, do you *think* it's your outfit?" persisted Chilkoot.

His companion took from its holster the walnut-handled .44, closing his big fingers about its worn grip. Unthinkingly, with reflex familiarity, he shifted the weapon from hand to hand. Directly he slid it back into its leather with

2

a flick of the wrist which left the old man's narrowed gaze a blink behind. Again he said quietly:

"I don't rightly know, old-timer. But she *feels* mine."

"Yes, I reckon she does," nodded Chilkoot, uneasy now. Then, after an awkward pause, "Well, that takes care of that part of it."

The stranger glanced up. "There was more?"

"Considerable. Say like the ten thousand dollars in new paper bills in that money belt I found around your middle."

"Partner"—the other smiled, treating Chilkoot to his first look at his quizzical, bright grin—"you are full of jimson juice. I never had more than five dollars hard money in my whole life. Excepting maybe it was Confederate."

"Yes," said the old man, "that's another thing. You *was* a reb, wasn't you?"

"I tell you I don't know; I don't seem to know anything about who I was—or what."

"Oh? I can tell you something you know. That's how to handle a gun."

"That's something?"

"In these parts it can be everything."

"I'll take your word for it, old-timer. Anything else?"

"Yes. I can tell you are *are* a reb. You got a boondock Texas drawl would give you dead away anywheres north of Red River."

"You're doing pretty good, old-timer. Keep telling."

The other had lost his quirky grin. The old man bridled at the change in temperature, bobbing his beard feistily.

"All right, I'll tell you this; if you can't remember nothing about yourself, how come you can say for certain that that money ain't yours? Or that you didn't come by it dishonest?"

"I just know. Where on earth would a fellow like me get his hands on ten thousand dollars? Honest or dishonest."

Chilkoot increased the angle of his whiskers.

"I can tell you one place. A mule-train owner from Orofino, over in Idaho, was murdered in his blankets not far from here and not long gone. They found him cut backjaw-to-backjaw, head damn near off, Indian style. He had sold off his trade goods in the mining camps up in

Alder Gulch, was packing his profits home in paper, figuring to ride and maybe get around the road agents."

"Road agents?"

"Don't play kitteny with me, boy. I'm too old. I said road agents."

"I heard you."

"Highway robbers, damn it! Thieves, murderers, cutthroats. The miserable sons been forgetting what the vigilantes done to Henry Plummer and his bunch only three years gone this January."

The stranger's warm gray eyes turned frosty.

"So I'm a road agent," he said softly. "Then what?"

"Then like this," said the old man. "A vigilante posse from Virginia run this here killer's track line square up to the edge of that slide which took out the Virginia-Salt Lake road; the slide which brung you down off the mountain and buried you where I found you. The posse never picked up the track line on the Salt Lake side of that break in the road, boy. Far as I know, they still ain't picked it up, and that's what makes it interesting for you."

"Why me, old-timer?"

Chilkoot studied him, head cocked to one side.

"Simple matter of mathematics. That feller from Orofino was carrying ten thousand in paper bills. In a money belt. Around his middle. They found him naked as a jay bird from knees to nipples. Now did they teach you to put two and two together where you come from, or didn't they?"

He let the cynical question hang suspended in the brief silence. But the younger man, when he replied, only asked in his gentle way:

"Old-timer, you figure I killed that man cold blood in his blankets? You think I'm the one that posse's after?"

Chilkoot wagged his beard quickly.

"No, sir," he denied. "If I had, you'd have woke up in the Virginia jail instead of my shack. Way it is, I don't know what to think. I just don't. Past giving you the benefit of reasonable doubt, like the jury fellers say, I'm stuck."

The stranger's dark face relaxed.

"Thank you, old man. I'm beholden for the trust."

"Name's Chilkoot," gruffed the other. "Chilkoot

4

Johnston. Spelt with a *t*. Some around here make it Crazycoot Johnston. I don't argue it none."

His companion grinned, the gray eyes warming again.

"Like the poet fellow says, 'What's in a name?' You tell me you're Robert Edward Lee or Ulysses Simpson Grant, I'll believe you. Meanwhile we'll make it Chilkoot —*Chilkoot*."

The old man studied him another lengthening moment. It was as though he were weighing the younger man against some difficult, long-delayed decision. When at last he spoke, the soft-voiced stranger knew that his simple words held some future promise—or menace—far beyond their disarming literality.

"You will do," was all the old man said and got up and stalked out of the one-room cedar cabin on Nameless Creek.

It was the first open weather of that remembered hard winter of 1867; a fine, wind-still day, the skies cloudless, the temperature already arise, the sun only just then brimming the high saddle of the Absarokas between Emigrant and Monitor peaks to the east. Ben Allison and Chilkoot Johnston knew what the good weather meant. They sat now discussing the prospect on a pine-plank bench outside the latter's shack.

Because the aging wanderer of the creeks had chosen his den with all the cunning of a timber wolf, and because the record snows and abysmal cold had closed the trails, Ben's presence in the country was yet unknown. But with the weather breaking and with eager men waiting on both sides of the landslide to resume their tracking of the missing ten thousand dollars, such anonymity could not continue. Any dawn past this one could bring the fatal first posse or solitary bounty hunter, probing Chilkoot's gulch to determine the source of the cabin smoke above the alders. It was this contingency which Chilkoot now considered.

"Ben," he said, "let's see how she stacks up. First off, there's you. Who are you, and where did you get that ten thousand dollars? Next off, there's me. What's kept me these past weeks from snowshoeing into Virginia City and reporting you and the money to the vigilantes? Boy, I'll sign you a grant deed that we don't need to go no farther

5

than that. Not with them damned stranglers from Alder Gulch. You would get the rope, and I would get more years in the territorial jail than I got left to give. It's a real problem, believe me."

Ben thought it over in his slow, careful way.

"Well, partner," he asked finally, "what do you suppose?"

Chilkoot bobbed his head quickly.

"Bury the money, boy. Dig it far under, belt and all. Give it time to work out its own secret."

"That's fine," agreed Ben wryly, "for the belt and the money. Now how about me?"

The old man looked away toward Rotten Rock Mountain. This was what he had been waiting for, and he was ready.

"Ben," he began, far-eyed, "you've been given a rare opportunity and rare tools to meet it with. You're young, steady, strong, watchful, a good, straight thinker. You talk a little slow, but there ain't a whisper of a doubt about the speed with which you lay your hand to that slick-butt forty-four. Better yet, you got a grin to thaw rim ice and a way about you which makes folks open up and talk to you where they wouldn't to a fee-paid lawyer. It's why I'm talking to you and why I'm hoping you will listen to what I've got to say."

Ben felt the stir of the words.

"Sure, Chilkoot, go ahead. But cinch her down all you can. I want to be gone before the sun hits the road up there on the mountain."

Chilkoot glanced upward, nodding. For a silent time he sat watching the pink flush of the sunrise creep downward toward the broken course of the Virginia City-Salt Lake stage line. Presently he looked back at Ben.

"In eighteen and forty-three," he said, "I started for Oregon in the first rush. I had a wife, three little girls, a rickety wagon, a double hitch of mules and whatever of a second chance in life lay ahead of me.

"When our train got beyond Goose Creek in Snake Valley, down in the south of Idaho, I thought that chance had struck sure enough. Some of the folks come to me with a idea about splitting off for California. They had heard I'd trapped that country in the early days, and their question was, did I know a way through it for wagons?

6

"Well, I told them that I thought there was a way angling south and west to hit the headwaters of the Humboldt and following that stream's grass and water across the Nevada desert to the Sierras. It was wilderness country, I warned them, with no wheel ruts to follow, no trading forts to fall back on, no army posts to hold off the Indians. But if they had the faith in me, I would take them on their trust and guide them to California the best way that could be found. That was it. We left the main bunch next morning, heading for the Humboldt.

"No need to say what my own hopes was. I was forty-seven years old, had never done a useful thing for others in my life, not even provided decent for my own family. Now I felt it in my bones that the Lord had sent me a brand-new chance. My heart was higher than timber line. I felt twenty years younger just for the belief those good folks had in me. I *knew* I would make it this time. Hope springs eternal, boy; it ever and forever does—"

He let it die away, sighing as though the full weight of Rotten Rock Mountain had been laid upon his shoulders by the memory now called forth.

"At the third night's camp," he continued, "a band of Utah Paiutes straggled into our fires. They was half a territory off their usual track, and when I asked their chief what the trouble was, his answer struck a fear chill into my belly which I can feel freezing me to this day.

"The 'spotted sickness' was what he told me.

"Well, we rustled them Indians out of camp like they was hydrophobia wolves. We burnt what we was sure they had touched, boilt and scrubbed with lye soap what we wasn't sure of or what we couldn't spare, no matter.

"Then we started on. We counted the days like they was numbers on the clock of doom. At Arapaho Wells, in the Nevada badlands north of Pequop Summit, Ethel Pearl, my eldest girl, complained her insides hurt her low down. That was the beginning. Within twenty-four hours she was fevered out of her mind. In another twenty-four the spots were showing. We all knew what it was, and I ordered a sick camp set up there at the Wells. It was none too soon. Within three days the smallpox was onto us full rage.

"There was fifty-nine people in that California train; thirty-seven of them was buried there at the Wells, my

7

woman and two eldest among them. When that happened, my reason left me. I turned like a rock inside.

"The poor folks that had been spared begged me, even quoting the Scripture of a man being his brother's keeper, to stay with them and to guide them on out of that wilderness. But I wouldn't listen. I took my gun and my woman's picture locket with the tintype of the baby in it. I give the baby herself to a young couple which had lost their own three tykes to the pox. With that, and with them still calling after me to wait, I walked off into the desert, never once stopping, never once looking back."

Chilkoot paused while memory scanned the back trail and cut the squint lines deep and haggard about his eye corners.

"Point is, boy," he concluded, low-voiced, "that I forgot God made me stronger and more able than the others for a reason . . . a reason of his own."

"Old-timer," broke in Ben gently, "all that was near a quarter century gone. It took place many a hundred mile from here. What's it to do with us today?"

The old man peered at him searchingly.

"Ben," he said, "it's like the Lord was saying to me, 'Chilkoot, I've sent you this tall boy so's you can have him to take up where you left off. He's you all over, excepting this time I've cut him a mite wider and higher to better suit the job. And he's yours to send out to finish that job, providing you can make him see the need for it and convince him to take up your journey on the right terms. You got to make him understand that he ain't never to turn his back on small folks in trouble. You got to get him to promise he'll always look out for them as ain't been give his size and heft to look out for themselves. If you do that, Chilkoot, then you can lay down your own burden knowing it's been took up by the man you ought to have been and never was.' "

The words faded again. Chilkoot sat staring at the sunrise on Rotten Rock Mountain, the mists of years unused and opportunities forsaken dimming his eyes. At length he placed a gnarled hand on Ben's shoulder. With the other hand he brought forth from within his frayed, wolfskin coat a tarnished, small gold locket and segment of chain. He gave the worn token to Ben. Ben took it, knowing that it and the tiny child's face within it were all

8

of mortal connection remaining with the trail Chilkoot Johnston had lost twenty-four winters ago; the trail which he now charged Ben Allison to find and to follow to its unknown ending somewhere beyond Arapaho Wells on the old California cutoff.

"Ben," he said haltingly, voice soft, gaze faraway, "I don't know where you'll go or what you'll do with this second chance that I say God has give to both of us. But wherever you go and whatever you do with it, you remember one thing I've told you, boy. There ain't but this single truth in the whole world. It's from the Scripture them wagon-train people called after me there in the Nevada badlands. Never forget it. boy; never fail it. It's God's law. You *are* your brother's keeper."

2

Joe Meeks's Map

THREE WEEKS and four hundred miles from Nameless Creek and the Virginia City vigilantes, Ben made the last night's camp at Arapaho Wells. Fire laid, coffee tin on, mount turned loose to forage, he sat back to wait for the water to boil. And to take belated stock, meanwhile, of his agreement with Chilkoot Johnston.

His errant memory, while it refused to yield up material details of his past, still served him sharply in matters of the spirit. Who Ben Allison had been before the old man dug him out of the avalanche, he could not say, Neither could he recall where he might have gone or what he might have done in that former life. Yet certain things he *knew* about himself. One of these was that whatever trust he accepted he would discharge. Having taken the locket from Chilkoot, he was bound to follow its trail as far from this point of its origin as human strength, wit, will power and the proverbial luck of fools would take him. It was quite a bargain. Glancing about the camp at the means available whereby he might keep it, Ben had to grin.

If this forlorn oasis in the endless sage were the outset of that rare second chance in life which the old man had considered such a God-given privilege, all Ben could say was, the good Lord protect him from many more such chances. The prospects looked to him like betting a pair of deuces, hidden, into three queens showing.

Assets: one ancient, on loan, off-eyed prospector's pack mule; one moldy, green grub sack eaten down to two days' remaining ration bannock flour and weevily beans; one 1860 Army Colt converted post-war to fire the new .44 Smith & Wesson metal cartridges; one rangy, raw-boned body seeming to be somewhere between twenty and thirty years tough.

Debits: one dented, soft gold locket, likeness baby girl, five months, inscription, "Amy Geneva Johnston, St. Joe,

10

Mo., May 21, 1843," plus one completely implausible promise to find the described child, if living, or if since departed, to determine the nature of her history beyond Arapaho Wells. And all this in a trackless desolation centered by the Great Salt Sink of Utah, bordered by arid desert waste and mountain ranges four ways around; the entire area, from Montana to Santa Fe and Tucson, from nomad Sioux in the north to Bedouin Apache in the south, the uncontested haunt of the admitted worst of the white-hating horseback Indians.

Again, it was quite a problem. But now, somehow, Ben had lost his grin for it. He took out the locket, let it spin slowly in the firelight on its slender chain.

"Whichever way she points when she stops," he said soberly to the old mule, Malachi, "that's the way we'll go—"

Malachi, pawing out the snow-buried grass nearby, halted and threw up his head. He wagged his ears, blew the snow out of his nostrils, eyed the man at the fire. If it were not a hostile glance, neither could it be called friend-ly. Malachi plainly had his doubts about Ben Allison.

When the locket had stopped spinning and was hanging dead still, its face cover pointed southeast. Ben shook his head, frowning slightly.

"Arizona Territory?" he asked himself aloud. It was a natural thing to do for a man much used to the lonely places. Where the only companion is the passing wind, one talks to oneself or to no one. Unless, of course, one is so fortunate as to have along a four-footed friend of unusual sensitivity. "What do you think?" he said to the old mule. "You ever been to Arizona?"

Malachi batted his one flop ear, laid back the other good one, walled his eyes, bared his worn yellow cusps. It was a mean look, and he meant it. The snort of dismissal with which he turned his back on Ben and any such mumbo-jumbo business as locket spinning was totally elo-quent. Ben nodded quick agreement.

"You're right," he said. "It's got to be a better guess than Arizona. Something that makes at least some sense when hooked to the old man's story. But what? What else is down that way that could put us on the trail?"

With the question his frown lightened.

"The map!" he cried. "Maybe it's on the map!"

He had forgotten Chilkoot's last gift upon parting, an heirloom trapper's chart of the region west and south of Salt Lake. This was reputed to be the work of the redoubtable Joe Meeks, done thirty years before when he and Bridger and Broken Hand Fitzpatrick and Crazy Bill Williams had planted beaver sets on every drainage from the headwaters of the Humboldt in Nevada to those of the Pecos in New Mexico. It covered a thousand-mile crescent of country still left blank and marked "desert" on the atlases even of Ben's day. And it was, for all its crudeness, more reliable than any modern cartograph purporting to trace the untraced wastes beyond the Rockies.

Further, Joe Meeks's map was annotated in a singularly useful manner not to be found on any sophisticated documents of later date. No shining light of literacy, Joe had scratched a series of symbols at strategic points upon his masterpiece. These had been listed in a key by some contemporary who could read and write or, at least, print laboriously. And *accurately*. If the symbol marking some crawling, green-scummed seepage translated "good water" in the key, the thirsting traveler could drink deep without fear. If a clear, attractive pool was marked "don't drink," the wise wanderer moved on unslaked. And if, above all, there appeared upon the map a symbol which in the key stated simply, "unfriendly, go around," the informed passer-by swung wide, stayed in the saddle, lighted no fires and traveled fast for forty-eight hours.

Upon all this old Chilkoot had laid great stress in giving the map to Ben. The latter, in turn, had judged the gift on looks, promptly filed it away in his war bag with a mental note that it might serve for fire starter at some camp where natural tinder was lacking. Now he put the locket away and dug out the grimy document. There was even— almost—a benighted sense of reverence about the great care with which he brought forth from its oilskin pouch the graphic last will and hand-scrawled testament of Joe Meeks, mountain man.

The delayed respect was well paid.

Frowning to make out its faded detail in the poor light of the fire, Ben fell to studying the map. After a long, quiet moment, his gray eyes went wide.

"Damn!" he said softly. "That's fair-to-middling creepy! Right square where she pointed—!"

12

His frown intensified. With big, slowly moving forefinger he painstakingly retraced the spidery course set down so long ago. It was an ancient Indian trail leading south from Arapaho Wells. Coming to Pequop Summit, it detoured the base of this oft-noted landmark, continued down a long valley between the Toano and Pequop ranges, thence eastward over White Horse Pass back to the Utah side and the Goshute country. Skirting twelve-thousand-foot Haystack Peak and the Deep Creek hills, it bore south once more, threading the salt marshes of Snake Valley, climbing the Conger range and crossing Ferguson Desert by way of Government Well to end at the foot of Sawtooth Peak in the Needle Mountains. At its terminus was one of Meeks's strange symbols. The key read, "Main Paiute Village," and it was when these three words leaped off the camp-soiled paper that Ben swore softly and knew where it was that he and Malachi would ride with first light tomorrow.

The Paiutes were the parent tribe of the band which had carried the smallpox into Chilkoot's camp at Arapaho Wells in '43. If any human being yet alive in all that vast silence out beyond Ben's fire had present, useful memory of what track the Johnston train may have taken away from its fatal halt at the Wells, the human being would most likely be some Utah desert Paiute. And one who was by now rheumy-eyed, his thinning braids touched by the snows of seventy and more winters. For Ben knew that among the Indians only the old ones remembered the things which happened long ago. The young people had trouble recalling what took place yesterday. They had no time for tribal history older than the last corn dance or most recent horse raid.

When this thought took Ben, he grew apprehensive. Why would he know what the Indian mind and manner was like? Why should it be perfectly clear to him what the old people did and the young did not? There was no apparent reason for such assumptions, yet their assertions continued to occur to Ben as naturally as his next breath. Why? Ben knit his brows and could not answer the question now any more than he could the hundred and one others like it which had arisen the past weeks to plague him about his past. Damn! What *was* the mystery of his feeling for these people? And, indeed, of theirs for him?

13

What could he have been to them that made him know the things he knew about them and their ways?

How was it that he could lay a fire with flint and steel, a not common accomplishment even on the frontier?

Why could he, as he had discovered from the first band of mounted red men met upon the long ride from Montana, understand and reply fluently to questions put in the Indian sign language of the high plains? Where had he learned this art? Under what possibly sinister circumstances?

Why was it that the ordinarily hostile red men looked carefully into his Indian-dark face and made the "brothers welcome" sign, instead of taking his mule, his gun and his white man's long blond hair back to their winter lodges? Was there some possible shred of hereditary truth in old Chilkoot's sometimes testy complaints that he "all the time looked and too often acted like a damned redskin?" No, that had been no more than cabin fever on the old man's part. The best of companions got edgy cooped up together through a hard winter. Yet Ben had seen his own face in the cabin's shaving glass, and he had felt his own feelings of response to the wild horsemen met upon the trail, and he knew that there was *something*.

What was it then?

Was he a half-breed? A renegade white? A despised squaw man? A white foundling from some burned-out wagon train, reared by the savage riders of the northern plains No, that could not be either, for he had no memory of the spoken languages of the northern tribes. He had met Piegans, Sioux, Shoshoni, Crows, Cheyenne, even a winter traveling band of Oregon Nez Percés. All had been friendly, yet none had used a tongue intelligible to Ben. So an Indian upbringing seemed unlikely, while having been a squaw man or renegade was simply one of those things he *knew* he could not have been. But what *had* he been? What in all the farflung wasteland ranges of the wild horse tribes had Ben Allison been?

He gave it up, as he always did.

Whatever the answer was, it had to lie somewhere down the trail. He would find it, as he would find Chilkoot Johnston's daughter, *when* and *if*. Meanwhile, given such inclusive odds, a good night's sleep was the best beginning for the gamble. In the morning he and Malachi would start south. With decent luck and likewise weather, the old mule not going lame under him, he ought to pull into the Paiute village in ten days. Until then, with beans and flour for but two days, his chief concern was finding food. In late winter, along the margins and through the rugged sub-deserts of the Great Salt Sink, this was apt to prove a pretty lean-bellied proposition all by itself.

Ben's rueful smile broke again.

Well, at least they couldn't say he hadn't taken on a chore cut to size. Ben Allison of San Saba or wherever, stood six feet four bowlegged inches above the floorboards, And that without benefit of his patched Confederate cavalry boots. Yet even if he towered life-size as all West Texas, the idea of merely *looking*, twenty-four years later, for a lost white baby in the blind gut of hostile Indian country, guided only by Joe Meeks's map and a cheap gold locket, came out considerably short of horse sensible. Especially when measured against a man's chances of going there and getting back with his hair in one piece.

Looking now southward across his fire into the black winter night which hid the Paiute Trail, he shivered and nodded consolingly to himself. Old Chilkoot better have been right about the length of the material sent him by the good Lord to finish out that second chance; that was a mighty *tall* job waiting down there in the Utah darkness.

Still, his grin widened. It was not that it was really funny; it was that Ben was inclined to grin more than to grit his teeth when trouble washed his way. As Chilkoot had observed, not infrequently and not altogether in admiration, he had a tendency to carry on as happy as though he had good sense.

To the old mule, Malachi, he now said cheerfully:

> "Early to bed and early to rise
> Makes a man healthy, wealthy and—
> Keeps his scalp stitched on straight."

Malachi regarded him with a mixed look of compassion and disgust. Why, the aging animal's patient stare seemed to demand, atop all his other onerous physical burdens, must an honest, hard-working, blue-eyed Montana pack mule be made also to bear this added spiritual insult of

15

having been delivered into the service of a stringhalted philosopher? What possible justification could exist for the imposition of this further injury of being forced to listen to the clear delusion upon the simple-minded part of this lanky young idiot that he had been dealt the gift of pithy observation? Or even of ordinarily intelligent comment?

The old mule grunted and sighed unhappily.

Life with the old man back on the creeks had never been like this. It was a sorry day for Malachi Johnston when the old man had made him pack *this one* home from the avalanche in Madison Canyon!

3

The Paiute Trail

ON THE NINTH DAY south from Arapaho Wells, the desert bared her sandstone gums to show the lone fang of Sawtooth Peak snagging the raw blue sky ahead. Topping a final rise of creosote scrub, Ben pulled in Malachi and sat him, sharp against the brilliance of the morning sun, looking down upon the Paiute village.

It was not much to see. These Indians, if they owned horses, were not horse Indians. Ben could make out the ragged geometry of the few irrigation ditches taken off the small stream which drained the saddle of Old Sawtooth. The irregular squares were marked by the wind-drowned furrows of last year's dead yields of corn, beans and rattlesnake melons. Startlingly, there in the broom sage and greasewood, a naked-armed platoon of eastern-seeded fruit trees stood at straggling attention along the flanks of the row-crop fields. These would be the undoubted, if dubious, bequeathings of the Saints up at Salt Lake, Ben thought. You couldn't beat those Mormons, by damn. You couldn't even tie them. They got into and out of places years before the Gentiles got around to discovering the country that held those places. Then the second thought took him—how the devil did he know anything about Old Brigham's band and their busy ways? Then the uneasiness about his past came on him again, and he put his attention back where it belonged—on the Paiutes.

Clucking to Malachi, he started the old mule down the slope. As he approached the brush and animal-skin huts, a gathering of the elders drifted cautiously out to meet him. They were gaunt, shy-acting, withered both by their many snows and by their chronic want of sufficient good food. Their dress was of poorly fleshed rabbit furs pelted without troubling to remove the feet. In some cases the dessicated heads of the untanned skins also still dangled from the wearer's garments. None of the oldsters carried a

17

weapon, but one or two of them bore rabbit throwing sticks and a third, obviously the shaman of the band, came armed with a gourd rattle and a feathered medicine stick.

When they drew closer together, they saw how poor Ben was. They came a little farther along, peering hard, making absolutely certain that he had with him nothing either of edible or tradable nature. Then their questioning half-smiles faded. They stopped and gathered in an orderless rank across the trail, as though they would bar him from their dwellings. Ben rode up to them, stopping Malachi at the proper distance. With great dignity he then made the hand sign of Indian respect for the elder person.

When the Paiutes saw the gesture—a graceful touching of the brow with the fingertips of the left hand—they whispered quickly among themselves. Almost at once the shaman stood forth. He put both hands out, palms toward Ben, using both hand signs and some considerable "mountain man" English.

"We are a poor people," he signified. "You, too, are poor. Come into our houses, then, and be welcome."

Ben made the sign which returned his understanding of the invitation, got down off Malachi and walked with the elders back to the council hut at town's center. There a fragrant piñon log was asmolder, its wondrous pungent odor putting the bite of its smoke into the clear wine of the dry air. The shaman waved Ben to enter. The latter dropped to hands and knees to gain ingress, his height being half again that of his tallest companion. Inside, while waiting for his eyes to adjust to the gloom, his nose was working on a marvelous odor he could not identify.

It proved, directly, to be boiled cornmeal with bits of cactus rat, including at least one complete tail with hair intact and a recognizable, beady-eyed skull, together with some sort of yucca or wild onion root, steamed *au jus* and served on the rare side.

This was the community breakfast, just being readied as Ben topped the trail across the creek. Starved as he was, he would greatly have preferred his hosts to have gone ahead without him. But the Paiute would not touch a morsel of the gray stew until he had taken his fill of it. Ben ate gallantly, keeping his eyes closed tight, in this manner feigning to evidence a delight of the gustatory

18

senses beyond that which sight might safely bear. The Indians were much pleased with this rapture over their simple fare. Ben was able at the same time to fortify himself without risking an abortive return to the dirt floor of the hut of any of the delicacies which he dipped so carefully from the iron pot which the shaman's squaw had set before him.

In the end despite his artful dodging, he very nearly ruined everything when a sidelong glance at his final hand-scooped helping showed him he had drawn the cactus rat skull. Sheer inspiration saved him. Noting that several of the old people leaned forward eagerly when they saw him dip the skull, he graciously picked it from his hand, touched it to his forehead, passed it over with a flourish to the shaman.

The latter made a brave show of refusing the tidbit, but when Ben made a series of flowery signs signifying that such a small gift was poor repayment indeed for the hospitality offered him, the old man gave in.

"My son's skin is white," he waved, "but his heart is red. He thinks like an Indian. His father thanks him."

With that, the old man sucked out the jellied brain and eyes of the rodent, tossed the emptied skull to his woman. The squaw caught it deftly. Popping it into her wide mouth, she ground it noisily three times with her bone-hard gums, gulped it down with an echoing belch and smiling nod of acknowledgment for Ben, the original donor.

Now the ice was broken. When, some minutes later, the council pipe of salt-marsh reed and piñon burl came out and was lighted and passed around, Ben's carefully introduced question about the white baby girl of Arapaho Wells was received in a friendly way and not with the stony silence which customarily would have greeted any such white inquiry concerning a white child who, presumably, had met an Indian fate.

In this case, though, however friendly, the red reply was not encouraging.

Yes, the white-haired shaman admitted, the Paiutes did know something of this girl child. And it was good that the Tall Son had come when the men of the village were away in the Conger Mountains hunting sheep and antelope. For in this way the old ones could tell their visitor

19

what they knew, and he could take his leave with the information freely. In the old days things had been different. Then the red man and the white had been friends. Now even the Paiutes, a peaceful people, were angry with what went on. But the Tall Son was of the old manners, and he should have what they knew and welcome.

"Thank you, father," motioned Ben. "What is it that you can tell me of the little one?"

"Only this," replied the other, hands moving to frame the words with eloquent clarity. "When the Spotted Sickness had passed from among our people, we went back to see how we might help those white people. We feared they would have taken the sickness from our visit, and it was but fair that we should try to find out and to help them.

"We did find them, and they were in a poor place. It was three suns along the Goose Creek Trail toward the big wagon road, the one that goes to the Nez Percé country. You know that road, don't you?"

Ben nodded that he did, gesturing, "Yes, what happened there?"

"It wasn't there; I said on Goose Creek."

"All right, what happened on Goose Creek?"

"On Goose Creek the Snakes found those poor wagon train people before we could find them. You know the Snakes? The Shoshoni? Washakie's people?"

Ben shook his head. "No, are they a bad people?"

"Well, bad to us and to the Nez Percés, whom they especially hate. But ordinarily they are like the Absarokas, the Crows. They get along pretty well with the white man. Indeed, Washakie, their great chief, is the friend of all white men and was the same at that other time, too. But the leader of this hunting band which had found that wagon train, he was a bad Indian. Also, he was much taken with the young mother of this baby that you seek."

"She was not the true mother," explained Ben. "The baby was given to her by the true father when the true mother died in that camp of the Spotted Sickness. Now it is this same true father who has sent me to find his small daughter, if she yet lives."

It was the old shaman's turn to shake his head.

"I do not see how she can still live, but the Great Spirit Father is strange in his ways. It may be that he will lead you to her."

20

He paused, summoning up the details scattered by two and a half decades of desert wind.

"That bad Snake chief tried to take the woman from her husband's wagon. There was a fight. The Indians got excited. You know how that is. When all was done, only the young woman, her husband and the baby girl remained living of the whites. The chief saw the husband trying to crawl away and hide. He caved in his head with the butt of his rifle. Then he took his hair, leaving him there as a corpse. The last that is known to us of this woman and the yellow-haired baby is that the Snakes took them off with them, back to their home in the high mountains.

"This much we were told by the husband, who was not dead and who lived by his deep heart alone, until we came along, and he could charge us with the story of the bad Shoshoni. We trailed the Snakes a few days. Maybe three. That's how we knew they were going home. So that's it; there is no more to tell."

He slashed his hands abruptly in the ending sign and Ben asked quietly:

"But the child was alive the last you knew?"

"Yes, we could hear it crying that third night before we turned back. It must have been a very pretty baby for the Snakes to let it cry like that. Or perhaps the mother was so attractive in her body that the chief softened and was not himself. Who can say? What would be gained by guessing? But, yes, you are right. The child was yet alive when we came away. It was a blue-eyed child, incidentally; did I tell you that? The husband made sure we understood that. And the color of the hair. He said it would be important when his people came looking for her; when the Pony Soldiers were told the Shoshoni had stolen a white mother and child, and they came to free them and to punish the Indians for the killing on Goose Creek."

Ben nodded, face darkening.

"Could you tell me, father," he asked after a moment, "what Shoshoni chief this was? Of what land? In what high mountains?"

The shaman's hands answered quickly.

"The chief was Crowheart. The Horse Creek band. Their high home place is called Mountains of the Wind. But how will this help you, my son? You don't know the

21

way, and we do not dare guide you upon it. Do you then have some magic you have not shown us? Something that will take you there, where we your friends cannot?"

"Yes, father, I have," replied Ben and brought forth the oilskin pouch.

The Paiutes had never seen a map drawn on paper. They crowded around Joe Meeks's pictographic chart with intense interest. It took a little patience on Ben's part but the old shaman was very bright and soon began to "see the land" as Meeks had set it down. Beginning with his own village and Old Sawtooth, he was able to show Ben precisely where he must go to find the Shoshoni country. Ben marked very carefully upon the map the place where the old man's finger stopped moving. He drew the symbol, cursing fervently under his breath.

His new destination was but a day's pleasant journey down Union Pass to Wind River in northwest Wyoming Territory—the better part of five hundred arrow-flight miles straight back toward Montana!

4

Blood Brother

MALACHI, his iron shoe plates long since ground away to nail-shank nothingness, could go but a certain gait, riderless. Carrying Ben, he refused to go any gait at all. The result was a working compromise. Ben walked. All the way to Wyoming.

It was mid-April before the comrades topped Union Pass, dropping down it to strike a tributary which led them to Wind River. At this point their luck changed. Bankside of the Wind they met Frank Go-deen.

Go-deen was a Milk River half-breed from the Canadian border buffalo country. Short, pot-bellied, legs bowed and muscular as a Barbary ape, he proved a ribald, sunny-natured rogue. Despite his forbidding appearance—a buffalo lance-blade slash across nose and mouth had left him with a perpetual leering tick—Ben had no choice but to trust him. Indeed, Go-deen left him little option in the matter. Assuming from Ben's dark skin and slanted eyes, and, despite his camp-barbered, coarse blond hair, that the newcomer was a brother outcast of the half-blood bar sinister, Go-deen was friendly by mistake as well as by instinct.

Ben, finding it to his advantage, did not argue the natural illusion. Why debate bloodlines when social acceptance might mean the difference in keeping and losing his scalp. This was Indian country. When in it, and given such a gratis opportunity to do so, *act* like an Indian. There was no single, better way to prevent falling hair on the frontier. Ben and "brother Frank" hit it off first-rately from the opening word.

As to Ben's quest, he had struck a bonanza in the garrulous breed. When innocently "started up" over that first night's fire by Ben's query as to the possible existence and whereabouts of a Shoshoni band called the Horse Creeks, Go-deen demonstrated himself to be a human talking machine with whom the taciturn Ben had no chance. Falling farther and farther behind in his attempt to stay within conversational reach of the Milk River gossip, and since he had set him going on the right track with his opening question, Ben simply sat back and kept his ears uncovered.

Ah! yes, indeed, his companion led off, there was a Horse Creek band of the Wind River Shoshoni. And, yes, indeed, Frank Go-deen knew a little something of them. Now if the Tall Brother would refrain from interrupting, he, Go-deen, would undertake to supply what he knew of those Horse Creeks. It was little enough, but if there were no more rude detours and a man were permitted the free flow of the conversation, he might get it said by bedtime.

Ben merely grunted, waving him to proceed.

Go-deen, scowling fiercely, warned that the grunt and the wave were absolutely the final interference with his story which he would tolerate. With which threat, and not waiting to see how it was obeyed, he launched into his tale with a will which would not have been turned aside by a buffalo stampede.

The Horse Creeks were a renegade family branch of old Washakie's main Snake Clan. It seemed that many years before, their chief Crowheart had broken Washakie's official word of peace with the white man. He had taken a comely white woman out of a small wagon train over on Goose Creek in the Idaho country.

When Washakie heard of this deed and demanded the woman for prompt return to the Army people at Fort McGraw ("that is just a ways down here on the Popo Agie River"), Crowheart brought the woman to Washakie with her left breast cut off and a skinning knife wedged to the blood guard between her kidneys. For this the old chief ordered him seized and taken to the big Pony Soldier fort at Laramie. But Crowheart was very cunning. He killed two guards and got away near Point-of-Rocks, a very famous place on the old Oregon Road. The one that went to the Nez Percé country by the easy way, by South Pass. Surely the Tall Brother would know of that way?

Ben felt constrained to nod an acknowledgment here and did so. Immediately Go-deen upbraided him:

"Be quiet! Will you not keep still? How is a man to

order his thoughts when another will not keep his mouth shut ten seconds?"

Ben kept his grin inside, enjoying its acid bite privately. Go-deen, interpreting his bowed head as tacit admission of surrender, swept graciously on.

"Anyway, from that time Crowheart and his personal following, a blood-knit family band of no more than five or six lodges, enjoyed the life of double outlaws, hunted alike by red man and white. As the charge was murder in either case, the fugitives lived like ghosts. For a long while they disappeared. It was thought they had died out or drifted apart. The Army still believes this, and Washakie no longer troubles to tell them otherwise. Yet the truth is far different, as you shall see."

He stopped, eying Ben and giving him a chance to say something. Ben held his head down. Go-deen nodded his satisfaction.

"Those Crowheart people are still together," he continued. "They live at a place known to me, in some very good meadows not far from here. You just go up Horse Creek to the shadows of the Red Tops. Those are the very high peaks you saw from the pass this afternoon. And I will tell you something else. I talked less than a week ago to the old chief himself. Yes, I mean Crowheart.

"He lives up there with his son, a bad Indian like himself. They have a few lodges and are waiting for the new grass to come high enough to fatten their pony herd against the summer business—horse stealing from the Nez Percés.

"Do you know the Nez Percés, Tall Brother? They are a strange people from Oregon and Idaho. Their name means 'Slit Nose,' and they raise those great spotted horses called Appaloosa. One of those leopard horses is worth ten Sioux ponies or fifteen Shoshoni. The Nez Percés raise them, and sheep and fat cattle, too, on ranches and in pastures exactly as the white men. At least it is said they do. For myself, I have never been to their far land. Indeed, I have seen but few Nez Percés, and those few from a good safe distance. Did I say they were a fierce people? *Wagh!* They're the best fighters there are. Proud? They won't sit at the same fire with a Shoshoni or a Sioux. They fear no Indian. Not even these tough ones here in the buffalo country, where the Nez Percés come to hunt

25

the curly cows. Even the Oglala Sioux, the great Crazy Horse's people, to whom I am related on my mother's side, fear them. As for the Shoshoni, who will otherwise fight a grizzly bear, just mention the name Slit Nose and they will leave you there standing in a cloud of horse dust."

Now if there were anything else the Tall Brother wished to know of the Horse Creeks, or of the Nez Percés for that matter, let him ask it. The answer would be prompt and complete; providing, of course, he could keep his mouth closed while it was delivered.

Ben was by this time almost afraid to raise his head, but the reported death of Amy Johnston's foster mother forced him to encourage Go-deen. Further, after the many weeks of conversing only by hand sign with the pure-bloods met on the trail or by pidgin pack mule in camp with Malachi, the half-breed's colorful command of English was not altogether harsh music on the hungry ear.

"There was a child," he said, "blue-eyed and with yellow hair. Perhaps six months old; a girl. It's known she was with this woman when Crowheart took her out of that wagon train. You know anything about that?"

Go-deen shook his head.

"I never heard of a child. Neither did Washakie, I can guarantee you. If he had, he would have chased Crowheart clear through the Land of the Grandmother. Excuse me, that's what we Milk Rivers call Canada. Anyway, Washakie never knew of any white child with Crowheart, or he would still be after him. No, there was no child. Not unless—"

"Unless what?" said Ben.

"Crowheart had one squaw from our Milk River band. A poor one, tough as a crow, all bones and no breasts. We called her Magpie. If I remember the price right, Crowheart paid six solid-colored ponies for her. The sale tells the tale. This Magpie never grew the Shoshoni's seed. Always wanting a child and twenty years trying in vain, she may have taken the white baby when Crowheart killed the mother. She may even have killed the mother herself. The breast gone sounds like squaw's work. And there was also an old story in that direction. But that Crowheart would take the blame to shelter a barren old Milk River hag smells of fish to me. I don't believe it. I know that old

26

devil. He would gut his own mother for a plug of tobacco. But, anyway, there's your 'unless.' If Magpie took the child, it may still be up there—"

He broke off to point into the night, north toward the joining of Horse Creek with Wind River. Then, he concluded abruptly:

"But I will tell you one thing; if you find her, you won't find a white woman."

"What—" said Ben, following a bit slowly.

Go-deen nodded, spat shruggingly into the fire.

"You will find an Indian." he said and turned his back on Ben, pulled up his blanket, broke wind and went at once to sleep.

5

A Beautiful Thought

"WHAT DO YOU THINK?" said Ben. "Ought we to risk it?"

Go-deen shook his head. They lay in the boulders at the edge of the meadow, slightly above the grazing pony herd and its lone watchman. "Ordinarily I would say yes, let's grab him and have a talk. But now I don't know."

"What's the trouble?"

"I recognize that fellow."

"Who is he?"

"He's called Iron Eyes; he's a bad one."

"He doesn't look bad."

"Neither does Crowheart."

"You talk in circles. How did we arrive at Crowheart?"

Go-deen looked at him witheringly.

"I brought you here, is that right? I told you those are the Horse Creek lodges yonder in the pines. There. Where we see the smoke. Do I lie? No. Also I pointed out to you that the ponies down there belong to the Horse Creeks. Already we understood that the Horse Creeks are headed by Crowheart, a very bad Indian, and that his son inherits from the sire. So again I say I don't know if we should grab him or not."

Ben gave him a bewildered glance.

"Grab who?" he asked. "Did I say anything about going after Crowheart or his son? Why don't we just worry about that horse guard for right now?"

"Exactly what I'm doing." Go-deen grinned, as quick with his crazy smirk as with his mock-savage scowl. "That's the boy down there. Iron Eyes. Crowheart's son."

Ben gathered the reins of his temper. Traveling with this off-centered Milk River mental case was about like sharing a bag with a good-natured rattlesnake—everything depended on the next shake of the sack.

"Thanks for telling me," he said acidly.

28

Go-deen shrugged.

"You talk too much. You don't give a man a chance to say anything. I could have told you that was Iron Eyes ten minutes ago."

"Except that *I* talk too much, eh?"

"Exactly."

"I see. Well, in that case I will shut up and let you talk a while. What I suggest you talk about is how the hell we're going to get any information out of these Horse Creeks without grabbing one of them. You say they'll kill a white man sure. And I'm not about to bank on them taking me for Sitting Bull. So if I vote down walking in and asking them nice about the little girl, and you veto the idea of blind-jumping the horse guard yonder, how do you propose to find anything out? Now take your time, I don't want to stampede you. I'm getting a great respect for the fine balance of that brain of yours."

Go-deen eyed him suspiciously. But Ben's expression was as cherubic as saddle-leather skin, slant gray eyes and Indian-high cheekbones would allow. The breed nodded, satisfied.

"I'm not so sure we couldn't pass you off for Sitting Bull," he said, "but I'm a reasonable man. I won't ask you to go with me."

"What? *You're* going into the lodges?"

"Certainly. The Horse Creeks respect my brain, too."

"More likely your tongue, I'd say. What do they pay you for spying on the enemy? For letting them know how the wind blows on the rest of the prairie?"

It was now Go-deen who fashioned the look of angels.

"You're wrong, Tall Brother. I don't deal with these Horse Creeks. You can't trust them. However, we Milk Rivers are another matter."

"How so?"

"You're forgetting Magpie. If she's still alive, and I can get a word with her—"

"But damn it," Ben broke in, "you told me yesterday that you had talked to Crowheart three days ago. How come you didn't ask *him* about Magpie, if she's kin of yours?"

"Why? Do I look foolish? She's a sore subject with him, I would guess. She's taboo. Like a mother-in-law. You just don't mention such things."

29

Ben nodded.

"I'm learning. Another two days with you, and I *will* be able to pass for Sitting Bull. Do all Indians think like you do?"

"No, not all. That's what is interesting about Indians. You can't win any bets guessing against them."

"I can see what you mean," said Ben, eying him. "And you're only *half* Indian."

"You're talking too much again. I'm going."

"Hold on," said Ben, as the breed slid back from the boulders and stood up. "What you expect me to do?"

"You go back and wait with our mounts. See that the wind doesn't change and carry their scent to the pony herd. Keep your finger wet till I get back."

"You take too long, and it'll be more than the finger. This is pretty close quarters here. I wouldn't want to have to run them Horse Creeks for the river through these rocks. Not on what we're riding."

"Squaw talk," grunted Frank Go-deen and stepped into the mountain undergrowth and was gone before Ben could launch any more orations.

Go-deen rode a gotch-eared white gelding, the easy match of Malachi for age and evil mind. Further, he was equally talkative. Ben spent a lonely two hours waiting for the sun to go down. With Indians he always felt more on even terms at night. Their dislike of the darkness was one of those things which filtered through to him from the blank page of his past. He simply knew it, as he knew all the other things about them. Knowledge, however, and despite the sages' brave claim to the contrary, did not always dispel fear. So while he waited for the night and for Frank Go-deen, Ben enjoyed many a fresh doubt as to the entire sanity of his being where he was.

Twenty-four *years!* Good Lord, that was as old, probably, as he was. And that was how long ago this little girl had disappeared from the Goose Creek burnout. She had been with the Indians since Ben was maybe two, three years old, and here he was sitting in the scrub pine and buckbrush of whiteless Wyoming—God knew how far from the nearest fort—holding his breath and the halter straps of two wolf-bait plugs, waiting for a half-breed he

30

had known twenty-four *hours* to come back and lead him out of these Horse Creek bulrushes!

"Well," he muttered aloud to his companions, "confidence is the main thing. That's what I always say. What do you always say?"

The gotch-eared gelding said nothing. Malachi flagged his ears and snorted contemptuously.

"Shut up, you damn fool," said Ben. "You think them Horse Creeks won't eat mule meat?"

For reply, and as though to show what he thought of the threat and the threatener, Malachi spraddled and began to urinate. His stream, striking a hat-sized rock, sounded to Ben louder than pouring a chamber pot out a second-story window. In the utterly still twilight, it carried with the force of a hydraulic mining nozzle. Ben cursed and drove a bony knee into his flank, literally moving him over into a foot-deep bed of muffling pine needles. In the process he came out not unshowered.

"You son of a bitch," he said quietly. "You want to make a noise to bring them Indians down here, I'll help you out." He drew and cocked the Colt .44. "Understand?" he asked, gesturing with the revolver. "One more hilarious prank from you, and you get it right between your china-blue eyeballs. Now you make up your mind and, by God, quick."

Malachi studied the gun with interest. Whatever his conclusions, he kept them to himself. But he made no more noise. Ben put the Colt away. He sat down on a nearby boulder, searching the forest gloom, now grown suddenly black as pitchblende.

"Damn!" he said uneasily. "I sure wish he'd get here."

At his elbow, squarely out of nowhere, a familiar rough voice growled softly.

"Wagh! Are you still talking?"

"Go-deen!" cried Ben. "Man, am I ever glad to see you!"

"You had better be, Tall Brother. Had it been a Horse Creek, he would have greeted you with a knife blade between your spine bones. I am beginning to wonder if you have any Indian blood at all."

"It comes out even." Ben grinned. "I'm beginning to wonder if you have any white. You're about as noisy as a drop of oil running down a gun barrel."

31

"We have a proverb, Tall Brother." The Milk River breed smiled. "Walk soft, live long. A simple idea, but it works."

"I'll remember it. What did you find out?"

"Many things. But for the sake of our situation, I will be brief."

"Wait a minute," said Ben. "Let me find a rock. If you're going to be brief, I don't want to be standing through it."

"Never mind the rock. Try your saddle."

"How's that?"

"Let's talk as we ride; I think Iron Eyes is behind me."

"You *think!*"

"Well, put it this way—I know he is. You like that better?"

"Much better," said Ben. "Here's your horse."

"Good. We'll go down the middle of the creek for a ways. It's a pretty fair bottom, and the noise of the water will cover our sounds as well as our tracks. *Hookahey!*"

"Hook a what?" asked Ben.

"*Hookahey,*" repeated Go-deen. "That's Sioux for 'let's get the hell out of here.' "

"A beautiful thought," said Ben, swinging up on Malachi and turning him for the stream bed. "Let us dwell upon it."

6

Away from Wind River

THEY FOLLOWED the tumbling, noisy raceway of Horse Creek out of the meadowland below the Red Tops. After what seemed to Ben at least twenty miles in a foaming, swiftly falling watercourse—and was possibly two and probably one mile—Go-deen turned the white gelding bankward. Here a shelf of sheet rock came down solidly to stream's edge, allowing them an egress which marked their mounts' trails only with hoofprints of clear creek water. The last of these had dried long before daylight.

With sunup they were back in their camp on Wind River, Go-deen satisfied they had, for the time, lost Iron Eyes. In consequence, and while they enjoyed a half-breed breakfast of buffalo jerky and stone-ground coffee, he gave Ben the substance of his conversation with Magpie.

Yes, the childless Milk River woman had reared the white baby. It had grown up, knowing no life but that of an Indian, precisely as Go-deen had predicted. The child, now a full young woman, of course, had actually been given the most severe of Indian training, for her foster father was a renowned hater of the white eyes, while Magpie had the typical half-breed's resentment of her white side—the side which would not accept her as one of its own. So the small one had grown to womanhood poisoned by the hatreds of her parents, trained in hardness by the life of the outlaw which Crowheart's people were forced to live, twisted in her mind and toughened in her body in a way that few even of the pure-bloods among the horseback tribes were conditioned.

Go-deen paused, scowling, the lance-blade scar across his broken nose darkening as he grew angry, or uneasy, with his thoughts.

"I don't know, Tall Brother," he said to Ben. "Perhaps the best thing is to forget about her. Go back and tell her true father that you couldn't find her. Or that you heard

33

she had died long ago. I have seen a few of these white children—especially the girls—who were with the Indians since their earliest memory. It seems that being suckled by a squaw is no simple thing to be weaned away from. Something seems to get into the child along with the red mother's milk. Something wild. Something very difficult to live with in the white way. Many have said before me that such ones are best left with their Indian parents." He looked at Ben, ugly face serious for a rare moment. "Tall Brother," he said, *"hookahey,* let's get out of here."

Ben's gray eyes shadowed over.

"No, Go-deen," he said, "I can't do that."

"Nonsense! Come with me. We'll go up on the Milk and run buffalo all summer. You'll meet my people. Maybe you'll like my sister. Younger and not so ugly as I. A little fat, but that is the best for cold weather. What do you say?"

"I have to say no. If that girl—that young lady—is up yonder with the Horse Creeks, I'm bound by my word to go after her. Damn it, I haven't got no choice."

"Well, that's another thing. Maybe you have."

"Such as what?"

"Well, you said it yourself—if the girl is up there, you've got to go up there."

"That's what I said. What of it?"

"Very simple. You don't have to go up there."

"What?"

"We can head for Milk River tonight. I know a good short cut by Cow Island. No Pony Soldiers that way."

"What in the name of hell," asked Ben, "are you talking about?"

"The girl." Go-deen shrugged. "The grown-up young white woman you seek. She's gone; she's not up there any more."

"Good Lord," said Ben, "she's gone? You mean she's dead?"

"We could find her easier if she was."

"For the luvva Pete!" said Ben. "Will you quit stomping around the brush pile and shoot the rabbit?"

"Sure." The squat breed grimaced. "But you won't like it. And I won't go with you."

"All right, I'm waiting," sighed Ben. "You can drop the other boot."

"The Slit Noses got her. Late last fall. Just before the big snows closed the trails."

"The Nez Percés?" said Ben. "I thought they were friendly?"

"They are. To the white man."

"Well, then, the girl will be all right."

"Yes, she would have been."

"What the hell you mean, *would* have been?"

"You remember I told you how the Sioux and the Slit Noses hate each other? Especially the Hunkpapa Sioux and the Wallowa Nez Percés? Now the Oglalas, my people, they sometimes get along with the other Nez Percés—say, like the Asotins of Looking Glass, the Salmon Rivers of old Toohoolhoolzote and the White Birds of Peopeo Hihhih; but if you take one of Old Joseph's Wallowa Nez Percé and one of Gall's Hunkpapa Sioux— that's Old Joseph now, not Young Joseph who is the white man's good friend—and you put that Wallowa Nez Percé and that Hunkpapa Sioux on a narrow trail face to face, you are going to have one dead Indian, perhaps two, for neither will turn aside for the other; neither will step back and give way."

Ben clenched his fists and set his jaw, restraining his urge to do bodily harm in the direction of Frank Go-deen.

"Listen, friend," he pleaded, "I don't give a damn about what one of Old Joseph's boys and one of Gall's bucks would do to one another meeting on a sheep path. That ain't my problem; it's theirs. What I want to know about is that girl; *she's* my problem!"

"Exactly what I was saying. This particular Wallowa Nez Percé who met this particular Hunkpapa Sioux on this particular sheep path of which I speak—if you will let me—was that same Wallowa Nez Percé who took the white squaw away from the Horse Creeks. *Now* whose problem is it?"

"Oh, Lord!" groaned Ben. "Don't tell me; let me guess: the Sioux took the girl away from the Nez Percé and they got her now!"

"As far as the Horse Creeks know, yes. They were trailing the Nez Percés when they, the Horse Creeks, crossed tracks with these Sioux—a large band, three times the number of the Nez Percés. They set the Sioux upon the line of the Wallowas, and they watched the fight that

35

followed. They say the Nez Percé were killed to the man, but the Hunkpapas claim the young chief who was leading the Wallowas got away. I don't know; I wasn't there."

Ben nodded, tight-lipped.

"There anything else you *do* know? I mean that you'd like to tell me about this girl before we shake hands and go our different trails? Like maybe where could I find these *particular* Hunkpapas that got this *particular* white woman away from these *particular* Nez Percés on this *particular* sheep path we was just *particularly* talking about?"

"Oh, sure, Tall Brother; do you have the time?"

"I'll take the time," said Ben. "Keep going."

Go-deen hunched his sloping shoulders in deprecation.

"There's really very little more to tell. . . . Let's see . . . the name of the young Wallowa was Aluin Ueukie, John Lame Elk; the Hunkpapa was Slohan, Buffalo Ribs; the head of the Horse Creek trailers was Iron Eyes, of course. That's about it."

"Why do you say, 'Iron Eyes, of course'?" asked Ben curiously. "Because he was the old chief's son?"

"No, because he was the Indian husband of your white woman."

"No!" cried Ben. "Not that mean-looking devil!"

"Well," shrugged Go-deen, "argue it if you want. But they shared the same lodge since her sixteenth summer. Eight years and all wasted. The girl was the same as the foster mother before her, the exact same. Like Magpie, she would not grow Shoshoni seed."

"Thank the Lord for small favors," sighed Ben. "At least I'm not trailing a mother."

"No, but Iron Eyes is tracking a wife. That's why he's following you. He knows you're after the girl; he thinks you may lead him to her. Eh? How do I know? Indian arithmetic. Very easy. Iron Eyes came in from watching the horses just as I was leaving Magpie's lodge. He saw me. And I, waiting in the pines, saw him. He dragged Magpie out of her lodge and beat the story out of her. I could read her signs of surrender. She told him about you. That's a certainty."

"Wonderful," said Ben acrimoniously, "just wonderful." He looked witheringly at the paunchy breed. "Any-

36

thing else you'd like to add before Iron Eyes cuts me down?"

"Yes. Good-by. Right now. I would add good luck, but it would be a waste of words. With Iron Eyes on your track—" Go-deen moved his shoulder again. "I will be merciful," he said. "I won't finish it."

He got up from the breakfast fire and went to his old white horse. Swinging up, he brought the bony gelding back to the fire. For a moment he studied the warming skies and growing light of the new day.

"I ought to wait until tonight," he mused, "but then he won't follow *me*. Here," he said impulsively, unhooking his grub sack from the saddle horn and handing it down to Ben, "you take this. You'll need it. Which way you going?"

"You haven't told me yet," said Ben. "Which way are those Hunkpapas of Buffalo Ribs?"

"North."

"Then I'm going north."

"Good. I'll go south."

"That suits me," said Ben. "I want to thank you for the grub." He eyed the greasy sack of jerky. "You sure you can spare it?"

"Good-by," repeated Go-deen. "I'm going south. You still talk too much. If I stay here listening to you, neither one of us will need any food." He gave the old white horse his head, heeled him around, down river. Belatedly, Ben thought of his full debt to the Milk River breed.

"Many thanks, brother!" he called after him. "I mean for getting me the story of the girl; guiding me in and out of that Horse Creek country."

"All very well," called back Go-deen, turning in the saddle, "except that you're not out of it yet. I mean the Horse Creek country. One more advice, brother. I said I didn't think I would wait for night to travel after all. Did you hear me? Think about it. Apply it to your own case. *Hookahey,* you understand?"

Ben grinned, albeit crookedly.

He trotted, he did not walk, over to Malachi and swung up on him. Suddenly he was as anxious as Go-deen to put the miles between himself and their Wind River breakfast fire. And for the same reason.

To the old mule he said sharply:

"Hee-yah, *Hookahey,* wolf meat! You savvy Sioux? Make tracks. Vamoose. Take out. Get scarce. *Move!*"

Malachi shuffled obediently into a spine-jarring trot. The unexpected obedience jogged more than Ben's backbone.

"Damn," he said, "that's dismal. You're scared, too, eh?"

Malachi's only answer was to shift from the trot into an even more punishing lope. Ben let him go the gait, nonetheless. Better to let his teeth rattle than to risk riding baldheaded, he told himself. Yet somehow the philosophy fell short of the situation. Especially when, at the first rise of ground, he looked back down the river and saw Godeen and the white gelding had already dwindled to a small black dot. Even as he held there watching, they turned a bend in the bank and were gone altogether. Then things really got lonely and quiet along the Wind. Ben looked around apprehensively.

"Malachi," he said, "if this ain't the Big Lonesomes, it will do till we find same. Meanwhile, I got a deal to make with you. You don't leave me, I won't leave you—other than between bounces on that lame-camel lope of yours. You game? Or you want to go your own way, like that mealymouthed breed yonder?"

Malachi seemed to consider the offer, and for a bad moment Ben thought he was about to decline it. But then he snorted to clear his nostrils, stuck his whiskered muzzle into the freshening morning breeze, took a deep sample of its upriver odors. Whatever he smelled, it was something he didn't care for so soon after breakfast. He took Ben's deal and also, in the bargain, the bit in his few remaining back teeth. Ben gave him no argument. When he turned inland from the river, his rider merely nodded and let the reins go slack.

"If that's your idea of north," he said, "you take it. Don't let nobody talk you out of it neither. Least of all me. I just come along for the education. And maybe also the mountain air. *Hookahey* any old way you want."

Malachi flagged an ear but did not look back.

It was a little late in the morning for idle conversation.

All that day Ben bore north, quartering away from Wind River, following the game trails upward through

38

broken, cut-up country. About noon he had struck a creek which he knew was not Horse Creek and had spent the afternoon following it to its headwaters, knowing that in this way he would find the top of the drainage and be able to pass over into the next valley east of the Wind and so be out of the immediate range of Crowheart and the Horse Creek band.

It was wicked going all the way. What wasn't rock was mud; what wasn't mud was rock. It was a country built on edge and tilted over backward. You went sideways or back two steps for every step you went up or forward. Had it been bare and open, it would have been bad enough, but it was tangled and matted and windfallen with a bristle of bull pine and alder scrub that would have discouraged drilling with a jackhammer. How Malachi got through it, Ben never had the nerve to inquire. He simply hung on for all he was worth, and when sundown came at last, the old mule had him over the divide and dropping down the eastern side. Here, in a small, dark glade of open grass, Ben called the halt. Within twenty minutes, weary as he was, he had the water boiled and the coffee beans rock-pounded and poured into the simmering tin. He had just tethered Malachi in a stand of last summer's hay near the spring which watered the pothole meadow when, back by the fire and through the thickening dusk, he spied a moving, ghostly white form that could not belong to two ancient Milk River plugs.

"Go-deen!" he gasped and stood there, never so glad to see anyone in his brief, remembered life.

"Come, come, Tall Brother," chided the breed. "Don't just gawk there looking. Ask me down. Offer me food. Ask me the news of the trail. You might be surprised."

"My God," said Ben, "I *am* surprised. *And* delighted. Get down, get down!"

Go-deen got off the gelding, moved to the fire, stood grinning at Ben.

"I couldn't do it," he said, widening his chronic leer. "Not to a brother of the blood."

"Do what?" said Ben happily, not much caring what it was and refraining from hugging the fat breed only for fear the latter might knife him for the effort.

"Leave you alone in the woods with that damned Iron

39

Eyes. I never did like him anyway. And besides he beat Magpie on my account. I owed him something."

"Say," said Ben, reminded of their Shoshoni shadow and growing edgy at once, "I guess we had best douse the fire. I'd forgot about him. Coffee's boilt anyhow."

Go-deen spread his hand magnanimously.

"No, leave the fire. It looks nice at night. Besides, Iron Eyes won't see it."

Ben glanced back up the darkening mountainside.

"You wouldn't want to guarantee that, would you, blood brother?"

"You don't like my word? It isn't good enough for you?"

"Somehow, no," admitted Ben. "In some vague way I get the notion it ain't. No hard feelings, you understand?" His wide, quick smile melted Go-deen's resentment before the breed could bring it to bear. "You know how it is."

"Yes, I do," said Go-deen. "But you don't."

"How's that?"

"When I give my word to a friend, I am no longer a half-breed." He was suddenly, somehow—short, fat, grotesque and villainous looking withal—touched with the strangely poignant dignity of his red forebears. Ben nodded awkwardly and lost his grin.

"I'm listening," he said. "Go ahead."

Go-deen went over to his old horse and got something out of his saddlebag. He came back to the fire and tossed the object to Ben. Unthinkingly, Ben caught it.

"There," said Go-deen. "Next time I tell you that I couldn't leave you alone in the woods with Iron Eyes, you believe it."

Ben felt his stomach flop over and pull in. He looked down at what he had caught in his hands and was still holding in the light of the little mountain fire.

It was a Shoshoni scalp.

7

Land of the Throat Slitters

ON THE SIXTH DAY north of Wind River, April twenty-first, moving east of the Yellowstone uplands and passing successively through the Pitchfork, Greybull and Elk Basin drainages, they crossed into Montana. They were now safely out of Shoshoni country, not yet into danger range of the Sioux. This was Crow country. While they were in it, a tall white man and fat half-breed companion could light fires and sleep easy.

Crossing the Clark Fork of the Yellowstone they bore northward, going over the main channel at the old Indian ford near Laurel. Angling to the west, Go-deen led the way through the Cayuse Hills to the Coffin Butte crossing of the Musselshell. Here, they camped and recouped for three days, for beyond the Musselshell lay the Land of the Throat Slitters.

In the "rest" camp, Go-deen regaled Ben with true tales—he said—of the Sioux. They were for the main part well calculated to keep Tall Brother mentally stimulated. Typical was the breed's meandering explanation of the manner in which his mother came by their high plains name. The way Go-deen told it, it took most of the second morning. But reduced to its least terms, it took about twenty seconds; as the Cheyenne were called Cut Arms by the other Indians, so the Sioux were named Throat Slitters. This was very uncomplicated really. Just Indian arithmetic again. The Cheyenne marked their enemy dead by hacking off the left hand at mid-forearm. The Sioux did it by slashing the gullet ear to ear. Ergo, Cut Arms. Ergo, Throat Slitters. Simple? But of course. There was absolutely nothing to figuring out Indian mathematics once you understood that in their system two plus two did not equal four but five. Or seven. Or three. Or whatever you wanted or needed it to equal in order to have things

41

come out even for you. It was clearly a superior system to that of the whites.

Lulled by such logic Ben regathered strength, but courage, no. With nightfall of the third day, May first, he was thinking of deserting as soon as the moon came up or Go-deen ran down, whichever natural phenomenon occurred first. But once more mere man triumphed over Mother Nature. Go-deen outtalked the moon. He was in fact just getting warmed to his subject, a rattling good account of an experience of his in which he had Indian-wrestled the great Crazy Horse and thrown him six falls out of eight, when Ben's head fell forward for the final time. He got a fair night's sleep considering that it was gained sitting on a pea-gravel bar propped up by a hard Montana rock, and the next morning he and the half-breed went on over the Musselshell.

Go-deen was at home now, and his moves were as certain as those of a migrant bird. He came on the second night to a wide place between the Little Belt and Little Snowy Mountains.

"Judith Gap," he said happily to Ben. "Tomorrow you will see something."

The following morning they went through the gap, coming out into the most magnificent high country game basin the white imagination could conceive. Ben simply stared; he could not speak.

"Judith Basin," announced Go-deen with marked pride. "The last of the great Indian hunting grounds. The Sioux own it, they say. Occasionally a foolish band of Crows or Nez Percés will question the title. But they do it only to build reputation at home. It's a very brave thing. To come hunt in Judith Basin is better than striking coup barehanded in hot battle."

Ben nodded, shading his eyes against the morning sun.

"And which one of the lionhearted lease breakers would you say that was coming yonder, Crow or Nez Percé?" he asked grimly.

Following his point, Go-deen's eyes narrowed.

"Nez Percé," he replied. "You tell by the feathers."

Ben squinted again.

"What feathers?" he said.

"The ones he hasn't got," answered Go-deen. "A Crow

42

would wear feathers, usually two in the back forked like two fingers." He held up his fingers in a V. "That dead one yonder wears a hat. Who ever heard of a Crow wearing a hat?"

"For that matter," said Ben, "who ever heard of a Nez Percé wearing a hat?"

"Oh, lots of times. I told you they had taken the white man's road. Even Looking Glass, their famous fighting chief, wears a hat instead of feathers. It's a black soldier hat with three balls of otter fur pinned on the front of it, exactly like the one that poor fellow over there is wearing."

"Come on!" complained Ben. "You may have good eyes, but you can't see otter fur balls on that hat from here!"

For reply, Go-deen reached under his leg. There in a rifle scabbard he carried one of his numerous strange treasures; this one a yard-long brass-bound telescope. He handed the unsheathed glass to his companion.

"Take a look," he said. "See for yourself."

Ben focused the telescope, swore softly under his breath.

"Damn, that's somewhat!"

"Sure, didn't I tell you? I would have thought the scalp I brought you back there would have decided the issue, but it's apparent you have a hard head."

Ben grinned tartly.

"Well, I won't bet into your openers again. There's three fur balls of some kind pinned on a black cavalry hat yonder. You want to say they're otter fur, it suits me."

"Thank you. What else do you want to know?"

Ben watched the fleeing Nez Percé a moment longer before answering. He moved the glass backward, studying his pursuers as well. Then he nodded.

"Those would be Sioux chasing him, I suppose."

"Yes, Buffalo Ribs and six Hunkpapas."

Ben lowered the telescope.

"Now listen, you're not handing me any of that. You might recognize feathers or hats or otter fur balls at that distance, but you're not calling personal face features."

"There's no need. I know the horse the leading Sioux is riding. That's Buffalo Ribs's horse. His bay paint war horse. Nobody rides a Hunkpapa's war horse but the

43

owner. You can bet on that all summer long. Also you can bet on the rest of what I said—that's a dead Nez Percé over there."

Ben looked at him, shaking his head. His stubborn jaw took a hard set. The good-humored lines disappeared from his eye corners.

"I'll take a little of that last," he said quietly.

Go-deen stared back at him.

"You're doubting my word again? What's the matter with you? I thought you were only obstinate. Are you really stupid then after all?"

"Maybe. What odds you giving today?"

The Milk River breed studied the cross-meadow race briefly, then shrugged.

"The same as the Sioux are giving that Nez Percé; seven to one. That all right?"

"It's all right. You stay here. But make those odds seven-to-two."

"What!" said Go-deen. "You wouldn't!"

"Wouldn't I?" said Ben, soft as new snow and easing the big .44 in its worn leather. "You watch me."

8

Lame John

BEN FOLLOWED along the rear of the ridge from which
he and Go-deen had sighted the outnumbered Nez Percé
riding for his life. It was a low, rocky crescent half-circling
the meadow across which the race for death was being
run. If a man could encourage Malachi to his best, he
ought to be able to come to the end of the crescent ahead
of the hunted and the hunters. For his part, the Nez
Percé was making for the rocks hoping to get into them
and die profitably by taking one or two or three of the
enemy with him. The latter, in turn, were urging their
shaggy ponies to the limit, just as determined to prevent
this achievement as was their quarry to effect it.

The first factor guaranteeing the latter a chance to
succeed was the quality of his mount, a rangy, big-boned,
bad-headed Appaloosa which appeared to cover the same
ground in one leap as did the Hunkpapas scrubs in three.
The second factor was Ben Allison and Malachi Johnston.
Ben cajoled and low-talked the old mule the best way he
knew, and for a wonder the willful brute took the spirit of
the thing gallantly. He responded with a calamitous gallop
which, while it very nearly unhinged Ben's jaw and fused
his vertebrae, did get over a surprising distance in a short
time. Happily, there was no need for caution. The ridge
hid both mount and rider from the Sioux. An early spring
shower had laid the dust but the night previous. The wind
was to Ben strongly, carrying any sound of his endearments
or Malachi's reactions thereto safely away from the
Hunkpapas. He and Chilkoot's mule made the tip rocks of
the crescent with seconds to spare. Ben sprang off his
mount and ran, bent double, to take cover. As he paused
behind the last rock out, the Nez Percé swept by on the
panting Appaloosa.

"Get down, get down!" Ben yelled at him but could not
wait to see if the command was obeyed. With the shout,

he leaped into the open meadow facing the onrushing Hunkpapa horsemen.

The latter were almost upon him, but he had timed it beautifully. Further, he had accurately foreseen the reception which would be given the appearance of a six-foot four-inch white man under their very noses by the wild Sioux ponies. The wiry mounts came loose at all seams in the same instant. They split away from Ben, bucking and squalling in their fear of him and his alien odor. Two of them actually brushed him in whirling aside, the contact upsetting his aim and saving their riders, one of whom was Buffalo Ribs. Others of the Sioux—three others of them—were not so fortunate.

The walnut-handled .44 boomed point-blank into the dividing mass of the ponies. Ben was not picking individual targets but firing into the group. The instinct was that of the practised gunman and the group no farther than fifteen yards to its outermost member. Even in the dust and violent motion of the ambuscade, Ben knew that two of the Indians were done for from the way their slack bodies struck and bounded among the jagged rocks before him. As if to confirm his opinion, a deep voice spoke calmly at his elbow:

"Good shooting; *kaiziyeuyeu, itu timnein.*"

The four surviving Sioux were now pulling away into mid-meadow. The third of those Ben had shot lay very quiet in the grass ten feet out from the rocks. Ben could and did take his eyes off the enemy. He turned to the Nez Percé, warm grin breaking quickly.

"I don't know what you added there in Indian," he told his companion, "but I reckon I'll second the motion regardless."

The other's return smile was as grave as Ben's had been cheerful.

"What I said was, 'Thank you, that was a thoughtful thing to do.' "

"You're a Nez Percé, aren't you?" said Ben.

"Yes, a Wallowa of Old Joseph's band."

"Well, my friend, doesn't that make you kind of a far piece from home?"

Again the Indian smiled and spread his hands eloquently.

"You have just called me friend," he said. "Can any man be far from home when he is with his friend?"

It was a graceful thing to say, and without thinking Ben touched his forehead in respect. The Nez Percé's face lit up. He returned the gesture.

"I see you speak the language of my people," he said. "That's a good sign. As I also speak your tongue, I hope we will truly be friends. What do you say?"

"Well, we've made a fair start," admitted Ben. "And speaking of tongues, you handle that Yankee English pretty good. Better even than the half-breed I'm riding with, and he's the best I ever heard up to now. What's your secret?"

"No secret. I was a Christian Indian. What my people call a Treaty Indian. The agent at Lapwai taught me from the age of ten. I am now twenty and one. Before the agent there were the Catholic black robes; they also taught me well. Good men. I learned much from them."

"You did for a fact," said Ben admiringly. "I never heard an Indian could talk like you."

"And I," cut in a disgusted voice behind them, "never heard a white man cou.. .lk like you. Now get out of the way; there's work to finish beyond you."

Ben and the Nez Percé turned at the first sound of Go-deen's words. They were in time to see the breed raise his rifle, a Sharps of .50 caliber and 473-grain ball, seemingly aiming it directly at them. Both dove for the ground as the big gun roared above them.

In the meadow, ten feet out, the wounded Sioux died soundlessly. The great chunk of lead struck him in mid-chest, as he lay reared on the elbow to which he had come in seeking to shoot Ben and the Nez Percé in their backs. Ben got up from the rocks slowly. The dying brave tried to say something to him. He could not make the words come. Instead, he touched his forehead in the respect sign, hunched his body like a snake with a broken back, slipped forward into the dirt of the trail and was motionless. Ben stepped forward and retrieved the rifle—a brand-new Winchester carbine—from his loosened grasp. Straightening, he found Go-deen's eyes. The breed lifted his thick shoulders, nonchalantly blew the white smoke through the Sharps's barrel.

"I could have shot him without bothering you two," he

said, "but I didn't want to alarm you. Besides, there was plenty of time."

"If that was your idea of plenty," said Ben sharply, "I'd hate to get caught between you and what you'd call short notice." He leaned to help the Nez Percé, just now arising. When the latter had come to his feet, he noticed that he limped badly. "Are you all right, friend?" he asked quickly. "I didn't see you take that hit."

"It's an old wound," replied the other, "not from to-day."

"Not from the same day possibly," said Go-deen, beady eyes alert, "but from the same Sioux, eh? Am I right? Of course I am. You're the Wallowa, Aluin Ueukie, John Lame Elk; the same one that took the white woman from the Horse Creek Shoshoni of Crowheart."

The Nez Percé moved forward. As tall as Ben Allison very nearly, he was the handsomest man, red or white, the latter had ever seen. He towered over the squat breed, voice soft as a woman's, dark eyes fierce and wild with that look of freedom seen only in the eyes of eagles.

"Yes," he said, "I am the one. My people and the white people at the agency call me Lame John. But don't fear; I am not awkward about the leg. I received it fighting for the white woman. To find her again, I would take another like it or far worse."

Ben frowned slightly.

"You mean you're back here looking for that woman?"

"Yes, I will always look for her."

"But do you know if these Sioux still have her?"

"No, I don't. These few you drove off just now, they jumped me as I was gutting a deer I had shot. I'll admit I didn't dream there was a Sioux within miles. If my people ever hear of it, I will never live down the disgrace. We don't regard the Sioux as much. We think of them as dirt, as less than dirt."

"Beware!" warned Go-deen. "I am half Oglala."

"Hah! The very name means Dirt Thrower. Do you deny it?"

Go-deen wavered, broke out his leering, lopsided grin.

"I deny nothing, cousin. But I would like to make a good suggestion. Since Tall Brother missed his shot on Buffalo Ribs, it might be a wise thing if we went away from here pretty quick. I don't know about you, but I'm

48

getting uncomfortable." He pointed across the meadow. "I have the feeling those four are talking about us."

Ben and Lame John looked at the Sioux. As they did, Buffalo Ribs upended his Winchester, another of the new carbines, and levered five deliberately spaced shots. With that he shook the rifle at the three companions, shouted something to his followers, wheeled his war horse and was gone swiftly into the fringing timber.

"Five shots," said Ben thoughtfully. "I'm not familiar with that sign apparently. How does she read, Go-deen?"

"Five, that's the Sioux bad medicine number," replied the other. "They put it on anybody they intend seeing again. Five. Slowly spaced, just like that. I'm glad Buffalo Ribs wasn't looking at me when he let off those medicine shots. Come on, let's go."

Ben took Malachi from Go-deen, swung up on him. Holding him in, he nodded.

"Just a minute. You mean to tell me that damned Sioux was looking at *me* in particular?"

The breed regarded him impatiently.

"Did *I* rescue this Nez Percé from him? Did *I* shoot three of his warriors out of their saddles? Did *I* jump out from behind these rocks yelling like a spirit wolf right in his face? Did *I* throw all those shots at him with that short gun you carry on your leg? Well—?"

"Well, no."

"No is right. Never fear, Tall Brother. Buffalo Ribs won't be confused between you and me when he meets us again. He will know you. Trust in that."

"Thanks," said Ben. "I would have worried if you hadn't of reassured me."

"Brothers," interrupted the Nez Percé, "let us do as the Fat One suggested. Let's get out of here."

"Fat! I like that! I really do like that—!"

Go-deen was sputtering, and Ben stepped Malachi forward, wedging him between the breed's old gelding and Lame John's rawboned Appaloosa.

"Hold on," he said, "let's don't waste time arguing weights. We're all here on the same business. Maybe we can show the best profit working together."

"What do you mean?" asked Lame John, puzzled. "I can't see how we are here on the same business. How is that? I'm after that yellow-haired white woman, I ad-

49

mitted that. But she can't be your woman, for she was Iron Eyes's. I *know* that."

"Wait up, friend," said Ben and, bringing forth the locket, proceeded to tell him the full story of Amy Johnston. When he had done so, Lame John looked at him a long, searching moment, then asked quietly:

"You do not want her for yourself then?"

"No, I just gave my word to her father exactly the way I said and no more."

"Then," agreed Lame John, "we do have the same business, and we are three against the Sioux's three hundred."

"Two only," corrected Go-deen at once. "I am along in the capacity of an employed guide. The Sioux are my brothers in blood. Don't think for a minute I will fight with you against them."

Lame John regarded him with some interest.

"What do you call fighting them? You shot that brave just now. Was that an act of brotherhood in the blood?"

"Bah! Don't question me. I am Frank Go-deen of the Milk River half bloods. Would I lie to an ordinary Wallowa?"

The tall Nez Percé leaned from the saddle, putting out his hand.

"I am John Lame Elk," he said, "and I do not question the man who shoots his own brother in my defense."

"It was only a half-brother," said Go-deen grudgingly.

Ben edged Malachi back into the meeting.

"Is this a private lodge," he asked, "or can anybody belong to it?" He held out his own hand toward Lame John. "I'm Ben Allison," he said. "Welcome to the Amy Johnston Rangers."

A light showed in the Nez Percé's eyes, but he did not smile. He took Ben's hand firmly, however.

"Come on," urged Go-deen, jerking his head toward Ben, "let's get going before our white friend here starts another speech. All white men talk too much but this one—eeh!"

Now Lame John smiled.

"I like the way he talks," he said. "I never heard such a beautiful tongue in my life as that with which he spoke to the Sioux just now."

"Bah! Any fool can jump out from behind rocks shooting helpless Hunkpapas with no warning. It was like lancing trout in a rain pool. Gun talk is always cheap!"

"Indeed it is," agreed Ben. "Let's move out."

They turned their mounts, following swiftly around behind the ridge again. After a while of riding in silence, Lame John shook his head.

"No, not cheap," he frowned. "In the Bible it says, 'All that a man has will he give for his life.' The white brother offered me his life back there. Is that cheap? No, never. So now I offer him my life here."

"Nonsense," said Ben, coloring badly. "Nobody owes nobody a thing. We're all square."

"That's not for you to say," replied Lame John softly.

"A life for a life is the Indian law. I would not change if it I could. From this place to the last end of the trail I go with you. There's no more to be said."

"Now you've done it!" growled Go-deen, eying Ben resentfully. "We'll never get rid of him. Three mouths to feed and one brain to do the cooking. Eeh—!"

9

Hookahey!

ALL THAT DAY they trailed the Sioux survivors, coming with day's end to the warning sign of lodge smokes spiraling above the trees ahead. Not denying Go-deen's advice, they cut away from the smokes, seeking higher country and safer from which to make their next decision.

With dark, they lay up among the wind-warped cedars of the Little Belts, high and cold above the camp of the Hunkpapas. The Sioux village was set in a lovely alpine grassland bordered by thick timber and drained by the beginnings of the South Fork of Judith River. There was no water upon the arid hogback they had chosen, nor did they dare make a fire. Their supper consisted of a few grainy mouthfuls of jerky forced down by muscle, not mastication. For after-dinner entertainment they studied the Sioux through Go-deen's telescope, holding terse court on the aspects of Hunkpapa community life as it might relate to their own present ambitions. The problem, according to Go-deen, was a simple one: to find out if the people of Buffalo Ribs still held Amy Johnston or, if not, what they had done with her.

However simple, though, said the breed, this might take a little doing, as there remained one small complication. Ordinarily his Oglala blood would gain him friendly entrance to the Hunkpapa lodges. But as Buffalo Ribs had almost surely seen him join Ben and Lame John in the ambush rocks, this kindness of kinfolk could not be counted upon. To this must be added the historical bad feeling between the Hunkpapas and Lame John's people. Then consider the fact that Go-deen knew, from first-ear listening in the Sioux lodges all during the months of deep cold, that there had been much talk of an early spring war with the whites. Go-deen could not say whether a subsequent vote for that war had been given. All he could say was that the winter talk had been of a big war with the

52

white man as soon as the new grass was coming first above the ground; and now the new grass had come, and Ben Allison was a big white man. In view of this, he, Go-deen, would have to identify that one small complication before mentioned. He would do it by asking Lame John and Brother Ben if they had any ideas for an approach to the lodges below which would not involve getting all three of their throats slit.

Ben and the tall Wallowa shook their heads. All right, then, said Go-deen, they would do it his way. Ben was almost afraid to put the next question but knew he must.

"And what," he asked, "might that be?"

"It might be any of several things, Tall Brother, but in fact it is only one. We leave this ridge by the back side before daylight. Once down it, we keep going as far and as fast as these miserable brutes of ours will carry us." He had the telescope up at the time, and Ben asked quietly:

"Why? You seeing something you don't like down there?"

"Indeed, indeed," said Go-deen. "I'm watching Slohan's lodge. There is a nice fire in front of it, and Slohan is talking across it with the headmen—maybe two dozen of them—with no squaws."

"No squaws? That's a war talk, eh?"

"Naturally."

"Slohan? That's Buffalo Ribs's Sioux name, isn't it?"

"I told you that."

"Sure, you've told me a lot of things."

"Good, then let me add this one more thing to all the others; don't let the sun catch you still sitting up on this ridge."

Ben, squinting through the darkness, could make out the small figures seated and standing about the fire below. But the distance was so great that, with the naked eye, he could see no movement in the group.

"Are you reading their lips?" he inquired crisply of Go-deen. "If so, tell me what they're saying about me. I'm dying to know."

"If you make a joke, it escapes me," said the breed, "but perhaps you are right anyway. You well might die from knowing what they are saying about you."

Ben's briskness wilted.

"Like what?" he asked humbly enough.

"Like they're speaking with their hands, as they always do in a serious council. So I'm not reading their lips but their signs. From this it becomes an easy matter to form an opinion of what is being said."

"Such as?"

"They did see me shoot their friend when you were talking too much back there in the rocks. They also saw you help the Nez Percé to his feet. They recognized me, as well. So the rest is easy. They will come after all three of us with first light."

Ben looked at Lame John, frowned, turned back to Go-deen.

"Anything about the woman we're after—Amy Johnston?"

"Nothing that I could make out through the glass." He lowered the telescope, collapsing it. "As far as I'm concerned that ends it. I have only one more thing to say."

Ben got wearily up off his belly.

"Yes, I know," he sighed. *"Hookahey."*

"That's it; let's go."

They started off, but Lame John stayed where he lay.

"You coming?" said Ben, looking back.

The Nez Percé did not move.

"You know that I'm not, brother," he replied. "I am here to get the woman back or die. If not the one, then the other matters very little."

"Look," said Ben, going back to him, "I want to find her, too. I've given my word to do it, same as you. But I don't think that us getting ourselves killed is the best way to go about helping Amy Johnston. Now, come on, get up and get going."

"No, never."

"I'll give you my word and hand to come back with you and try again the minute we can get some decent help to bring it off. We just can't swing it alone."

"You go on, Brother Ben. I must stay."

"The hell you must stay!" exploded Ben. "Now, damn it, come on. Don't just lay there like a damned—" He stopped himself but not in time.

"Like a damned Indian," finished Lame John quietly. "No, no," he went on as Ben stammered his apology, "it's all right, brother. We don't think in the same ways. That's
54

only natural and right. Our hands may meet but not our minds. One is red, the other, white."

"The hell!" said Ben firmly. "I don't shake hands unless I mean it in my mind. Get up. We're not leaving without you."

"Speak for yourself, Brother Ben," dissented Go-deen. "This Milk River is leaving with or without that Wallowa!"

The breed began to move away through the windy darkness, but Ben was after him instantly. Seizing him by the collar, he hauled him back to where Lame John still lay upon his stomach watching the Sioux fire.

"Oh, no you don't!" he said. "We're not splitting up. In fact we're going to hold a little war talk of our own right here and presently. There's been two too many chiefs so far. You understand?"

Go-deen wrinkled his lance scar, refusing to answer. But Lame John's soft voice took up the matter.

"What do you propose?" he asked.

"Number one," said Ben, "that we decide whether the finding of Amy Johnston is my job or yours. It can't be both. Number two, and depending on number one, are we going to run this trackdown white or Indian style?"

Go-deen took a pose of outright hostility, or the best imitation of it which he could manage with Ben's big hand still holding him firmly by the shirt collar. But Lame John got slowly to his feet and stood facing Ben, dark eyes burning.

"Well spoken," he said, putting out his hand. "Neither do I accept a man's hand lightly."

Their hands met quickly and were quickly released, but with the grip Ben knew the Nez Percé had surrendered his most prized Indian right—the freedom to make one's personal decisions without regard to his fellows. His next words sealed the concession.

"Back there this morning," he told Ben, "I said I would go with you to the far end of the trail. Now I say I will follow you to it. What do you want us to do?"

Ben answered him with a wordless grip of both hands on his shoulders.

"First off," he said, "we'll do just what Go-deen advised; be long gone before sunrise. Next we'll do what I suggested; go round up reinforcements and come back.

That's the best I can think of, looking at it long-haulwise."

Lame John bowed his head, a feeling almost of sadness lining his dark face.

"It's the difference between the red man and the white," he said. "It is why the Indian must lose, and you whites must win in the end. It is exactly what Young Joseph has always told us."

"Young Joseph," said Ben, "must be a pretty smart cookie."

"He will be a great man one day; he has the power to see ahead."

"Yes, well then," said Ben, correcting the drift of the exchange, "we're agreed. We'll play it my way from here on."

"Right," answered Lame John. Then he turned to Go-deen with one of his grave smiles. "What was that Sioux word, brother?"

The halfbreed regarded him balefully.

"Hookahey," he grunted.

Lame John wheeled back to Ben, the smile giving way to a sober-sided nod.

"That's the one, Brother Ben," he said *"Hookahey!"*

"Bah!" said Go-deen, throwing up his hands. "Both crazy! One red, one white, and each as wild as a wolf with his bowels full of poison bait. *Eeh!* What's a man to do when his own comrades go mad?"

Angry growls aside, when Ben led the way to their tethered mounts, the Milk River breed went shoulder to shoulder behind him with John Lame Elk, the Wallowa Nez Percé. And from that time there was no serious question of final voice among the Amy Johnston Rangers.

10

The Gray-eyed Oglala

JUST BEFORE DAYLIGHT they rounded a switch-back in the mountain trail they were following through the Big Snowy range, east of the Sioux encampment. Ahead lay a small pothole meadow similar, save in extent, to that wherein Buffalo Ribs had pitched his lodges. They were out into the grass, free of the timber, before any of them realized *how* similar was this new meadow. Go-deen, riding the lead, cursed and hauled in his old white gelding. Ben, immediately behind him, nearly fell off Malachi when the latter bumped the haunches of the white and was bumped in turn from the rear by Lame John's Appaloosa. Awakened by the collison, the dozing Nez Percé, his view blocked by Ben's wide shoulders, asked sleepily:

"What happened? What is it, brother?"

Ben's two-word reply—"More Sioux!"—brought him sharply awake.

The light was still poor, but there could be little doubt they had blundered into a second party of Throat Slitters. After the Indian habit on the trail, this band of red travelers was early adoing. Hence the weary night riders had no chance to withdraw gracefully from the unwanted meeting. In fact, eight or ten Winchesters were pointing their way before Go-deen got his discovery curse well out. The *click-clink* of these rifles being put on cock provided an effective suggestion to stand where they were.

Two of the red riflemen now arose from beside the breakfast fire and came forward. One of these was slender and sensitive looking, no more than five seven or eight in height. The other was quite tall, narrow-faced, very dark-skinned. It was not until they drew near that Ben noted a racial peculiarity in the taller Indian. He had startlingly gray eyes. It was at the same time that Go-deen discovered something even more notable about the smaller Sioux.

"Tashunka!" he cried. *"He-hau!* It's you, it's you!"

The slender chief, plainly less pleased than the Milk River half-breed with the meeting, held up his hand and asked a blunt question in the native tongue. The tall, hawk-faced Indian stood by saying nothing. Go-deen replied effusively in Sioux, then turned delightedly to Ben and Lame John.

"It's Crazy Horse," he told them, "my Oglala cousin, the half-uncle of my mother, three times removed. These are my people. We're saved!"

"From what?" asked the tall, dark-skinned Oglala, startling Ben with his clear English.

"From that damned Buffalo Ribs," explained Go-deen.

"Slohan?" said the other. "Tell us about it."

When Go-deen had complied, including the information as to Ben's and Lame John's reasons for being in the country, the tall Sioux turned to Crazy Horse and spoke rapidly to him in Oglala. The latter scowled but nodded in apparent consent. He then went back to the fire and sat down. The tall one waved quickly to Go-deen.

"Get down and come eat, Frank. Your friends, too. You're in luck; Tashunka's in a good mood. No spirit dreams last night. He says you can join us at the fire and listen to the news, if you wish. He says your two friends will be all right—maybe."

"Thanks, Cetan," said the breed, Ben noting the patent respect he paid the other. "It was good of you to talk for us. Yes, and for the woman, too."

"What could I do?" asked the Oglala. "You told us she was a white woman."

Ben thought the comment a little strange from a high plains hostile. He wondered about it as, with Lame John and Go-deen, he followed the English-speaking Sioux to the fire. Here they squatted on their heels in polite and proper imitation of their savage hosts. Directly, fresh strips of deer loin were cut and put to broil over the clear pine flames. While the fat from the venison spat and hissed into the fire, Ben watched the tall chief. He was even more interested in him than in Crazy Horse, an Indian seen at such range by no more than a handful of white men before or later. It was not the fact that he spoke English, but the particular way in which he spoke it, which dug at Ben's mind. He could swear he detected a

58

slight drawl, very much like his own Texas accents, in the other's speech. Lame John and Go-deen both spoke English, of course, but they continually reverted to Indian phrasings and ways of saying things. This gray-eyed Ogla-la talked as straight as Ben Allison. Indeed, his grammar, Ben realized, was superior to his own, marking him obviously as an educated man. Here was a puzzler for sure, but since he was unmistakably second-in-command to the famed Crazy Horse, he had to be a Sioux of reputation. Ben determined to find out about him from Go-deen at the first opportunity.

Meanwhile the talk over the breakfast fire had begun. Ben and Lame John sat silently through its course, glad enough to be ignored by these fierce horsemen who were their sworn enemies. After about half an hour, during which time Ben caught the war sign over and over again. Crazy Horse stood up and made the departure sign. His tall subchief came over to Ben and Lame John.

"You two keep as quiet as you can," he advised them soberly. "Just come along as you're told, and try to keep out of the way as much as you can. I've spoken for your safety and been promised it. But with these people of mine you must be extremely circumspect at all times."

He threw a glance at the mounting Sioux.

"Did you understand any of what was just said?" he asked Ben.

"Enough," answered the latter. "Neither of us speak or savvy Sioux, but we both read hand signs."

"Then you know the talk was all of war. I am doing my utmost to prevent it, but I'm in a peculiar sort of a position and can do only so much."

Ben wondered what that position might be but dared not ask just yet.

"What about the girl—Amy Johnston?" he asked. "Do you think they mean to get Buffalo Ribs to turn loose of her?"

"I'm going to do what I can in that direction. I've already spoken of it to Tashunka. He said only that we would see. I left it there. You don't push Tashunka."

"That's right," said Go-deen, coming up with their mounts in time to hear the last sentence. "Not if you want to see the buffalo come again, you don't. Here's your animals. Get on them, and shut up."

Ben took Malachi and legged up on him stiffly.

"Whereaway we going?" he inquired of Go-deen, as the tall subchief went off to get his own mount.

"With them, naturally." The breed shrugged. "You think they'd turn us loose in their rear? Me, perhaps. But you two? A white man and a Nez Percé? Hah, that's a good one! I'm laughing."

"All right," said Ben, showing a patience he didn't feel, "where are *they* going then?"

"Why to see Cousin Slohan, of course. Where else?"

Ben gritted his teeth. He looked around to see if the Sioux were watching. They were not. Out of the side of his mouth he said to the grinning Go-deen:

"Listen, you crackpot breed, it may tickle your funny bones something fierce, but I ain't laughing with you, you hear? I killed two of those Hunkpapas yesterday and put down a third that never got up. Likewise, I made Buffalo Ribs look bad in front of his braves. That don't add up to any welcome mat for me up there to that village. Neither does it for old John here."

He checked the Sioux again, swept on.

"I ain't going, you understand. I'm pulling my .44 and bluffing my way out of here right now. If the bluff don't work, I'll try blasting. You coming with me, John?"

"Yes," replied the Nez Percé. "Those Hunkpapas will kill us no matter what these Oglala say. But the Oglala may let us run if we start from here. Let's go."

"Wait!" hissed Go-deen. "You've got these Dirt Throwers wrong. They won't let you run. The only thing keeping them from opening your throats is that big devil with Tashunka; the one that just now talked to you. You think he was warning you for fun?"

Ben held up, alerted by the unusual seriousness of Go-deen's manner.

"That tall rascal must have pretty strong medicine," he said, watching the Sioux brush away with pine branches all sign of the campfire and of the picket line where the ponies had stood during breakfast and since being brought in from the meadow and the night's grazing. "Ordinarily one Indian won't listen to another like that."

Again Ben didn't know how he knew this. It simply flashed into his mind blindly from the blind past, as had everything else since the snowslide in Madison Canyon.

60

He accepted it intuitively, and in this case the instinct proved as accurate as his previous ones about these nomad people.

"That's right," agreed Go-deen matter-of-factly. "Ordinarily one Indian wouldn't listen to another like that."

Ben watched him, sensing another of his queer spells.

"But what?" he asked guardedly.

"But this other Indian isn't an Indian," leered the breed happily. "He's a white man."

On the way back through the Big Snowies Ben found his chance to query Go-deen about Crazy Horse's gray-eyed companion. The breed knew surprisingly little of the white Oglala. What he knew, he told straightly enough.

He had been a government scout or Army guide, wounded in the big fight at Fort Phil Kearny the past winter. That had been in December, but a few months gone, in the ambush where Colonel Fetterman had lost all his soldiers to Red Cloud, Long Fox and Crazy Horse. Well, this tall white man had been picked up unconscious from the field, his life claimed by Crazy Horse who had admired the way in which he fought. The Oglala chief had taken him back into He Sapa, the sacred Black Hills hunting country of the Sioux, there nursing him to health. Given an Indian name, Cetan Mani, Walking Hawk, he had married an Oglala girl and taken up the life of the tribe.

Ah, no, you could not call him a squaw man. He was a full Sioux, a true blood brother in Crazy Horse's own White Fox Lodge. His dark skin was only partly from wind and sunburn. He had been, in the beginning as dark as many high plains Indians. The Sioux had accepted him as one of them. His great skill with rifle and pistol had led them to name him chief hunter of the band. Because Crazy Horse had personally adopted him into his own lodge, he also stood high in the war command of the Oglalas. But as to where he had originally come from, who he was or what his white name might be, nothing was known. His former life, like Ben Allison's, led only into a box canyon. If Ben would inquire further into it, he would have to do so of Cetan himself.

Accepting this, Ben turned the inquiry to the Sioux

61

members of the party. Here Go-deen was prepared to speak with more detail and, plainly, more enthusiasm.

Hah! Now Ben had asked something. Did he have any idea at all of the power of the company in which he rode? Of course not. But look—that handsome chief on the bay pinto—American Horse, called Iron Plume by the Oglalas, one of the great fighters of all time. Then take the shaggy-haired grizzly of a man on the stout black—Charging Bear—a very famous warrior. And the dangerous looking skinny warrior who rode with him—Little Wound—as bad as they came.

Then going down the line front to rear, there were Low Dog, Crow King, Fast Bear, Little Big Man, Old Bull, Red Shirt, Swift Bear and Big Road. These were not all Oglalas by any means, but members of various other Sioux families going to the big council at Slohan's meadow.

Coming also to that meeting would be the Cheyenne of Crow Necklace, Hail, Two Moons, High Wolf and Yellow Hand. Yes, and even the Blackfoot of John Grass. Oh, it was going to be some war talk, all right. And what a lot of fun as well to see what all those white-haters would do when Crazy Horse spoke up and told them to give the white woman to Ben and Lame John and to let her thus go happily free with a white man and a Wallowa Nez Percé! *Eeh!* That would be some laugh. Especially since High Bear and Gall, the war chiefs of Sitting Bull, were going to be there to speak for that old Hunkpapa head devil, the greatest white-hater of them all!

Ben found small trouble suppressing any inclination to join Go-deen in the walleyed cackling with which the breed relished the thought of this Indian joke. He stared at him, instead, with a dubious frown.

"You," he announced accusingly, "ought to be in the booby hatch."

"The what?" Go-deen scowled defensively.

"The place where they keep crazy people," said Ben. "A nut house. A loony bin. You're as cracked as grandma's pet thundermug."

Go-deen nodded, lance-scarred grin suddenly back in place. He pointed up the line of war-feathered Sioux.

"We'll see who's crazy," he said, "and pretty quick, too. Do you recognize that rise in the trail ahead?"

Ben peered through the late afternoon shadows.

"Well, maybe not. It *was* pretty dark when we came down there last night."

"Damn!" said Ben. "So soon?"

Go-deen didn't answer and didn't need to.

Ben looked around, feeling a chill from more than the long blue shadows of the bull pines. There was no denying it. The dry rocks, the steep rise, the warped straggle of the cedars breaking the skyline where the trail went up and over the hogback spur. This was the place. Beyond that rise lay the lovely alpine meadow which held the lodges of Slohan's Hunkpapas—trail's end or journey's beginning for Ben Allison and Amy Geneva Johnston.

Whatever came of the war talk in Slohan's meadow, Ben and his friends were not to know of it. They were held prisoners in a spare lodge set up upon their arrival. Their guards were two each of Hunkpapas and Oglalas, the four chosen as much to watch one another as the three hostages. Darkness came quickly. With it the council fire was lighted. Ben could see its flare from the entrance flap of the prison lodge. He could see, too, the excited reaction of the Hunkpapas to Crazy Horse's brief opening speech. But he could not make out what that speech concerned. Since Go-deen could not see the speaker from his position, there was no translation of the Oglala's remarks. However, the transcript arrived soon enough. Bearing it was the tall white Sioux. With him was an Indian of peculiarly dangerous look, armed to the ear lobes and aloof as a buffalo wolf.

"Zinciziwan," said the tall white man, indicating his companion. "Yellow Bird. He will take you out of camp and set you on your way. The Hunkpapas are afraid of his personal medicine; they'll let him through."

"There was trouble just now?" asked Ben, as the other cut him loose.

"Yes, more than a little." He was working now to free Go-deen and Lame John. "You won't want to waste any time."

"What about the woman?"

"She's gone. They traded her to some visiting Cheyenne last month. They were Southern Cheyenne, Black Kettle's people. The Hunkpapas say they heard—don't ask me how they heard; it's one of their secrets I haven't discovered yet—but they say they heard 'by the wind' that the Cheyenne didn't keep her. They are supposed to have gotten rid of her down on the Arkansas. That would be up near the headwaters, as they haven't had time to get down on the main stream. Anyway, 'the wind' says she had a mean mind and wouldn't lie quietly with the chief. So they palmed her off on the Kiowas. They got eight spotted horses for her, a high price; especially from Satank."

"Satank!" groaned Go-deen.

"Is that bad?" asked Ben quickly.

The breed threw up his hands helplessly.

"Bad? Anything to do with Satank is bad. He's mean as a boar grizzly with a sore sheath. He's head man of their toughest warrior society, the Kaitsenko. They're all murderers and Satank the worst of the lot. If he's got her, we may as well forget the whole thing and go shoot summer meat on Milk River."

"That's not far from true," admitted the white Sioux, "but if you're determined to go down there on the Arkansas after that poor girl, there's one more thing I've been able to arrange to help you."

"We owe you a plenty just to be getting out of here in one piece," said Ben. "But we'll take any help we can get as far as going after Amy Johnston. I mean to find her if she's alive."

"I thought as much," said the other, "or I wouldn't have given those ten mares and my best buffalo horse for you. Not to mention the '66 Winchester and eight boxes of shells the Kiowa boy cost me."

Puzzled, Ben started to question him about the Kiowa boy, but he waved hurriedly for them to follow him and ducked under the rear skins of the lodge. They crawled after him and went off through the dark, keeping the high cone of the prison lodge between themselves and the council fire. Looking back as they went into the timber, Ben noted that the guards were gone from in front of the lodge and that the meeting at the fire had grown suddenly noisier. He didn't need the tall Sioux's anxiously called, *"Hopo, hookahey,"* to speed him at this point. His Indian intuition was working fine, and it was telling him to lean on the white Oglala for all he might be worth right now

64

and to worry about paying him back for the favor later; preferably much later.

Some half mile into the pines they came upon a murky glade formed by one of the small creeks of the Judith's origin making a horseshoe loop free of timber. In the hollow of the loop they saw a shadowy clot of horses and, upon drawing close, saw they were tended by a lone Indian youth not appreciably bigger than a bear cub.

"Little Tree," said their tall guide, putting his hand on the boy's shoulder, "your Kiowa passport. The Hunkpapas took him in a southern raid last fall. They were holding him for a hundred and fifty horses. Tashunka got them to see where it might be a good way of getting the Kiowas to join the Sioux in their war to send the boy back."

"Damn," said Ben doubtfully, "that skates like pretty thin ice to me."

"It does," admitted their rescuer, "but I'm hoping it will hold up under you until Yellow Bird can get you across the Musselshell."

"*Little* Tree?" wondered Go-deen belatedly and with obvious concern. "Is the boy by any chance of the blood of *Big* Tree, Cetan?"

"Very much so, I'm afraid, Frank. That's why the high price and the agreement to let him go home."

The answer was echoed by a second groan from Go-deen, and Ben asked resignedly:

"Now what?"

"Oh, nothing, nothing at all. Just that there are two other Kiowas who go hand in hand with Satank for bad reputations, and Big Tree is one of the two."

"Oh, well, I'm glad it's nothing serious. For a minute there you had me worried."

"Not serious, not serious at all!" piped up the Kiowa boy in sudden, unexpected English and backed it with a grin bright enough to light a candle by. "Not unless you also arouse great-uncle Satanta."

"No!" cried Go-deen, covering his ears. "It's impossible. I won't hear it. He didn't say it; he didn't say Satanta. He couldn't have!"

"He said it, sure enough," nodded Ben. "What of it?"

Go-deen ignored him, voice rising.

"Where's my horse. Lead him out here; show me the trail. I'm going. Good-by, good-by!"

Ben grabbed him, putting a rough hand over his mouth.

"Shut up, you featherhead! You want to get us winged before ever we get over the ridge? What the hell's the matter with you!"

"Satanta, that's what!" answered Go-deen with the third groan. "He's the other one of those three Kiowas! I won't do it! I'm going back to Slohan. Eeh! My mother should have been an Osage."

"I think she must have been an O-sap," said Ben. "Get the hell on that white plug, and quiet down."

They found their mounts and got on them. When they had done so, Ben noted for the first time that the Kiowa boy was leading two spare ponies.

"For you and Frank," explained the tall white Sioux. "Your own mounts couldn't go the gait you'll need to get out of Hunkpapa country. You had better use your old animals through the night, but change over first thing in the morning."

Ben put out his hand and the other white man took it.

"Don't waste time you haven't got," he told Ben, as the latter started to express his gratitude.

"All right," agreed Ben. "You want to give me your name?"

"You wouldn't know it," said the other, shaking his head. "Just say I'm a Southerner like yourself." He paused, looking off, then said with lonely softness, "Some of us take strange trails. I suppose we shall all blame it on the war—" Then, quickly, "Ride out, friend. Trust Yellow Bird to the river and Little Tree beyond it. You've got your guns and good horses. You will need both. And much luck beside."

Unconsciously, Ben touched the fingers toward him. He smiled, a little sadly, Ben thought, and returned the gesture.

"God bless you, mister," Ben muttered and kicked Malachi around and sent him into his ungainly lope after the other horses following behind Yellow Bird and Little Tree. At his side Lame John reined down his long-striding Appaloosa and looked back toward the tall figure still standing in the starlight of the creek loop.

"Go-deen was wrong," he said quietly. "That's no white man back there."

Ben twisted in the saddle, taking his own long, thoughtful look.

"Maybe you're right," he finally nodded.

Yet somehow he felt compelled to stand in the stirrups and wave one more farewell to the motionless figure behind them. He could not be sure if his salute were returned, or not, but he fancied he saw the lean arm lift in hesitant, mute reply.

It was the last he ever saw or heard of the tall, gray-eyed Oglala.

11

South to Salt Fork

YELLOW BIRD took them to the Musselshell by a new route strange even to Go-deen. It passed through the Little Belts west of Judith Gap, came out above the Coffin Butte crossing. The distance was approaching forty miles as near as Ben could reckon, and the hard-faced Sioux got them over it with the last of the starlight. Not pausing even to breathe the horses, he plunged his lathered mount into the stream where it narrowed between banks of sheet rock. It was swimming water all the way. Ben thought Malachi was going out from under him time and again, but the old brute kept going. He was a dripping last out on the far bank, and the look he gave Ben would have withered anything that was not wet with Musselshell snow water. When Ben reached to give him a rewarding pat, he bit him angrily on the forearm. Ben let it go. There were times when even a mule was right.

Their Sioux guide now pointed south and said something to Little Tree. With that, and not even a look at the little group he had captained through the night, he put his pony back into the river. They watched until he had made the crossing and disappeared into the far-side timber. Then Ben turned to Little Tree.

"What did he say?" he asked.

The small Kiowa shrugged, grinned engagingly.

"He said, 'Ride like hell.' "

Wondering where this button-eyed imp had picked up his civilized ways, Ben returned the grin.

"I think he said right," he nodded. "Lead out."

Go-deen was at once offended.

"Now wait!" he demanded. "This papoose may be of some possible use down on the Arkansas, but as for a guide to that country, don't be foolish. I have been down there more times than he has birthdays. We've got to go through Arapaho, Ute, Cheyenne and Pawnee country to

68

get to Kiowa. This is a bad spring for traveling. There's a war summer coming. You want to ride seven hundred miles behind a boy? Pah! You wouldn't get to the Republican River or the Smoky Hill, let alone the Arkansas. You wouldn't even get to the North Platte following this child of three evil bloodlines. And if he did get you down there, he would only lead you right into an ambush. You can't trust a Kiowa. It's an old saying of the plains. Now why don't you just quit all this talk and follow a man?"

Ben winced wryly. "You're right, Frank," he said. "When will I learn to keep quiet. Lead out."

The breed gave Little Tree a punishing look, swung the old white gelding into the lead.

"We will go a little ways into the timber," he said, "then change to our fresh horses and keep going. We won't stop for food until the sun goes."

There was no dissent, not even from the demoted Kiowa youth who now chose, for reasons of his own, to ride beside Ben. The boy, however, did have a comment on the new order of things. Examining Go-deen curiously and for a head-cocked moment, he said admiringly:

"You know, Tall Brother, at first I was much taken with the size of his paunch. Now I see it is nothing compared to the bigness of his mouth."

Ben looked at him, suppressing his grin.

"Little Tree," he said soberly, "you'll do."

It was a pleasant journey. Go-deen knew where he was going, and the luck held good. They met no hostiles, saw only a few parties from far off. They saw no wagon trains either, for Go-deen was right there, too. It was a war summer. The Army was stopping all movement which it could control west of Laramie in the north and below Fort Bent in the south. After a few safe days on the trail, the little band relaxed and sought company in one another's conversation.

The Kiowa boy proved as bright as he had seemed and in no way reluctant to admit that his education in the words and ways of the white brother had come from spying for his tribe by attending the Washita Agency School outside Fort Cobb. He had hung around the soldiers all he could, and it was their rough manners which had impressed him most. As he put it to Ben, "I didn't learn a damn thing at the school, except to say 'excuse me' when I used a cuss word." He had been expelled, however, not for profanity or failure to learn, but for having been with a patrol of his friends from Fort Cobb who rode into a Kiowa trap for which it was quite generally understood—although never formally proved—he was the tender and tempting bait.

It was for this reason the Army had refused to take any action when Big Tree asked the soldiers to go after the Northern Sioux who had seized his favorite heir with an eye to fat ransom. "Good riddance!" had snapped the harassed commander to Big Tree's loud cries of Hunkpapa trespass. "Tell the Sioux I'll pay them fifty horses *not* to bring the boy back!" So, at least, ran Little Tree's story of his chief claim to reputation among his people. Ben accepted the boy's Texas-size history, wanting to get out of him other and more pertinent information—namely, what he might know of Amy Johnston. Wisely, Ben let the journey run on well toward its end before broaching this matter, figuring, meanwhile, to have won the boy completely over.

Yet when he finally asked about her, referring to her as "the white woman with the Sioux," the boy only looked at him in an odd way and said, "What white woman?"

Ben made it more explicit, wanting to know how many of the Hunkpapa squaws Little Tree had noted who had blue eyes and yellow hair?

"Oh, that white woman," said the Kiowa youth at once. "Well, there's nothing to tell of her."

"What do you mean?" said Ben, curious to learn how the boy could so easily accept the presence of a non-Indian among his haughty captors.

"Look at it this way," said Little Tree. "You know that white man who rides with the Oglalas; the one you waved to twice when we came away that night?"

"Sure, what of it?"

"Well, he's been with the Indians six months."

"What's that got to do with the woman?"

"She's been with them twenty years. More, even."

Ben nodded slowly.

"Go-deen was right then," he said. "He warned me I wouldn't find a white woman."

"You won't," promised Little Tree. "On a cloudy day

70

or across a smoky fire at night, you couldn't tell her from a Kwahadi Comanche."

"Thank you," said Ben a little wearily and got up to rake out and bury the coals of the coffee fire they had paused to build on a nameless tributary of the Salt Fork of the Arkansas River, one hundred and twenty miles north of the Washita-Canadian buffalo pasture and the home hunting ground of Sitting Bear, the Sarsi-Kiowa chief known to the white frontier as Satank.

There was some change now, an indefinable something difficult to describe but impossible to escape.

The country grew quieter with each mile. Each new sunrise was greeted with apprehension, each day's end met with gratitude. On June fifth, thirty days out from the Musselshell, they sighted the North Fork of the Canadian River. Crossing by the old Indian ford downstream of famed Gypsum Bluffs, they went on into the even greater stillness beyond.

It was a brilliant morning, bright with sunshine, keen air and the sweet songs of meadowlark and prairie quail. Yet the onus of foreboding rode with Ben as closely as the sun dance of his shadow on the short curl of the buffalo grass. After the day was only an hour gone but the silence already wearing its blunt saw cuts deeply into his taut nerves, he reined in his Sioux pony and said quietly to Little Tree, riding with him, "How far now?"

The Kiowa boy, who had been fresh and friendly as a newly minted penny all the way from Montana, suddenly looked at him as though he had never seen him before.

"*Ouchita* one more sun," he answered, blank-faced and abrupt as any adult hostile.

Ben looked at him sharply but said nothing. Go-deen, riding directly behind them, caught Ben's eye and made a sign of warning. At coffee fire an hour later, Ben got the breed aside.

"What the hell was that all about?" he asked him. "Did you hear the little devil? He froze up on me like rim ice. Last night he's chatting away like a magpie; this morning, out of the bright blue, he starts grunting like a damned blanket buck. What's it mean?"

"It means he's home. North of the Canadian he's still on enemy ground. That's Cheyenne and Arapaho country

71

up there. On this side it's pure Kiowa. The kid knows it; he feels it. Last night he's a little boy having a fine time with older men. This morning he's a Kiowa brave."

"We'll have to watch him then."

"Like a hawk. If he gets away, our hair won't be worth worrying about."

"You're not serious?"

"Not unless you'd call a Kiowa ambush serious."

"Oh, come on, Frank! This kid has been with us a whole month. We've been closer than sow bugs under a buffalo chip. We're his friends!"

"Sure we are. So were those cavalry soldiers from Fort Cobb."

Ben looked at him quickly, but Frank Go-deen was not making half-breed jokes that morning.

"By the Lord, I think you mean it," he told him.

Go-deen nodded acidly. "Don't waste time thinking," he said. "Take it for a fact."

"All right, I'll keep an eye on him. Let's get back on the trail."

"No, wait a minute, brother." Go-deen put out his hand, touching Ben on the arm. "One more thing. When he goes, shoot his pony. If you don't, I'll shoot the boy. He's our last chance now."

"What do you mean 'now'?" asked Ben uneasily.

"We've had Indians on our trail since daybreak," said Go-deen. "They're not Arapaho or Cheyenne."

Ben glanced covertly at Little Tree.

"You think he knows it?"

"No, he's looking ahead, not behind."

"What do we do then?"

"Keep going. As long as we're heading for the Washita, we're going right where they want us to go. They won't start anything till they've got us both ways, dear brother. That means front and rear."

"That means when we hit the Washita, in other words?"

"Something like that."

"Ah, consistency!" said Ben. "Thou art a jewel!"

"Do you insult me again?" growled his companion.

"No, I merely comment favorably on the even temper of your ways—always cheerful and full of hope."

"Bah! You're crazy like I always said."

72

"No," said Ben, "for a fact I'm not. Truth is I'm one hell of a lot daffier than you *ever* said; I'm going on with this crazy chase. If that don't prove it, they'll never get me committed."

"What?" said Go-deen.

"Nothing," answered Ben. "Let's brush out the embers and get along. I can't wait to see how glad Little Tree's daddy is going to be to see his boy."

They rode on, nor had Ben too long to deny his curiosity. It was not quite an hour after noon halt, the sun only beginning to wester when, five miles ahead, they made out the shadow-green line of tree growth marking a major watercourse. At once the half-breed raised his hand in the halting sign. In the bit-champing uneasiness which followed, he began uncasing his brass telescope.

12

The Loyalty of Little Tree

BETWEEN the motionless travelers and the river, the gray waves of the prairie rose, fell, rose yet again before sloping off to stream's edge. The short-grassed swales thus put across their line of approach and out of their line of sight could be hiding all the hostiles south of the Smoky Hill. Knowing this, Ben waited tensely for the breed to put down the telescope. When at last the latter had done so, he asked, low voiced:

"Now what?"

"Now," replied the other, "we get ready to shoot the kid's pony—or the kid."

"More Indian arithmetic?" inquired Ben anxiously.

"Yes. If Satank is ahead of us, he will be between us and that water yonder. You can count on it."

"That's the Washita already, you figure?"

"There's no doubt of it whatever."

"But Little Tree said one more sun."

"Well, call it a short sun," snapped Go-deen impatiently. "That's his precious *Ouchita* yonder. We've been pushing the ponies."

"All right, how do we figure to ride it from here?"

"There's no use trying to circle. Our best chance is to go right on ahead as though we smelled nothing."

"And what is it we do smell?" asked Ben.

"Kiowas," answered Go-deen. "Right over that last rise between us and the river. You want to bet, Tall Brother?"

"Not hardly. You think we ought to tie the kid? Put his pony on lead?"

"No, we got to wait for the kid to make his move. He still might stick with us. It's a hundred to one the other way."

"If he does stay by us, then the Kiowas will be friendly, though. Is that it?"

74

"Sure. They're Indians. If they think they owe you something, they'll pay it—either way."

"It's up to Little Tree then."

"Yes."

"Anything else?"

"Yes, you can't trust a Kiowa."

Ben nodded tightly. He looked back at Lame John, riding with the Kiowa boy and alerted to drop him or his pony if he made a break to get away upon sighting his relatives. Lame John caught Ben's look, nodded quickly. Ben waved to him, and they all started forward again.

Twenty minutes later they topped the first of the two rises between them and the river. The swale beyond it stood empty. Nothing moved in it. Not bird, not beast, not even breeze. Ben relaxed, sighed audibly.

"One down," he nodded to Go-deen.

The breed shrugged. "I said the last rise, not this one. Don't let your air out yet."

"Frank," said Ben, "I believe you'd ought to turn Christian. Jesus needs you for a sunbeam."

Go-deen glanced at Lame John and Little Tree, just then pulled up beside them. He ignored Ben, speaking to the Nez Percé.

"How do you feel, brother? Good, bad, in between?"

"I'm not well," answered the Nez Percé, straight-faced. "This southern air disturbs me. It's too close. I don't care for it. What do you say?"

"The same. Let all ride together from here to the river. Real near together. My people have a saying: 'When ill, don't get far from the fire.' How about your people?"

"They have a saying, too," agreed Lame John. " 'Un-happiness fattens on solitude.' " They both looked at Ben, as though expecting some confirmation from the white camp and got it.

" 'Misery loves company.' " Ben grinned. "That's the way my folks put it, and I'm not about to argue the idea. Let's stick like glue." He caught the averted eye of Little Tree and added quietly, "How says our Kiowa cousin?"

Little Tree bowed his head. Ben could see the blood come into his dark face. After a long moment of staring at his saddle horn, the Kiowa boy raised his eyes and faced Ben, his expression at once defiant and uncertain.

"I say nothing," he declared.

"You sure, kid?" asked Ben. "We been pretty good friends, you and me."

The boy's fierce gaze faltered under Ben's steady regard. He jutted his small jaw, turned his face away from the tall white man. Ben waited him out, but Little Tree only looked over the prairie and would not turn around.

"All right, Frank," Ben said at last, "let's go."

They went quickly riding down and across the swale and up the far rise—the last rise short of the Washita. It could come as no great surprise when they saw what they did beyond it, yet Ben's stomach pulled in like green rawhide in the hot sun. There were upward of fifty of the hostiles sitting their shaggy ponies across the trail where it sloped down to water. Their long buffalo lances with the dyed horsehair tassles and their unique cart-wheel war bonnets stamped them Kiowas past question. And Frank Go-deen, squinting hard at their short-bodied, big-headed chief, grunted the final identification as he gathered his reins.

"Satank," he said and threw a swift glance to their rear. Ben saw his eyes go narrow and turned hurriedly.

"Oh, that's just great," he breathed, eying the second blossoming of cart-wheel bonnets along the rise behind them. "That the bunch you spotted trailing us?"

"Yes, that's Satanta. The tall, gaudy chief on the bay paint. He's like you, a real big talker. Down here they call him the Orator of the Plains."

"Thanks. It's wonderful to have the opportunity to learn on the job."

With the curt comment, Ben fell to studying the situation, eyes darting desperately right and left. Upstream on their right, the country roughened within the mile, its piling up of sharp rocks and water-cut prairie earth, trapped with willow scrub and cottonwood saplings, making horseback escape in that direction a certain snare. To their left downstream, the land lay more open, and Ben's eyes lighted up for a moment as he saw a possible racing avenue in this parallel course. But only for a moment. As he started to point out the route to Go-deen, a third band of Kiowas pushed their ponies out of a willow grove flanking the downstream way. They held up their horses, sitting them in the same silence as Satank and Satanta, waiting for the cornered enemy to commit himself.

"Don't tell me," said Ben; "give me one guess."

"You're right," growled Go-deen. "Big Tree."

It was in that same instant, when his harsh sounding of the name was still on the breed's lips, that Little Tree cut viciously at Lame John's Appaloosa with his Kiowa quirt and drove his borrowed Sioux pony like a shot arrow down the eastern slope toward his savage father.

Lame John, fighting his nervous horse, could not fire. But Frank Go-deen, lance-scar leer set hard as Arkansas bedrock, slid out his heavy Sharps and laid its needle-eye sights in the small of the fleeing boy's back. In the instant of squeezing the trigger, Ben flung out his arm, skying the Sharps's barrel, sending the deadly lead wide and high of its mark.

"You fool!" screamed the breed. "Now what do you think you're going to do? Talk them to death?"

Before Ben could reply or even before he could think to tell himself why he had saved the traitorous Kiowa youth's life, Lame John brought his mount up beside theirs. On his handsome features they saw the play of the sober smile he saved for such precise, blind turns in the trail.

"The Nez Percé have another saying," he told them gravely, "Would you care to hear it?"

"By all means," said Ben, easing his Winchester free of its scabbard. "Philosophy's my long suit."

" 'When in doubt,' " said the young Wallowa, " 'ride for the river.' What do you think?"

Go-deen bobbed his bullethead.

"I think your people are pretty damn smart. *Hook-ahey!*"

He struck his pony with the rifle's steel-shod butt. The little brute snorted and jumped like a rabbit, bombarding down the decline in wild leaps. Behind him came the pounding mounts of Ben and Lame John. And behind them, free of lead ropes or any other encouragement to follow and stay faithful, lumbered Malachi and the old white gelding.

Even so, it was a thin charge. Its makers knew they had no better than a ten-to-one chance to wedge through Satank's line. Providing they did, they would have no remaining chance whatever of beating the angry Indians to the tangled cover of the small island in mid-river, which they now saw behind the Kiowas. This tiny sanctuary, sticking out with sore-thumb lonesomeness from its dead-level surroundings of shallow water, bank sand and buffalo grass, loomed as their one forlorn hope for a fort-up. Yet Ben was certain they would never reach it. His reaction, looking around as he saw Malachi come puffing abreast of his Sioux pony, was to laugh and yell at the old mule.

"Come on, goat-head! Last one into the water's a pea-green cow chip!"

Malachi, walling his off-color eyes, pulled ahead of the Sioux pony, passed him lurchingly by. Here was no time for histrionics. If idiots wanted to play games with the Kiowas on three sides and sharp rocks on the fourth, well that was fine for idiots. But china-eyed Montana pack mules knew better. Malachi pinned his ears, took aim on the island, let out the last notch.

He went past Frank Go-deen in a bony blur, smashed headlong into the massed Kiowa ponies. He struck their bunched line with such an iron-skulled jmpact and start-lingly hideous, brass-lunged bray, that the thin-nerved Indian mustangs shied off uncontrollably. In the grace-note of opportunity so provided, Go-deen, Ben and Lame John drove through behind him and broke free for the river.

13

"Big Bat" Pourier

THE KIOWAS, who had held their fire hoping to take the strangers alive, now began shooting to get their horses down before they might make the island in the river. In the excitement many of the shots went wild, but with so many rifles at work it was only a question of seconds before some of Ben's party took lead. And it was almost an equal certainty that none of them or their mounts would get under cover unwounded.

Ben and his friends rode hunched over the withers of their ponies, no thought of anything but getting the last ounce of speed out of the little animals. As for firing back at the closing Indians, this would have been worse than a waste of time. Go-deen and Lame John knew it consciously, Ben, instinctively. If they could make the island, of course, all odds changed. Aimed fire was another matter entirely.

The three friends drove their horses, yelling and shouting them on as wildly as the pursuing Kiowas. But a hundred yards from the riverbank Ben could see they would not make it. Satank's band, directly behind, was less than arrow shot away, a fact announced by the sudden cessation of the Indian rifle fire and the commencement of the deadly sibilant hissing of the fletched shafts past the fugitives. Ammunition on the South Plains was always too precious to burn up needlessly. Where the arrow or lance or knife or ax would work, why blow up bullets? As the thought of the meaning of the Kiowa shift to "silent fire" flashed into Ben's mind, it was confirmed by Frank Go-deen.

"They've got us!" he shouted to Ben and Lame John. "When they start using arrows, the next thing out is the scalping knife! Get ready to take a few of them with you!"

Ben and Lame John dropped their looped reins, twisted

in their saddles, brought up their Winchesters. But before either could pull a shot or Go-deen unlimber his ponderous Sharps, a steady bark of carbine fire began to cut into the Kiowas from the island ahead. Amazed, the three comrades again crouched low over their horses and sent them full gallop through the sunlit shallows of the near channel, the friendly fire continuing to stream over their heads into the close-packed Kiowas. Never of a military mind to press the attack in face of well directed resistance, the hostiles split off and pulled away from the pursuit. The fugitives splashed ashore on the sandy spit in mid-stream, spurred their mounts into its tangle of red willow and cottonwood, leaped off them and ran back to help their hidden ally hold off the red horsemen. But the action at Sand Island was over for that afternoon. This information came from a mountainous figure which now reared up from behind a fortress of flood-lodged tree limbs, as they blundered up through the brush behind him.

"Compliments, mes amis"—the bearded giant waved—"but there is no more requirement for haste. We have driven off the red devils si très bien." A white-toothed grin split the black immensity of his whiskers. He reached over and fetched Go-deen a clout on the shoulder that would have parted the withers of an ox. "François!" he bellowed. "You have grown a little something here since last we met." He whacked Go-deen across the paunch, staggering him two steps backward. "You better take it off, I think. You have nearly lost that race just now."

Go-deen rubbed his belly.

"I might have known it was you." He glowered. "Who else would be crazy enough to be down here in a war summer. I mean, beside myself."

The huge French-Canadian shrugged.

"Cherchez la 'squaw'." He smiled. "You know me, François. But you should have seen this one. Ah! What a creature!"

"Brothers," said Go-deen, turning disgustedly to Ben and Lame John, "this is the great Baptiste Pourier. He calls himself the best scout on the plains. Actually, he's not bad for a Canuck. Works for the Army when they'll trust him, which isn't very often."

Lame John limped forward.

"You are the one they call 'Big Bat'? The one the Sioux fear so much?"

"I am he," admitted Pourier. "Though why the Teton should fear me, I have never understood."

"It might have something to do with the number of them you have laid on the grass." Go-deen scowled. "Just like those damn Kiowas over there."

They all turned to look at the four bodies sprawled along the bank of the Washita, as Big Bat shrugged again.

"I never shoot an Indian unless I have to, François, you know that. Would you have me let them ride over you just now? You, an old friend of the better days?"

"Bah!" said Go-deen. "I would rather have been saved by somebody with a full brain. I already have two crazy ones on my hands, and now you make it three. I think I will go home as soon as it gets dark."

Ben stepped forward, nodding anxiously.

"I think we'd all best go somewheres as soon as it gets dark," he suggested. "It looks to me like four's a crowd for this sandspit."

"The Tall One is right," said Big Bat quickly. "What do you call yourself, *mon ami?*"

"Ben. Ben Allison."

"You claim to be a white man? With that face?"

"Far as I know," said Ben. "Which ain't far."

Big Bat put out his hand.

"Baptiste Pourier," he said. "I, too, claim to be a white man."

Ben took his hand, then introduced him to Lame John. After he had shaken hands with the Nez Percé, the giant French-Canadian scout waved them into his driftwood fort.

"Come in and sit down; we'll make a little fire. You brought some tea, of course?"

"No tea," said Go-deen. "A little coffee only."

"Coffee?" The big man's disappointment showed keenly. "I saved you—I risked my own fine hair—for *coffee? Zut!* It's no use. There are days, positively, when it is preferable not to have left the blankets. Give me the damn stuff. What a blow of fate. *Voilà tout!*"

While Big Bat laid the fire, and Ben brought the coffee can full of water, Go-deen ground the beans. Nothing was said until the water had come to a race, and the breed

81

carefully rationed in the powdered beans. Then Big Bat sat back against the riverside wall of his barricade, eying them all for a long moment before nodding.

"All right, *mes amis*, now let us talk."

Big Bat did his part of the talking first. He was down there in Kiowa country for the Army, sent from the north because he would not be so well known on the South Plains as would be the local scouts and buffalo hunters who served as the Army's eyes and ears out beyond the fringe of forts garrisoning this restless frontier below the Arkansas. A rumor had been blowing all spring that the Kiowas were working up a deal with the Comanches, their blood cousins directly south, to make the war summer a real success. These negotiations were principally suspected of the Satank group, including Satanta and Big Tree, and the Kwahadi Comanches of Quanah. This Quanah was the son of a Kwahadi chief and a white woman stolen from the Texas settlements. This latter was named Cynthia Ann Parker, the fact leading to the whites calling her red son Quanah Parker. The Indians used only his Kwahadi name, and though still young, this tall, half-white Comanche was already a chief of reputation and a fighter against the whites more dangerous than his full red tribesmen brothers. Next only to Satank, who was the more purely vicious because old and ill, Quanah was the most feared Indian on the South Plains.

Now Big Bat's job had been to drift down into Comanche country seeking to find a nomad people called the Comancheros, a half-Mexican, half-Indian band who hunted buffalo commercially for the white and Spanish-American markets in Santa Fe, Albuquerque and Taos. Finding this band, which was led by a Kwahadi-Sonora Mexican breed named Soledad Dominguin, had been a nice thing. A matter of delicate judgment. A situation of the very keenest judgment. But Baptiste Pourier had brought it off.

Having seen Dominguin and having determined from him, with the aid of the small bag of Army gold provided for the purpose, that the Comanches did indeed have thoughts of joining the Kiowas in a clean-up of the settlements from the Rio Pecos to the Panhandle, Big Bat was easing his way back toward Fort Cobb when he had, late yesterday, been caught in the middle of a considerable

Kiowa movement in the local vicinity. He had been lucky enough to avoid detection, but to do it he had been forced to turn his horse free. The animal, unshod after the Indian fashion, would attract no attention if seen riderless and with all saddle-sweat stains removed, as Big Bat had removed them, with spring water and dried buffalo grass. Big Bat himself had made it to the Washita under cover of darkness, burrowing into the brush of Sand Island to lie up and wait out the Kiowa activity.

Since the island was much too small for an Indian campsite, and since he had no horse with him to be seen or heard or smelled by either the Kiowas or their nervous mustangs, he would have been entirely safe except for the thoughtlessness of his present guests in getting themselves jumped under his very nose.

Now that all was as it was, however, why, *naturellement,* he would need to look after them. In turn, they would need to allow him this necessary privilege *sans argument.* If this arrangement was understood, he would be happy to continue giving them the benefit of his many years experience in slipping out of such warm quarters as the present ones. *N'est-ce pas?*

Ben didn't know who Nez Say-pah was or what he might have to do with their possible escape from Sand Island. He didn't even know what tribe he belonged to. In consequence, he kept quiet, always a safe bet in a strange game. Go-deen, however, who spoke some of the Canuck patois from his Milk River upbringing, replied quickly to Big Bat, *"Oui si fait,"* and urged him to please go right ahead and unburden himself of any such wisdom as was his in regard to making four friendly fellows from Montana disappear from a fifty-foot sandspit in the middle of a hundred feet of water so shallow a short cow could wade it without getting her teats wet; that water, moreover, surrounded on three sides by seventy or eighty Arkansas Kiowa Indians and on the fourth side by sharp rocks and steep gullies that would discourage a Wyoming mountain goat; and, as well, to do all this with such dispatch and lack of sound as would guarantee no great loss of life or livestock among the departers.

At this point Ben felt compelled to interrupt and restate briefly his own business along the Washita. He reasoned that it might have some bearing either on Big Bat's decisions or those of Go-deen and Lame John in response to what Big Bat was about to propose. Accordingly, he retold the Amy Johnston story for the latter, ending it with the inevitable query as to whether the new listener had, in his own travels throughout the Indian country, seen or heard anything of the missing white woman. To his delight, Big Bat's eyes struck sparks, and his gleaming teeth flashed from their dark ambush of beard.

Ah! That one! *Sacristi!* By God and damnation, yes, he had both heard and seen her! He could, as well, tell them precisely where she was at this moment. Indeed, he could lead them directly to her, had he not more pressing business—his own life—to concern him. *Zut!* That woman had a body, though! The remembering of it made a man doubtful. For anything less than his life, he might be tempted to go back with them. That body she had was better even than that of the young Kiowa squaw he knew over at Fort Cobb—the one the memory of whose gifts upon the blanket had induced him to take the Army's risky offer in the first place; the one who had told him where to find the Comancheros of Soledad Dominguin; the one who waited for him, even now, over at the fort; the one whose breasts were like the famed cantaloupes of Colorado's Rock Ford country, whose buttocks were a round mellowness more beautiful and shining than the moon's, whose soft belly was silkier and of a greater sheen than prime beaver, whose sweet thighs had the perfume of fresh prairie hay, whose movements when the moment approached were of a madness to drive—

Here Ben, plunging in manfully, succeeded in halting the full gallop of Gallic enthusiasm. He managed, also to guide the narrator of Kiowa charms back upon the wanted track of Amy Johnston. With due apology for the detour, Big Bat sobered frowningly.

Well, all right, if they insisted on knowing, here was the way it was with that poor damned once-white girl, he told them. First, it was true Satank had bought her from the Cheyenne. But the old Sarsi-Kiowa was no more a match for her on the buffalo robe than the senile Cheyenne chief before him. He had, in turn, passed her off on Soledad Dominguin who wanted her for the Apache trade: probably for the Mimbrenos of Mangas Coloradas, although Dominguin had said nothing as to that. It would be an

84

excellent guess, however, that he had meant her for them because, since the treacherous killing of old Mangas, the Mimbrenos had been wolf hungry for white prisoners. At any rate, the last Big Bat knew of her, she was camped down on the Clear Fork of the Brazos with the Comancheros of Soledad Dominguin, waiting for the New Mexican Apaches to show up and look her over for possible purchase. That was the headwaters of the Clear Fork, way, way out in the buffalo country under the shadows of Double Mountains, four days pony ride from the nearest Army post.

Reaching the end of his grim reply, the huge Army scout looked squintingly at Ben. Slowly extending his arm across the fire, he tapped him on the chest with a forefinger the size and authority of a rail-splitting wedge.

"If you, *mon ami*," he concluded, all trace of ribald banter gone from his bear's growl voice, "or any other white man have the least idea to see this unfortunate Amy Johnston while she is yet a human being, it must be in the camp of the Comancheros. Once the Apaches have taken her, there is no more to be said of her in this life. She is worse than dead. I say it in God's name; in twenty years I have not seen a woman come back from the Apaches. *Voilà tout,* that is all."

14

The Escape from Sand Island

"WE ARE ALL from the north," said Big Bat, "so which way will the Kiowas expect us to take away from this place? *Exactement,* north. So which way do we go? South, *naturellement.* Now then, consider this other matter also: *how* do they expect us to go; in what manner? But of course, you are right. They will think to find us leaving frightened and furtive as the small field mouse with the coyote waiting for him to squeak. And how shall we actually depart? That is easy: with all the noise and excitement—including the bonfire—of a Bastille Day. Have you followed me to this point, *mes amis?*"

He looked around at them, swishing the dregs in his coffee tin, black eyes snapping in the firelight. When the others had no answers, Ben spoke slowly:

"You suggesting we do just the opposite of what they expect us to do, Bat? Is that it?"

"If you do what the Indian expects," answered the other, "the Indian will do what you expect; he will take your hair. But if you do something he does not expect, especially the last thing he would dream of doing in your place, then you have him in the corner. The Indian has no intestines *pour l'imprévu.* Am I not correct, François?" He turned to Go-deen, and the latter nodded.

"That's right. If they think you're up to something, they'll hold off. They're worse than a cat for curiosity, yet will shy off like a wild horse at a piece of paper blowing." He scowled at Big Bat. "But I don't trust you on a dark night either, *canadien.* What do you have in mind?"

"We will make a big fire, burn up this whole pile of flood wood here. While we get ready our horses, we laugh and sing. The Nez Percé there, he can make a few war sounds in his own tongue. You and I will furnish some Oglala talk. When prepared to leave, we will fire the Sioux bad medicine signal into the air with all three of our

86

repeating rifles. Then we will splash right out into the water, going for the south bank and chanting a Kiowa death song which I happen to know. *Sacristi!* It ought to scare the hell out of them."

"And if it don't?" said Ben.

Big Bat grinned, spread his post-oak arms.

"If it don't, *mon ami,* then we have no problems at all: and no scalps either. *Non, c'est vrai?*"

"If you say so," grudged Ben.

"But of course. François? Any objection?"

"I'm ready; how big do you want the fire?"

"Jean, mon ami?" He turned to Lame John, putting his huge paw on the tall Nez Percé's shoulder. "What do you say? Are you angry for what I have claimed of your people; that they will fight a grizzly bear and flee from a strange shadow on a windy night?"

"What you say is true, brother. The truth should not anger a man. I'll get the horses up."

"C'est tres bien; brothers—" He turned to Ben and Go-deen, seizing up a cottonwood log as big as a man's body in the action and throwing it atop the drift jam of their fort. "Let us labor in the name of *Le Bon Dieu;* or at least in the name of Baptiste Pourier. Come, help me burn the island down." He scooped up another tree limb, tossing it after the first. "Now as we work," he said, "we sing. Very softly at first, while you learn the words. *Allons!* Follow after me pianissimo in the key of middle C. Are you ready? So. To the death song of the Sarsi Kiowas:

> *Iha hyo oya iya iya o iha yaya yoyo,*
> *Aheya aheya yaheyo ya eye heyo eheyo . . ."*

Ben, looking at Go-deen, said awkwardly, "Frank, I feel silly as hell."

The breed shrugged unsympathetically, suggesting that under the circumstances he could well afford to look or feel a little foolish. Ben could see the point.

"True," he admitted; "true as the bore of Old Betsy," and with the agreement fell to singing and pitching on firewood as fervently as any fresh Christian. Directly, they had the pile large enough to suit Big Bat.

"Enough," announced the latter. "Who has the matches? I left mine with my saddle. I knew I would be lighting no fires before Fort Cobb. Now see how wrong I was!"

Ben gave him the matches, just as Lame John shadowed up through the brush with their mounts. Big Bat lighted the pile, fanned it furiously with his wide, flat-crowned hat. In seconds the bone-dry driftwood was licking hungrily at itself, within a minute had caught deep and was beginning to explode showers of fat sparks. By the time Ben had the coffee tins stowed in Malachi's packsaddle and Go-deen had scrambled up on his old white bareback, giving over his saddled Sioux pony to Big Bat, the fire was roaring in flames fifteen feet high.

"Voilà tout," said Big Bat, swinging aboard. "Let us sing once more. Everyone. After me. Fortissimo!"

With the order, he sent the Sioux pony splashing into the south channel of the Washita, his companions strung behind him, his bull's baritone leading the chorus in its dissonant rendition of the death chant. With the wild light of the burning island glaring behind them and the bellow of Big Bat's voice guiding them from in front, Ben and his friends made a weirdly impressive exit. The five signal shots of the Sioux bad medicine sign fired in slow-tolled unison from the three repeaters they possessed, as their mounts walked under close rein through the waters of the flame-lit Washita, would have puzzled less simple minds than those of Satank's rudely awakened braves. Satanta made a brief speech about the differences in men and squaws as to the iron in the heart, but he was heading for his own horse while he talked and when he got on him made no move to send him farther than the nearest rise from which he could get a good view of the strange exodus from Sand Island. Big Tree had already gone home to show Little Tree to his long-sorrowing mother. Moreover, it was clear to all or any reasonable Kiowa minds that the four northerners moving off through the night singing the Sarsi death song and walking—not running or loping—their mounts were all bereft as black loons. Accordingly, when old Ten Bears, seventy that past summer and secretly a friend of the white man, suggested that they had won enough in getting back the boy and that, further, the four fools yonder were bound right straight into Kwahadi country, the remaining braves were prone to agree and to go back to their blankets.

By morning Big Bat, having found and retrieved his cached saddle enroute, had brought his three companions to the agreed point of *au revoir et bon voyage*. This was the beginning of the Double Mountains buffalo trail, forty miles through rough Washita Hills from Sand Island. Here he was to take Go-deen's Sioux pony in payment for his services and depart on his own way back to Fort Cobb. Ben and his comrades were to continue on to Double Mountains and the camp of Soledad Dominguin.

Over their last coffee fire together, the giant French-Canadian took a stick and began to draw in the fireside earth the lay of the Double Mountains trail for the three "crazy ones." Three times he cursed and threw away the stick, selecting a new one which possibly might better enable him to delineate the faint track they must follow to find the Comancheros. Midway through the fourth drawing he growled, *"Bois de vache!"* the Canuck equivalent of "Cow dung!" and jammed the stick into the prairie loam with a helpless Gallic palming of his great hands.

"I cannot do it," he admitted unhappily. "Get on your damn horses; I am going with you."

15

Beyond the Brazos

MOVING CAREFULLY as they must, looking out to fore and aft and both sides all the while, it was a week's tense work getting to the headwaters of the Clear Fork of the Brazos. This was Comanche Country. The dread *Tshaoh,* the Enemy People, as the Sioux called them, were to be avoided, warned Big Bat, as was syphilis or smallpox. The Comanches were swift, sure death to all alien Indians, a slower but not less certain end to all adult white males. The Kwahadi, and particularly this damned Quanah, were the elite of the *Tshaoh* killer pack. If their eternal vigilance against the empty space surrounding them were to be relaxed for the one hour, or one minute, which it took the Kwahadi to detect them marching through their buffalo pastures, then they all might far better have flung their guns in the Washita and pleaded Christian mercy of Satank.

As it proved out, Big Bat brought them in off the endless ocean of prairie with sundown of the seventh day, barely two miles downstream of the target landmarks of Double Mountain. They had not seen a Kiowa or Comanche feather in the whole distance, not even at the heavily Indian-traveled Cashe Creek crossing of Red River—a remarkable feat of plains navigation on the part of Baptiste Pourier.

Ben was not slow with his praise for this seemingly impossible feat, but Big Bat waved him down frowningly.

"Mon petit," he explained, "any child of the prairie can play a week of Kwahadi hide-and-seek. Until we have back the woman, we have accomplished nothing. I suggest you save the flattery for Soledad Dominguin. His Mexican side may be lulled by it long enough for us to put a gun in his belly and strike a bargain."

Ben studied him a moment, looked around then at the

90

others. They said nothing. He turned back to Big Bat, sunburned squint deepening.

"It's your fandango." He nodded. "We'll dance it your way."

Big Bat's white teeth flashed.

"That way will be across the river here at this point, then up the other side, *tres attentivement,* to the fires of the market hunters. When we have arrived there, you will do exactly as I say. Otherwise, I can wait here and allow you to make you own moves. The Comancheros ordinarily are a timid people, smiling out of both sides of the face, the one to the Indians, the other to the Americans. But this Dominguin carries bad blood on his red side. He is little more popular with the other Comancheros than with the Americans and even the Mexicans who call themselves Spanish-Americans in self-defense. Soledad is more a bandit than a buffalo hunter. The Army tells me they have a price on his head, so you see we are not dealing with simple, native people here."

"This Soledad is a killer, eh?" said Ben. "A real *hombre duro.*" He did not know from whence the Spanish phrase had popped into his mind but said it as naturally as the English words before it.

"Worse than that, *mon ami.* He is a trader in the human flesh, standing between the settlements and the wild tribes which make use of white women, either as slaves or concubines or, in the general case, both. This is why the Army wants him, but of course they will never capture him." Big Bat palmed his hands. "Does one catch a puff of smoke with a cavalry patrol? Or execute a shadow with a company of riflemen? Ah, no, *mes amis*"— he included the others with the second palm lift— "Soledad Dominguin is in no danger, but *très* dangerous. So I will do the talking. *Etes-vous d'accord?*"

Frank Go-deen entered the discussion with a twist of his lance scar and a return of the hand gesture.

"Having come this far, the choice is about as attractive as a Mandan squaw. We agree."

Big Bat nodded, looked at Ben. He pointed to the .44 Colt on the latter's thigh.

"You wear that gun where it can be used *promptement.* Is that the fact?"

Ben was standing three-quarters facing the giant French-

Canadian when asked the question. He didn't seem to move, but Big Bat grunted and pulled in his belly, looking down toward it in amazement. It was nothing less than natural that he should do so, for there is something compelling about the rifle-sized bore of a .44 Colt. Particularly when it is buried to the front sight blade in a man's navel. Big Bat's beard split once more to the gleam of his beautiful teeth.

"It is the fact," he said. "Now please to put it away, until I give you the sign in the camp of the Comancheros."

"What?" said Ben, holstering the Colt with a puzzled look. "What sign?"

"The one I will give you when it appears we are not going to proceed around Soledad's Mexican side. That is to say when we have run out of time, and I have run out of talk."

"If it's a matter of talk," broke in Go-deen, "let Brother Ben handle it. I am thinking to make a match with him and this Satanta to see who is the real Orator of the Plains. The Tall Brother is a tall talker, Bat. You can't hope to beat him. I recall one time when he and I were scouting the village of old Crowheart up in the Wind River country. It was late afternoon and—"

His recounting of the adventure was shut off by the fact of Big Bat reaching over and picking him up bodily and clamping a hand the size of a haunch of venison over his mouth.

"François," he was reminded gently, "in your advancing years you grow forgetful. It is I, Baptiste Pourier, remember? I know you like a brother. If there is to be any contest with Satanta to determine who blows the longest wind, then it will not be Petit Ben that we enter. *N'est-ce pas, mon frere?*"

Furious, but not feeble-minded enough to mention it, Go-deen was set back upon his feet. Big Bat turned again to Ben.

"The sign in the camp of the Comancheros will be when I shrug and say to Soledad, 'Well, *mon ami,* if you will not listen to reason, we may as well say no more.' I will then turn away from him, and in that instant of the turning, when his attention is upon my back, you will place the pistol in his *estomac* precisely as you have just

92

done for me. François," he put a mollifying arm about the injured half-breed's shoulders, "when Petit Ben places the pistol, you are to be in the rear of Soledad. As he pulls in from the bite of the gun barrel in front, you are to greet him with the touch of the knife blade in the kidneys. Is it not simple?"

Ben and Go-deen looked at him, the former the first to recover.

"There is just one question which comes to mind somewhat naturally," he said. "What are Soledad's friends going to be doing all this time?"

Big Bat pulled from his saddle scabbard the little brass-framed Henry carbine with which he had greeted the Kiowas back on the Washita. He patted the yellow metal of its receiver lovingly.

"You remember this small one?" he asked. "She talks faster than François. Sixteen times, as quick as one can work the lever. She will be looking at Soledad's friends while you and François have flanked their leader. Those Comancheros know this gun. They say the same thing of it as the Sioux; that you load it upon Sunday and shoot it all week. Enough? You are satisfied?"

"Oh, completely," said Ben with a wry grimace. "What more could a man ask."

"*Joli!* Let us then proceed with the business."

They had been standing, afoot, at the ford, letting the horses drink and stretching their own weary limbs. Now they climbed back into their saddles, Big Bat leading the way over the crossing, Go-deen next, Ben, Lame John and old Malachi bringing up the rear. As they came out the far side and swung to the right upriver, Ben turned to Lame John.

"Well, brother," he asked, "you still want to find Amy Johnston as bad as you did back of those rocks up by Judith Gap?"

"Worse, Brother Ben," replied the tall Nez Percé. "The thought of her has ridden with me like war medicine, growing stronger with each mile that we draw nearer to her. I told you she was in my heart."

"How about her?" said Ben. "You think you're in her heart?"

"I don't know. We never talked."

Ben looked at him, startled.

"You mean to tell me," he said incredulously, "that you two never said a thing to each other?"

"Not a word, brother."

"And you mean to tell me you come all this way, run all this risk, for a woman you never even talked to?"

"I *saw* her, brother."

"She's that much to look at?"

"We all see with different eyes."

"Could be; seems to me, though, that you've come a powerful long ways on just one look."

Lame John shook his head, that hint of almost sadness Ben knew so well by this time invading his dark features. He reached out through the gathering dusk and placed his hand gently on Ben's shoulder.

"If the first shaft pierce the heart," he asked, "how many more arrows are required to kill?"

Ben, not able to say anything, said nothing. Both men rode on into the night. Perhaps they rode a little closer together than before, though. It was hard to say in the deepening shadows of first starlight.

16

Soledad Dominguin

THEY CAME into the camp of the Comancheros as the fat hump ribs, juicy tenderloins, rich tongues and tasty livers of the nomads' evening meal were being pulled from the broiling spits. After only a fleeting moment of uncertainty, during which their surprised host exchanged his discovery snarl for a bowing grin as white-toothed and overwhelming as Big Bat Pourier's, Dominguin bade them dismount and be welcome to a share in the feast. Ben, his eyes sweeping the camp behind those of Big Bat, saw nothing of the white woman. Wondering if they were once more too late, he watched Big Bat to see how he should play his own reaction to the invitation.

The French-Canadian appeared no whit concerned over the patent absence of Amy Johnston. Stepping down off his Sioux pony, he returned the Comanchero's smile tooth for tooth.

"*Mon ami*, we are honored!" he boomed. "We have come far to talk a little business, but that will wait." He turned to Ben and the others. "Come, I want you to meet Soledad; he's the most important man in this country."

Getting off his pony, Ben had time to tell himself that such adventurous spirits as Frank Go-deen and Baptiste Pourier required many talents to stay alive in the high plains. It wasn't just a simple matter of being a good shot, quick with a knife or having the constitution of a grizzly bear. A man had to have the morals of a stray dog, the cunning of a coyote and the guts of a government mule as well. Going toward the swarthy Comanchero, he suddenly got a better angle at the latter's face in the nearer glare of the fire. When he did, he wanted to pull back the hand he had just extended. But it was too late.

"This is Mr. Ben Allison," Big Bat was saying. "He is the one who has the business with you."

Soledad took his hand, and Ben felt as though he had

just picked up a live cottonmouth. He stood holding on, afraid to let go, afraid not to. The Comanchero had no such compunctions. He wrung Ben's hand heartily, flashed his fine smile again, swept a gracious arm toward the seat at fireside which he had vacated to greet them.

"*Señor* Allison, please to take my place by the fire. A matter of business is always a matter of pleasure with Dominguin." He pointed to the various spits propped in the ground before them. "What will you have, *señor?*"

"Some of the ribs," nodded Ben, sitting down uneasily.

Dominguin pulled a stick with six hump ribs impaled upon it—approximately four pounds of meat—and handed it to his guest of honor. To the others he waved a general invitation to be seated and advised them to choose what they would and eat well. No more was said for twenty minutes, while the famished travelers wolfed down their first fresh meat in over a week. The other Comancheros watched them from other fires, the women and children seeming particularly curious and friendly in their regard. The men appeared nervous or at least more reticent to stare than their mates or offspring. The four tough-looking hunters who had been with Dominguin when they rode up had drifted off to dine elsewhere and were now nowhere to be seen. Such was the sauce of hunger, however, that Ben, Lame John and Go-deen thought nothing of these missing henchmen, murderous looking as they had been at casual glance. Big Bat, just as famished but more familiar with the situation, kept his shoe-button eyes busy while his great teeth tore at the foot-long chunk of fat loin meat he had selected.

Ben, first pangs of the need for fresh meat dulled by five minutes of silent wolfing, would have liked the time to study the Comanchero camp. From what he could see of its endless strings of drying buffalo jerky, its quaint old Spanish wooden-wheeled *carretas*, narrow-bedded oxcarts for the hauling of meat and camp gear, its Arab-style desert tents, tethered buffalo-running horses, *caballada* or *remuda* of pack mules, its hordes of yapping, spotted mongrels and, above all, the raffishly attired Comancheros themselves in their part Indian, part Spanish, part American cowboy garb. The *campo* of these colorful half-breed buffalo hunters would have been worth a full day of friendly investigation.

96

Such time and temper was not to be given, however.

When Dominguin had gorged himself and inquired of his guests as to their state of satiety, he clapped his hands and a dark-skinned woman, looking for all the world like a gypsy hag from a Romany caravan, came from the outer darkness with earthen mugs and a great, steaming pottery urn of roast chicory beans and Mexican coffee. The mugs poured full, the woman asked in Spanish if any of the Senores would care for *leche* in their beverage?

To his complete surprise, Ben found himself replying in the same tongue and with equal fluency:

"Por favor, señora; un poco, no más."

The hag seemed pleased with his ability in the tongue and went off into the darkness to return with a potbellied mustang mare towed on a frayed tether. The mare was sided by a suckling colt which squealed and bit at the Comanchero woman, as she milked the mare directly into the hot mug taken, before he could object, from Ben's hand.

A bit rattled but up to the occasion, Ben took the cup back, raised it gallantly to the seamy harridan.

"Yo saludo usted," he smiled. *"A su hermosura, mocedad y prudencia."*

The old woman cackled like a stew-pot hen who had laid an egg just in time to avoid the ax. She slapped Ben on the back with one bony hand, stabbed the crooked forefinger of the other member into Dominguin's chest.

"You hear him?" she said in Spanish. "That's a goddam good man there. You take care of him. You hear me, *hijo*?"

"Madre mío," said Dominguin, "you get the hell away from here and keep your mouth closed. Do *you* hear me?"

"Bah!" snorted the elder witch, who Ben was left to guess was the mother of the Comanchero chief. "You don't frighten me, Soledad. Mind what I say. I mean it."

With that she was gone into the night again, and Dominguin was smiling and lifting his shoulders in apology.

"When they get so old," he explained, "they say foolish things. In her day she was something, though. When I was small, I have seen her peel and flesh seventeen skins, daylight to dark. *Ay de mí*. It is different these times. You can't find a woman to do five hides, and then they

leave more meat on the skin than they do on the skeleton.
Mierda!"

With the curse, he spit into the fire, laughed good-
naturedly, turned back to Ben with his bright smile.

"*Mil pardones, señor.*" He gestured humbly, dropping
his dark eyes a moment, softening the smile almost to
shyness. "It is a rough life out here. We forget our training. Our good manners escape us. Forgive me the over-
sight. There was a matter of business with Dominguin I
think you said?"

"Yes," said Ben. "Is it all right if we talk in English?"

"If you will," agreed the other. "Though your Spanish
is better than mine. Where did you get it, *señor?* I am
curious to know."

"So am I," said Ben. "Up to tonight I didn't know I
could speak a word of it. But then there's a lot of things I
don't know about myself. That's one reason I'm down
here in this south country—looking for answers."

"Ah, yes." Ben was aware now that Dominguin's eyes
had the flat glitter of a snake's. He hadn't noticed it
before, and it made him suddenly edgy. "Well," continued
the Comanchero, "what answers are you looking for,
señor? That is to say that you believe Dominguin can
help you to find? I am waiting, but don't hurry yourself.
There's time."

Suddenly Ben felt the short hairs at the nape of his
neck begin to rise. He knew they were behind him then
but had to look to make sure. He reached as though to
put his emptied mug upon the flat stone by the fire, the
movement allowing him the imperceptible, eye-corner
glance he needed. He straightened, looking across the fire
at Big Bat. The latter jogged his beard a quarter inch in
the affirmative, his black eyes staring at Soledad Dominguin as he answered for Ben.

"*Oui, mon ami*, you are right there is time. But let's
don't waste it talking to those who do not carry the gold.
Am I not right, Soledad, *mon frère?*"

"You have gold, Big One?"

"Oh, come now. Was it some other Comanchero I gave
the other bag to last week?"

"You have *more* gold then?"

"All that is needed. Shall we talk?"

Dominguin spread his hands. And his lizard's gaping smile. His warmth would have melted buffalo butter.

"Gold always talks. What do you want?"

"The woman," said Big Bat Pourier. "The one you stole from Satank for eight spotted horses."

Dominguin's smile died stillborn.

Behind him his four returned lieutenants closed a soundless step. They were so near Ben now that he could smell the rank odor of buffalo offal and dried slaughter blood on their filthy buckskins.

"It is most unfortunate," declared Soledad Dominguin, "that you have said what you have said."

The silence set in.

Ben felt that his tensed muscles must crack. He saw Go-deen and Lame John look at him for a sign and knew that they would follow where he would lead. Moreover, he knew the lead was his; the others, after prairie protocol, had leaned their rifles against the nearest *carreta* before squatting to the fire. He wore the only weapon.

Across the fire, Big Bat was watching Soledad Dominguin.

"I have asked about the woman," he said carefully. "Why do you say that this is unfortunate, *Frère* Soledad? Has she died? Have you let her get away? Have you already given delivery of her"

Dominguin's features thawed a little.

"Oh, no, none of these things."

"What then?"

"I have given my word."

"On what agreement?"

"A matter of my own arrangement."

"You will not tell us about the woman then?"

"What is there to tell?"

"What you have done with her. You know we carry gold to buy. Now I will reveal to you another power we hold."

"Oh?" Dominguin glanced around at his four ruffians. "I see my power, but I do not see yours. Where is it?"

Big Bat pointed to the north.

"At Fort Cobb. The Army has commissioned me to tell you that if you do not deliver the woman to us, they will send a hundred soldiers down here and shoot out the buffalo in this one summer. They will make a shambles,

99

an abattoir, of the South Plains. Now, *mon chèr*, how does that sound for power?"

Ben could see that Dominguin felt the thrust of the blade. Apparently the threat to destroy the hunting from which his people made their livelihood was more of a practical menace than any personal fears he might hold for his own head.

"*Malo*," he said to Big Bat, "*muy malo*."

"But of course." The huge scout shrugged. "Now what about the woman?"

"What about the gold?"

"I have the gold."

"I want to see it."

"I want to see the woman."

The silence returned. During it the four shadows behind Dominguin separated at a lift of his hand. Two moved out to flank the fire, giving themselves a line to shoot clear of Ben. The third stayed behind Ben. The fourth glided completely around the fire, to the *carreta*. Picking up the leaning rifles of Go-deen, Big Bat and Lame John, he dropped them one by one over the sideboards into the empty bed of the buffalo wagon. The muffled, metallic *thunking* of their hidden falls seemed to Ben to put Fort Cobb farther away than the hinder surface of the moon. Dominguin's grin returned for the first time in three minutes.

"You still want to see the woman?" he said.

For answer Big Bat reached inside his elkskin jacket. He reached with exquisite care and slowness, and the bandit Comanchero leaned forward with intent, sudden interest. When the hand came forth again, Ben's eyes went as wide as Soledad Dominguin's. The leather poke, even in Big Bat's enormous paw, looked swollen enough to hold a queen's ransom. Big Bat held it by the rawhide strings, letting its weight sway like the pendulum of some invisible clock ticking off the moments of wordless greed in the Comanchero's slitted eyes.

Ben swore to himself in soundless admiration. He had not dreamed that Pourier had the gold to back his boast about the Army. It had seemed like the most undressed sort of a cold-deck bluff. Obviously Dominguin had read it the same way. Now the entire temper of the matter

100

altered abruptly. The bandit chief's smile almost set his mustache afire.

"With old friends," he laughed, "one always enjoys a little joke before getting down to the agreement." He turned to Ben, waving the gunman behind him to step back. "*No es verdad, patrón?*" he asked unctuously.

"*Sí, hombre,*" replied Ben, unwarmed. "*A dónde está la mujer?*"

Dominguin laughed again, rattled off an order to the man by the *carreta*. The latter went off into the dark, returned moments later leading by the hand a slim, graceful Indian woman in the soiled camp dress of an Oglala squaw. It was only when she had come into the full firelight and raised her bowed head to stare at the four strangers that they saw her eyes were a startling cornflower blue, her waist-long braids a dull gleaming copper-gold.

"*Amy Johnston—*" breathed Ben. "*My God.*"

None of the others said anything.

17

Lost Sister

THE WOMAN, girl really—looking more seventeen than twenty-four—was an eyeful. Big Bat had not exaggerated her form but had neglected to mention her face. It was striking. Dark as Mexican saddle leather, angular and beautifully drawn, with oblique eye-set and straight, full mouth, it was a face to both haunt a man's memory and hold his heart still at first sight.

Ben could only look after his involuntary gasp of recognition. In turn, the captive studied each of the newcomers with her cornered-animal stare, searching to find among their number a friend. Big Bat she had seen before. She lingered on him only long enough to catch and seek into his snapping eyes. Go-deen she dismissed in passing as though she sensed he was not present in her account. Moving to Ben, her gaze hesitated. He felt the long, deep probe of her regard and stood tongue-tied under it. He wanted to speak out but could not. The girl appeared to wait for him a hopeful moment; then when he said nothing and made no sign, her glance dropped, shifted hesitantly to Lame John. There was an instant's doubtful peering, then Ben saw the anxious, brilliantly blue eyes come alive. As they did, the tall Nez Percé youth stepped forward to stand in front of her.

For perhaps the drawing of three breaths neither of them moved. Then Lame John reached and took her right hand in both his. Carrying it to his breast, he placed and pressed its palm over his heart. Then, stepping back, he signed to her in the Plains language.

"We are your friends; we have come to take you home." He pointed to Ben. "This tall one is of your own people. He has come from your true father, who is still alive. Will you listen to his story? He wants to tell you who you are and why you must come back with us."

The girl looked from him to Soledad Dominguin. Dom-

102

inguin shrugged his consent. Big Bat, voice rumbling deep with feeling, added his encouragement. Ben, eyes unable to leave the wild-thing compellingness which marked each movement of her body, each expression of her slender face, made the signs which told her that Lame John spoke the truth. Even Frank Go-deen, that Milk River man of few words and no sentiments, as he saw it, offered to break his well-known rule of golden silence long enough to serve as interpreter in the matter of conveying the Tall Brother's story of her true birth. Since he alone of those present spoke her Shoshoni tongue, it was the least he could do, and despite his dislike of long talking, he would be happy enough to do it for her, his lost white sister.

Hearing Go-deen speak in Shoshoni brought a second light to her averted face. Replying to Go-deen but staring straight at Ben, she murmured in a voice as guttural as any Wind River woman's.

"My ears are uncovered; I will listen to the half-blood brother."

Go-deen told the story with unusual astringency. And speed, too. It was clear he wanted to get it done with and be gone from the Comanchero camp. Throughout the recounting—well presented, if somewhat short—the listening captive remained impassive. From time to time she would nod, from time to time shake her head. When the breed had concluded with a rather eloquent brief for the dangers risked by Ben to bring her back to the love of her aging white father, Ben received his second jolt of the evening. Still looking at him, she barked a quick string of Shoshoni at Go-deen, motioning finally to herself, then to Ben, the first of the terminal gestures proud and defiant, the second—to Ben—cold-faced and disdainful.

When she dropped her moving hands, she stood, head down, as she had before, her expression returned to its original blankly hopeless stare.

"Do you want to know what she said?" asked Frank Go-deen in the lengthening silence.

"Yes," said Ben, "every word of it."

"It's not good."

"For God's sake," said Ben, "tell it."

"All right. She said to tell the Tall One that he lies. She has no white father. She is Shoshoni. Suckled on a Horse Creek squaw, weaned on a stolen Sioux pony. She says she is the daughter of Crowheart and the Milk River woman, Magpie. She says to say to you that she is *Shacun*, Indian woman; you are *Wasicun*, white man." Go-deen made the cutting-off motion with his right hand. "She says to tell you, 'that's all'; that she is already *katela*."

"*Katela?*"

"Yes, dead or fallen."

Ben looked over at Big Bat Pourier.

"She knows about the Apaches," he said.

"*Oui*, it would seem so." He waved to Go-deen. "Tell her not to worry about the Mimbreno of Red Sleeves. We have the gold to buy her first. Tell her we must hurry, though, to be gone before the Apaches arrive to make their offer."

As Go-deen nodded and began to apprise the captive of what had been said, Soledad Dominguin got up slowly from the fire. Instinctively, Ben followed him up.

"It would seem," said the Comanchero, "that you do not understand the situation. It is no longer a matter of who comes first with the price."

"What do you mean?" rasped Big Bat, heaving up like a buffalo, rump first, to stand glaring across the fire.

"Very simple." Dominguin shrugged. "The Apaches have already been here."

Ben's stomach shrank, as Big Bat said softly, "You didn't sell her to those *fils de chiennes*, Soledad? Be very careful with your reply."

In the instant Dominguin's face went blank.

"*She is sold*," he said.

There was a heartbeat of dead stillness before Lame John struck like a red wolf for his throat.

18

Mark of the Water Horse

As LAME JOHN'S BODY hurtled across the fire, Ben leaped back and drew the .44. But he could not fire before the Nez Percé had struck Dominguin, and then he dared not. He thought of the murderous lieutenant standing behind him and whirled to get him down. Again he was too late. Midway through his turn, the snarling bandit slashed him across the skull with the barrel of his rifle, and Ben went down as though every bone in his body were dissolved.

Big Bat, roaring like a buffalo in rut, charged the *carreta* and its armed guard. The latter fired directly into his face. Big Bat bellowed, staggered, pawed at the spurt of blood from the bullet crease above his eyes. Blinded, he crashed into the side of the *carreta*, spun off it, lost consciousness. He fell with the earth-jarring force of a giant pine and lay, as Ben had, where he struck and without moving.

Frank Go-deen did not move except to elevate his hands and loudly call out his neutrality. His plea was honored for the reason that Dominguin's four lieutenants were all leaping to rescue their desperately struggling chief. In the golden opportunity thus provided, the Milk River breed sat down at the fire and reached hurriedly for a buffalo rib and refill of his coffee mug, in the act claiming the age-old immunity granted by all nomad peoples to those partaking of their bread.

Dominguin, meanwhile and inadvertently, was saving Lame John's life. The converging lieutenants, because of the snake-like threshing and coiling of the combatants, could not shoot the Nez Percé without endangering their leader. Accordingly, they pulled the battlers apart by the hind legs as they would have two fighting dogs. Then with methodical viciousness they rifle-butted Lame John into a human pulp. In the space of time required for Go-deen to reseat himself and pour his cup, the Comanchero *jefe* and his winded aides stood panting above their bloodied victims. Seeing but three bodies upon the ground, their narrowed looks leaped at once to find the fourth. When these ranging glances swept to Go-deen, the breed elevated his palms and gestured helplessly.

"What would you have me do, my brothers? I am here only in the capacity of a paid guide. I am of the half blood, the same as yourselves. Could I fight my own blood? Never. So here you see me, a man of peace, sharing your fire and your fellowship. *Also your food,*" he reminded hastily, as two of the lieutenants started toward him with lifting rifles. He raised the coffee mug hurriedly. "To your health, gentlemen! And my own—"

He put coffee to lips, kept it there, his tiny eyes watching over the pottery rim of the container. Looking at him disgustedly, Dominguin snapped at the two aides to put down their guns and take the Apaches' woman away.

"Get this offal out of sight before the Mimbrenos come," he ordered the other two, pointing to the bodies on the ground. "Tie their hands and throw them in the *carreta*. Better put in gags, too. I don't want any noise when I am delivering to the Apaches. Cover them up with some of those green robes. I will take care of this fool at the fire. *Andale!*"

The four lieutenants jumped to his commands, the two leading the girl back across camp, the other pair scooping up Ben and his companions, dumping them into the empty *carreta* and starting to whip ropes and gags into place.

At the fire Dominguin squatted down again, refilled his own cup. Go-deen gave him his very best twist of the old lance scar, raising his own cup again.

"Your health," he repeated hopefully.

Soledad Dominguin stared through him.

"You said that already," he informed him unblinkingly.

"Oh, I did? Well, you will excuse it, brother. My memory grows short."

"Your future, too."

"What is that, cousin?"

"You heard me, *Gordo.*"

"What? Me, fat? You joke, of course!"

"Of course," said Dominguin blankly. "I'm known for my good nature."

106

Go-deen swallowed with some obvious difficulty.

"You're not going to kill me, Cousin Soledad? Maybe those two Wasicuns and that Slit Nose in the cart, but me, Frank Go-deen, your own flesh and blood? I'll never believe it!"

Dominguin continued to regard him with his unhooded stare. Finally, he nodded as though with a decision.

"I'm a business man, *Gordo*. Why should I kill you or your friends when I can sell you?"

"My God!" gasped Go-deen, shocked out of his perspiring pose. "You wouldn't trade us to the Apaches with that poor white squaw over yonder? *Wagh!*"

Dominguin smiled, shook his head, somehow managing to do so without altering his reptilian stare.

"No, I wouldn't do a heartless thing like that. Not with a brother of the mixed blood. But I do have some other sources which will occasionally pay a pony or two for good healthy captives. I mean whites, naturally. As for the Slit Nose, I may have to throw him in for good will. It doesn't hurt to be generous now and again; good for business in my trade, as a matter of fact."

"Brother," sighed Go-deen, "God bless you. For a minute, there, I thought we were going to the Apaches for sure!"

"No," said Soledad Dominguin, blinking at last. "I could never be guilty of such a dreadful thing. You are going to the *Comanches*."

When Ben regained consciousness, the moon was straight overhead, and by the set of the stars he was jolting due south in the *carreta* of Dominguin. On one side of him lay, or rather huddled, Big Bat Pourier, while Lame John hunched miserably on the other side. At the head of the cart sat Frank Go-deen, hands free but ankles collared by the same type of ancient Spanish leg irons which the Comancheros had had fastened upon Amy Johnston. The cart was half full of stinking green buffalo hides; the night was hot, the quarters close. Ben almost fainted from the fetid odor of rancid fat and rotting meat before his head was well cleared. But Go-deen reached over and hauled him up to a half-sitting position against the sideboards, and Big Bat growled for him not, in God's name, to lose consciousness again as he was hungering to hear a white

107

voice. The thrice-damned François had been too busy whining for mercy of Dominguin every time the latter rode by, and the heathen Nez Percé hadn't been able to say an understandable word in any tongue since coming to. Therefore, please, for the love of the good Christ, would not Petit Ben say something cheerful? Or even dismal? Anything at all. The immediate present sound of a friendly fellow Christian's voice was of more importance to Baptiste Pourier than the possibility of his next breath being cut off. How else could a white man feel in view of what Dominguin and his *enfant naturel* had done with the woman and planned to do with them?

"My God!" cried Ben, sitting straight up. "The girl! What did they—" He broke off, looking at Big Bat. "By God, they didn't!" he said.

"But they did, *mon ami*," answered the other. "François tells me it was directly after Dominguin and his small playmates put us all to sleep."

"Oh, Jesus," groaned Ben. "The poor thing."

"She's gone," rasped Go-deen. "Forget her. There's no use even thinking of her any more. But we had better do a little thinking of ourselves—Dominguin is going to sell us to the Kwahadi."

Ben looked at him, shivering, but would not believe it.

"No! what the hell good would we be to them?" he said. "It don't make sense. They ain't after men prisoners."

"Well," explained Go-deen, "it depends upon what a man means by sense. Now what the Kwahadi mean by the word is one thing, and what we—but then it's no matter; we'll learn soon enough. Why hurry it?"

"They will buy us to torture," said Big Bat. "They won't pay much, but anything is a profit for Dominguin after tonight's disappointments."

"What are you talking about?" Ben scowled irritably. His head hurt something fierce, and his mood was for anything but long trips around the spring looking for water.

"About showing some small gain in spite of great loss," shrugged Big Bat. "You see, the Apaches came back and cut the agreed price in half. They said Soledad could take it or not, as might please his fancy. *Naturellement*, he took it. The alternative was even less attractive; they would

108

have wiped out the whole camp, beginning with him and his four vultures."

"That's hard to believe." Ben frowned. "From what I know of Indians, their word is as good as the next man's money. It ain't like them to double-cross anybody."

Go-deen grunted unhappily.

"The claim they made was that Dominguin did the double-crossing, not them. They said they bargained for a pure white woman, and he delivered them a damned *mestiza*, a mixed blood. They said she didn't even look half white but that they were honest men and would give half a price for her. This was because of her extra fine body and the fact she looked strong and was not afraid when they examined her. They said Mano Roto—that's Broken Hand, the Mimbreno who wants her—likes his women tough and mean as cats in heat. They thought your Amy Johnston had that look about her. So they took her."

"Yes, and that," continued Big Bat, grinning as hugely as though he had just heard the Seventh Cavalry Band playing "Garry Owen" over the near hill, "brings us to *la pièce de résistance;* a natural child of my own genius. *Voilà tout!* It was wonderful, simply wonderful!"

"No doubt of that," grudged Ben, holding his injured head as the cart jolted bangingly across a prairie dog town. "But tell me about it anyhow; I'm already as sick as I can get."

"But of course it was the poke of gold, *mon ami*, the money which I provided to offer for the good woman's life. You see, I awoke in time to witness the weighing of its precious contents."

"Somehow, Bat, it don't depress me you losing your poke at this stage of the game. Weighed against all the good we done poor Amy Johnston, it might as well have been six pounds of wet sand."

"*Oui!* Almost to the ounce, *mon cher! Sacristi!* I thought the half-breed son of a dog was going to choke. I surpassed myself even for me."

"You mean," asked Ben, slow to grasp it, "that it *was* sand in that poke? My God, you could've got us all killed."

"*Oui,* but in place of that, *voilà!* I have got us all saved. What? You don't believe it? Listen to Baptiste. Do you

109

think Dominguin would still be bothering to haul us down to the Kwahadi if there had been gold in the bag? Ah, no, not at these prices. As it is, we have a chance to breathe through the rest of the night, and who knows what good fortune tomorrow may bring?"

"Goddam it," said Go-deen, "why could I have not been born with an empty head like the rest of you? Here we are six hours north of Quanah's camp, and the talk is of good fortune greeting the sunrise. *Eeh*, Jesus!"

"Quanah's camp?" asked Ben uneasily. "Ain't he the one what—"

"The very one, Petit Ben," answered Big Bat cheerfully and before he could finish. "But don't worry about it; Baptiste Pourier will think of something."

"Sure he will." Go-deen scowled. "Like what? Another six pounds of wet sand?"

"*Zut!*" exclaimed Big Bat. "You have no sense of humor."

"But you do, is that it?"

"*Exactement.*"

"Yes," said Go-deen acidly, " '*exactement*' like Soledad Dominguin ... Sonofabitch, I wish I was back home on Milk River running fat cow or down on the Popo Agie chasing Shoshoni squaws."

The night wore on, the captives talking guardedly of escape but finding no holes in the Comanchero arrangement. Up on the driver's seat of the *carreta* the old mother of Dominguin sat hunched against the morning chill. With her, ox whip in one hand, rifle in the other, rode one of the four lieutenants. Directly behind the tail gate of the creaking cart, two others of the lieutenants followed on horseback. Leading the cart and the night-long exodus of the Comanchero camp, rode the remaining lieutenant and Soledad himself. It was plain the half-breed buffalo hunters were in a hurry. When, after the first fruitless hours of escape plans and Comanche guess talk, Ben asked the old crone why her tough son was in such a rush, Andrajosa Dominguin croaked a disquieting reply.

"Because, *hijo*," she said, "he wishes to be far from that fire back there by the first daylight. You know, *niño*, that no one, not even we Comancheros who trade with them, are beloved of the Mimbreno Apaches. They are danger-

110

ous to everyone. Not even the Lords of the South Plains are easy in their company."

"Mother," said Ben, "who are these 'Lords of the South Plains'? The name calls up a memory in me, although I will swear I do not know why. *Por favor, Madrita, quién están?*"

"Why, they are the Comanches, *por supuesto.* And don't think to get around me by calling me Little Mother either. There is nothing I can do for you or would if I might. You know that Soledad is half Kwahadi and half Sonora Mexican. Well, I am his Kwahadi half, *comprende?*"

"No!" said Ben. "You, a pureblood Cōmanche? With such a fine face and figure for your years? Nonsense!"

"Give me that whip, Alvarez," he heard her say to the driver. And then ducked belatedly as she cut at him with a backhand swipe of the heavy thong. "I will not miss next time," she promised. "See that you try no more of your clumsy *yanqui* tricks."

Ben laughed and told her decidedly that he was no Yankee, whatever he might be, and that for some reason he did not pretend to understand he was honestly interested in the Comanches. At this she peered hard at him and nodded.

"Yes, that may be sō. I find myself interested in you for some reason I cannot explain, also. Could it be that you have Kwahadi blood?"

"Well," grinned Ben, "nothing is impossible, as the steer said to the heifer. But I doubt it very much. It just seems that I'm plain interested in Indians."

"Talk Spanish if you want to talk to me," directed the ōld woman peevishly. "And remember I am a lady; no more of your poor jokes, you hear me?"

"Yes, mother," said Ben, straightening his smile, "a thousand pardons. How far is it now to this camp of the Kwahadi?"

The old wōman looked up at the stars, then over to the east where the horizon was paling visibly. She held up a bony forefinger, sampling the quickening breeze.

"Maybe an hour," she said.

"Mil gracias," replied Ben and fell silent.

After an impatient moment, Big Bat, who did not understand Spanish, said, "All right, all right; what did you

111

learn? You intend keeping it to yourself? I caught a little of it with my French ear but heard nothing of any great sense."

"Neither did I," said Ben. "The old lady is pureblood Comanche and wanted to know if I was a breed. Thought I looked a little Kwahadi, I reckon. I like that, with you two black-skinned sons sitting here alongside." He looked at Frank Go-deen with the jibe, but the Milk River breed was not amused to be included.

"I always said you didn't act pure white to me," he growled. "Nor look it either. You're mixed some way. So's Bat; he can't fool me. He's a dirtier color than I am, and the Sioux hate his guts. That's a sure sign."

Big Bat returned the growl compounded.

"It is the good thing for you, *métis*, that my hands are tied behind me. Otherwise—"

"Sure," interrupted Go-deen undaunted, "otherwise I wouldn't have said it. Shut up. You and Brother Ben make my buttocks ache with your eternal blabbering."

"This cart is making mine ache," said Ben. "I'll damn near be glad to get out and be stretched by the Kwahadi."

"You think you make fun, don't you?" asked Go-deen. "Let me tell you that you do not. That is precisely what the Kwahadi will do to us when they take us out of this wooden coffin with wheels."

"Eh?" said Ben. "What's that?"

"Hang us up by our thumbs," said Frank Go-deen, and they all fell silent after that.

The sun was an hour down. A full day had passed for the captives in the camp of Quanah, the half-white Kwahadi. It had been a long day, a merciless day; a day spent stretched by the thumbs from a Comanche waiting pole could scarcely be called less than these things.

Fortunately it had not been a hot day, the wind bringing in a summer rain just as the rising sun was becoming intolerable. Yet the sheer exhaustion of the ordeal and the paralysis of pain set up in shoulder, elbow, wrist and spine by the hang of their bodies against the thumb bonds was overwhelming. Adding to their misery Go-deen developed uncontrollable dysentery from his gorging of half-raw buffalo liver the night before, and his helpless condition drew the blue-green bottle flies by the tens-of-thousands to

112

swarm over the four men on the stretching wrack. With the stones and dirt thrown interminably by the Comanche children and the spittle of the squaws, augmented by occasional voidings of an old warrior upon them to draw the laughter of his wrinkled cronies, the captives were again bordering the unconscious when darkness and another cool shower momentarily revived them.

Momentarily was the exact word.

With full night the actual, the active, torture would commence. Dominguin had sold very cheap—five ponies and a Sonora mare with a mule foal—and the ceremonies would not be elaborate. Even so, and even with the victims in such poor physical condition to start, there would be something doing until nearly midnight, especially if they drew it out waiting for Quanah to get back from a horse raid on the Texas settlements along the Concho River, as had been indicated would be the case. Unless, of course, the damned white men died too quick or the Nez Percé Indian collapsed prematurely from the beating Dominguin's coyotes had given him. Actually, the Sioux breed seemed the only good chance to go through a decent course, and even he had worn himself pretty well out by crying all the day for mercy when he had not been so much as touched yet. Well, that was just the way things went on some days. And, after all, Dominguin hadn't exactly gotten wealthy on the deal.

So speculated the hard-faced loungers about the hanging wrack, as they waited for the fires to be built up and lighted and the fun to begin.

The thoughts in the minds of the four men on the pole had long since ceased to dwell in speculative channels. Deadening half-consciousness had drugged three of them. The fourth, Lame John, had fainted an hour gone, was not revived even by the cold gustings of the rain.

About seven, supper out of the way and the wet weather having blown off inland toward the settlements, the flints were struck, the damp kindling fanned into smoky life. Before the wood was well caught, Quanah rode in from the southeast. At once the camp was in an uproar.

The raid had been a good one. Over seventy head of fine horses ran in the loose herd driven by Quanah's braves. And the gods had been good in more regards than

113

the quality of the animals. The feared *Tejanos*, the Rangers, the Devils in the White Hats, had run them hard and close as far as the Kickapoo Fork. But there this lovely summer storm had met them, moving against the Rangers. Its downpour had drowned out every pony track on the *liano*. *Wagh!* With luck like that, who could complain about a little wet and a little weariness? *Tsh-t!* Raise the victory whoop and get on with the work at the waiting pole.

A hurried meal wolfed down, Quanah inspected the prisoners and ordered them stripped to the waist. This was for the delicate first procedure, a cutting of the torso in the nerve-ending places designed to produce the maximum of pain with the minimum of blood loss or debilitation. It was at this point that the particular old squaw who had stepped forward to rip Ben's shirt away paused for a searching look at the tall white man with the Indian-long shock of coarse tawny hair and the slanted, light-gray eyes. For a moment it appeared she would question him. But she did not. Shaking her head as if something hung in her mind which would neither divulge nor dislodge itself, she reached upward and tore Ben's rags from him. It was when she did this that her rheumy eyes opened wide and she stood back pointing dramatically at the odd, penny-sized discoloration on his left breast.

"Sa'm-bou!" she cried out. "Look at this! The mark of the Water Horse!"

19

Quanah Parker's Cousin

THE COMANCHES gathered around in greatest excitement. Ben and the others were cut down. A robe was spread for Ben, the headmen summoned to question him. Their tongue sounded oddly familiar to him, but he could make no answerable sense of it. Hand signs were tried with some better, but not enough, luck. An impasse loomed. Then someone recalled the remark of Dominguin's Kwahadi mother that the tall white man might carry some of the true blood in him. How had she found that out? Perhaps Dominguin had found a way to talk to the tall one. At once riders went after the Comancheros who, Ben was partly able to determine from the swift Kwahadi signs, had departed scarcely an hour since, waiting only for nightfall to put more ground between themselves and the Apaches of Mano Roto. Should Broken Hand decide, the signs continued, as had his Cheyenne and Kiowa brothers previous to him, that the northern woman was no bargain, Dominguin apparently wanted to move the complaints department as far south as he could. With any other Indians, the Comanches, the Lords of the South Plains, would have welcomed a clash. But between them and the Mimbrenos of Mangas Coloradas, the infamous and already legendary Red Sleeves, there existed a truce of mutual understanding; the understanding being that both were such merciless fighters that warfare became pointless. Why start anything when neither side would quit? *Bou'ou*, clearly there was no point in such wastefulness of warriors. So likewise, if fearless, pit bulls, the Mimbrenos and the Kwahadi looked the other way when one passed the other upon the prairie. Of course, if one band were far stronger than the other, that was a different matter, and it was then understood that life belonged only to the swifter riders among the outnumbered group. But

115

by and large the people of Mangas and those of Quanah avoided seeing one another where possible.

So it was that Soledad Dominguin and his aged mother, the one cursing, the other croaking, drove their oxcart back into the camp of the Kwahadi sometime after eight o'clock that evening. The young braves who had galloped out to return them had said nothing of the reason for their order. The Lords of the South Plains were not in the habit of explaining commands to Comancheros. Hence, the first idea Dominguin drew of his forced delay's motivation was when Quanah pointed out to him the mark of the Water Horse on Ben's breast and growled at him in guttural Kwahadi that he, Dominguin, was to serve as interpreter, since the *Ta'k'ae-kiH* spoke no language save his own, despite the Comanche symbol on his body.

"You mean, don't you," said Dominguin acidly, "that he doesn't speak your tongue?"

"Why, yes," replied Quanah. "Is it not the same thing?"

"Yes, it is *not* the same thing," gritted the Comanchero. "Did you ever think he might know another tongue? How do you think my old mother talked to him?"

"Do you mean the hand signs? We tried those. He is pretty good with them, but we couldn't get him to understand what it was we wanted. We don't use the signs as much down here as they do up north where he came from."

"No," snapped Dominguin, "I don't mean the hand signs. I mean my own tongue, my father's tongue."

"Spanish?" said the surprised Quanah.

Many of the Comanches spoke the Mexican language, both from their contacts with the brown-skinned traders of the Sonora country and with the Spanish-speaking white settlers of Texas. But it had not occurred to them to try it on a captive from far Montana.

"Yes, Spanish!" Dominguin now declared. "Your precious *Ta'k'ae-kiH*, your damned northern white man, speaks better Spanish than do I. Go ahead, ask him, see for yourself. Goddam, even with a Kwahadi mother it's difficult for me to follow your thoughts, Quanah. Now why wouldn't you have thought of a simple thing like trying Spanish on him?"

116

"Perhaps because I had a white mother," answered the Kwahadi chief. "I was thinking of him as a white man."

"Well, think of him as you like. He's your purchase and your problem. Now how about me? What are you going to do about me? Here you have dragged me back, and I have lost two hours on the trail and those Apache devils only twenty miles away when last seen. *Wagh!* You have got to do something for me."

Quanah had so far spoken with the utmost gravity and dignity. Ben, recovering sharpness of mind during the questioning period, had been amazed at the famed chief's gentleness and soft-voiced tolerance of the Comanchero's petulant responses. Now he saw the steel come into Quanah Parker's level gray eyes.

"Yes," he said, "I will do something for you, Soledad. I will give you until daylight to be across the Pecos. *Comprende usted?*"

"The Pecos? You must be having a Kwahadi joke. That's Apache country."

"Sure, that's the Kwahadi joke of it."

"But, Quanah—"

"Soledad, the choice is yours." Ben had never heard a man put more menace into such innocent words. "You asked me to do something for you, and I am doing it."

Dominguin lost several shades of his saddle-leather color. He licked his lips, quick and flicking as the lizard he resembled. He glanced at Ben, then back to Quanah.

"It's almost certain death, cousin. You're ordering me to go kill myself very nearly."

"You have the choice. You earned it with your own big words. No man talks to Quanah in the tones you used just now to me. Not in front of Quanah's people."

"Por Dios!" cried Dominguin. "I didn't mean anything! I was only angry at being brought back here for such a stupid rea—" He checked himself but far too late. In desperation, he wheeled to Ben.

"Listen," he pleaded in English, "see if you can't do something. You realize the choice he has given me? You're a white man; you can't let him do this to me."

Ben, still working to loosen and restore the life to his numbed limbs, shook his head.

"I don't follow you, Soledad. What does being a white man have to do with it?"

117

"He has said to me that I must cross over into Apache land before sunrise. That's almost sure to get me killed. But if I stay on this side in my own country, there's no *almost* to it; I will be killed—by him, Quanah. He's just promised it."

"I didn't hear him. He just told you to get out of his sight by daybreak. That don't sound deadly."

"Goddam it, *patrón*, don't argue it with me! Please! Use your influence with them. Quanah will listen to you. He's got to."

"What in the name of hell," asked Ben incredulously, "are you talking about? Have you gone daft?"

"*Por Dios!* Don't you know? Haven't you followed this talk of the mark on your breast? You're a Water Horse. That's the family mark, there, that you have on you. The Water Horses are the rarest Comanche secret family there is."

"Secret family?"

"Sure, they're like the hidalgos in Old Spain—you know, the rulers behind the rulers. The Comanches have maybe eight, ten, who knows how many of these family bands. There are the Wasps, the Wanderers, the Yap Eaters, the Antelopes—my mother is an Antelope—the Liver Eaters, the Burnt Meats, the Wormies—some others maybe. But the Water Horses, they are the most powerful and feared of all. And you have their mark on you."

"Well, good Lord, even if I do," said Ben, completely puzzled by now, "how's that give me any edge on this here Quanah?"

"You fool! He's a Water Horse, too. The head one."

Ben stared at him, the idea too remote for ready acceptance.

"You mean to say—" he began, but Dominguin cut him short.

"Yes," he said, "I mean to say just that; you're the same blood as Quanah. My old mother was right. You're a Comanche."

"My God," breathed Ben, "it ain't possible." But he turned, none the less, to Quanah and put the question to him in halting Spanish.

"Is it true what he, says," he asked, gesturing toward Dominguin, "that you and I have the same blood?"

118

Quanah's calm eyes studied him a moment. Then he nodded slowly.

"Yes," he said. *"Mira."*

He opened his shirt. Ben leaned forward, a strange feeling growing within him. Then he felt the small hairs lift at his nape. The blue mark on the Kwahadi chief's left breast was the same as that on his own.

"T'ou Tsei," said Quanah Parker, indicating the symbol. Then in Spanish again. "The Water Horse. We are true cousins, you and me—what the Indians call near-brothers. What I have is yours."

"Lord, Lord," said Ben, "I can't believe it."

"Cómo se dice?" asked Quanah politely.

"Oh." Ben grinned. *"Dispense me, usted.* I'm still a little confused from being strung up. I said I couldn't believe that I was part Comanche—Kwahadi, that is."

"Our grandmothers were sisters. It is as I said; we are near-brothers, once removed. You are welcome in this camp for the length of your life, and who is your enemy cannot be my friend."

Ben looked at Big Bat, Frank Go-deen and Lame John where they lay beneath the waiting pole. He pointed to them, inquiring anxiously.

"How about those who are my friends?"

Quanah glanced around at the reviving captives. It was clear he had forgotten them entirely. He turned back to Ben, making the apology sign.

"Now it is your place to forgive me," he said. "I am weary. We came many miles this day. Rode very hard. Be at rest in your mind. Your friends are the guests of my people. They will be restored quickly." He wheeled to bark some Comanche orders at the old women standing near. From the hand signs accompanying the commands, Ben understood he had instructed the squaws to care for the exhausted men and thanked Quanah in Spanish for the courtesy. The chief shook his head, saying it was nothing and asking Ben to follow him to his lodge where they might talk in confidence and at ease.

"I want to know why it is that you did not tell us of your Kwahadi blood," he said, turning to lead the way. "If Soledad's mother had not made the remark to old Spider Woman," he waved to the squaw who had discov-

119

ered Ben's tattoo, "we would have killed a true cousin; a very bad thing to do."

"To be honest," said Ben, catching Go-deen's eye and throwing him the "all is well" hand sign, "I didn't know about my Comanche grandmother." He twisted his wry smile at the somber Kwahadi. "To tell you the entire truth," he added, "I still don't know about her."

Quanah stopped.

"What do you mean by that?" he asked. "Do you call me a liar?"

"Por Dios!" protested Ben. "Never!"

"Well, then?"

"It's a long story," said Ben, "and I, too, am weary. May I tell it to you resting in your lodge?"

"Yes," replied Quanah Parker, eying him closely, "you may do that." He looked at him a moment longer. "Indeed," he added softly, "you *will* do it."

20

Comanche Compliment

As THEY ENTERED the lodge and Quanah busied himself bringing sitting robes, two pipes, tobacco and, to Ben's amazement, producing and lighting a fine Rochester hand lamp brought from the Texas settlements at what price of life no white man would want to speculate, Ben studied the Kwahadi chief whose evil reputation had filtered even as far north as Big Bat's and Frank Go-deen's Montana.

Quanah was first of all surprisingly young. Ben guessed he could not be more than a few months either side of twenty. He was very tall for a Comanche, a race inclined to short, wide bodies and huge heads, and, like Lame John, an extremely handsome man. His skin was quite dark, his teeth white, strong, perfect, his hair raven black and worn braided in two rolls wrapped with red cloth. Upon his forehead he wore a dollar-sized swirl of hair puffed and tangled in the Plains Indian sign manner which indicated, as nearly as it might in white translation, "If you want a fight, you have come to the right place." His body was muscular, straight, deep-chested. His legs were bowed and his toes turned in like any pureblood horseman of the prairie tribes. Positively the only sign of white blood which might be detected in his physical appearance was the light-gray color of his fine eyes.

Surprising Ben's glance, Quanah smiled quickly, setting those gray eyes alight with friendly warmth.

Seating himself beside the small lodge-fire's clear flame, he waved his left hand gracefully in the beginning sign.

"First, cousin, let me tell a little about myself; then to you and your life since you were known to the Kwahadi."

He paused, thinking, his dark face seeming to grow more shadowed with the thoughts.

"I am of less years than yourself, as you can see," he resumed. "I have never seen my mother since the Rangers of Captain Ross captured her and killed my father, Peta

Nocona. This was on the Pease River in 1860. The Rangers killed seventy-seven Comanches on that day, other than the chief, my father. You can see how my heart turns against them. I will always hate the Rangers.

"I had a younger brother and baby sister when my mother was taken, both since dead. Prairie Flower, the little girl, I loved more than my own life. She died like a small wild bird of a broken heart in those ugly settlement camps. They killed her like the Rangers killed my father. First they wounded her; then they finished her.

"I won't burden you with all this, though. You will excuse it, please. Also please forgive it that I cannot speak your tongue better. I am learning it, for I know I must. But it is slow work. Many think my mother taught it to me. That is a lie. She was but nine summers when taken by my father from the settlements. She spoke no English at all when I knew her. See how these white lies get started?

"So that is enough of me, Cousin Ben. Now for you."

Ben thanked him, told him briefly of his loss of memory in the Montana snowslide, his saving from a frozen death by old Chilkoot Johnston, his subsequent promise to the old man and his long, frustratingly near-successful search for the Indian-reared daughter. The tale completed, he made the returning-to-you sign to Quanah, who accepted it gravely.

Fascinated, Ben leaned forward. Quanah spoke in slow, deliberate Spanish, mixed in with frequent hand signs and occasional usages of the few frontier English phrases at that time within his command. His manner was entirely assured, his mind plainly superior. His humor, if subdued, was nimble and ready. Ben found himself immediately lost in listening; and the time flew like ghost arrows.

The name Ben had found burned upon his gun belt, Quanah said, was his true white name. And his people lived where the belt stated, over east of Kickapoo Fork of the Little Colorado River, near the tiny settlement of San Saba. That is, they had lived there. Now after the great war among the white men, no more Allisons were known around that place.

Ben's Kwahadi grandmother, the older sister of the squaw Spider Woman, had died long ago. Her daughter by a white captive from Arizona, Ben's mother, had been

122

caught by the Rangers when but six years old and reared in the Texas settlements. The grandmother had kept in touch with the daughter through the years, even when the girl had married Ben's father, an Army lieutenant from the *Tejanos'* war with Mexico. The latter, at the last, had been stationed at Fort McKavett to the south of San Saba, his family staying in the settlement for safety. Ben and his one younger brother, Clint—Quanah said, "Klee-n't," but Ben understood him to mean the common Texas name— had come not infrequently to see their Indian grandmother. These visits had been in secret from the Army father, conducted by the half-Kwahadi mother at the old grandmother's urging.

In this way the boys had been taught some of the Comanche life. Although Ben had forgotten what little he had known of the difficult spoken language, he had remembered its sound and also the signs and the general knowledge—the blood-brother instincts—of the South Plains Tshaoh; this memory explaining, no doubt, his good ability to get along with the other horse Indians on his long search for the missing white girl.

Now all his white family were gone and he was home with the people of his grandmother and of his dead mother. They were glad to have him with them, but Quanah would suggest that it would be safer for his friends to travel on as soon as they were able. Ben, himself, it was hoped, would stay and make his home on the plains. He could live with his great-aunt, Spider Woman, and as a Water Horse could ride with Quanah and the picked braves in the great war that was coming that summer. Naturally, Quanah understood that he might not wish to fight his other blood, and if this were the case, he would furnish an escort of warriors to take Ben and his friends into the Texas settlements or even back north through the lands of Satank. Quanah had just now made war plans with the Staked Plains Kiowas of Eagle Heart and White Horse, western cousins of Satank and Satanta. They were his strong friends, as was Lone Wolf, the chief Kiowa fighting man of all tribes. With their help Quanah could promise Ben and his companions a safe journey to the Arkansas.

What had the Texas Brother to say to all of this? the Kwahadi chief concluded. Would he stay with Quanah and fight on his grandmother's side? Or would he go back home and fight with the soldiers, with his father's people, against his red cousins?

Ben thanked him for his good heart and for his promises of safe conduct. He could assure him, he said, that he had no intention of joining the soldiers to fight the Indians. Not that summer or any other summer. He knew now that they were partly his people, something which he had felt all along. Knowing this, he would never fight them. Not unless he had to do so to save his own life or to keep his own word.

When he made these two exceptions, Quanah looked up at him quickly.

"Why do you say that?" he asked. "About your life and your word? I have already said your life would be in my hands, that I would guard it with my own."

"Where I am going," smiled Ben tightly, "it will not be in your hands to guard my life."

"What is that? Where do you think to go?"

"To keep my word."

"Ah? And what word is that?"

"To bring back to that old man who saved my life in the sliding mountain his only child, that yellow-haired woman Dominguin sold to Mano Roto."

"No! By the gods! You don't mean it?"

"Would you go if you had given your word to the old man?" Ben asked quietly. Quanah looked startled, then frowned a little.

"Of course I would go. What has that to do with you?"

"You said it yourself." Ben shrugged with a grin. "We're near-brothers, once removed. Yes, and both of us Water Horses, too. My word is the same as yours."

"Well spoken," said Quanah, a glint of humor showing in his gray eyes. "But as to my word, how am I to keep it if you go over into Apache country? Beyond the Pecos, I can't help you. If I could go along, it would be different, but there is this war; I cannot leave it, for I have already given my word to Eagle Heart, White Horse, Lone Wolf and many others."

"I understand that," said Ben

"Then you did not expect me to go with you?"

"Of course not. You would be doing us a great favor to put us safely across the river, let alone worrying about what happens to us on the other side. In this life nothing is certain. My white people have a saying about that, if you'd care to hear it."

"Naturally," agreed Quanah. "Don't forget I am half-brother to your white side."

"We say, 'You pay your money, and you take your chances,'" answered Ben. "How's that?"

"Pretty good. You want to hear how the Kwahadi says the same thing? 'Spit in the wind, and smile when you get splattered.' You think that fits as well?"

"Better!" laughed Ben. "You people are wonderful!"

"Well, realistic anyway." Quanah smiled a little sadly. "When will you want to go, cousin?"

"If we could rest a day and leave with darkness tomorrow, it would be good, I think. What do you think?"

"The sooner the better. But, yes, you do need the one day's rest. We will give you everything we can."

"We don't need anything that twelve hours' sleep and plenty of fat cow won't cure, cousin." Ben grinned, already feeling immensely better. "I've never been too much of a believer in whoever lives up there," he pointed to the cluster of stars showing through the lodge's smoke hole, "but having that old woman spot that Water Horse mark when she did has very nearly convinced me."

"I don't understand the gods either." Quanah frowned. "Isatai, our medicine man, the chief priest of the Kwahadi, he has been telling us for many moons how badly we shall beat the white man. Yet each year we lose more ground and more buffalo. Each year the white settlements come farther out along the streams, into the plains. They are a week's travel closer than they were in the time of my father; indeed, even since my own youth."

He paused, shaking his head, handsome features a study in pagan frustration.

"I pray harder all the while; Isatai rattles the gourds and shrieks upon the eagle-bone whistles more fiercely all the time, but it doesn't seem to matter. The white man can't hear it. He keeps coming."

Ben nodded, watching him a moment.

"You know that he will always keep coming, don't you?" he finally said.

"Yes, I know this. I have known it from the first. But

125

Isatai keeps promising these wonderful things, and in my heart I want them so badly—"

He let the words trail off, and again Ben nodded.

"We have another saying for that," he told him. "It's a hard saying. You want to hear it?"

"These are hard times. Say it."

" 'Wish in one hand, urinate in the other—see which fills up first.' "

Quanah sighed deeply, returning the nod.

"It's a good saying. Especially for us Indians."

"It's a good one for anybody," said Ben. "Wishing won't buy a bag of mesquite beans."

"No," said Quanah, "and it won't get you and your friends across the Pecos either. You had better close your eyes. I will take care of all else while you sleep; fresh ponies, food, blankets, guides, everything."

"We will want the old white horse and the mule with the gray whiskers," said Ben. "They have been with us from the first mile."

"A Kwahadi understands this," replied Quanah. "One has brothers with four legs as well as with two. It will be as you say."

Ben stood up, touching his fingertips to his forehead.

"God be with you, Cousin Quanah," he said.

Again the Kwahadi chief gave him his slow, sad smile.

"I would rather have you with me, Cousin Ben," he said. "I think you would be a better fighter."

Ben stood staring a long, thoughtful time after the proud figure of his Kwahadi kinsman. It was well that he did so, forming thus a lasting picture of him for his scrapbook of memories. For after he had disappeared, as with the mysterious gray-eyed Oglala benefactor before him, Ben Allison never saw Quanah Parker again.

21

The Apache Road

THEY TRAVELED light and fast, moving by night and the illumination of the moon in its third quarter. Their guide was Short Dog, a middle-aged Comanche who knew the country across the Pecos. The identity and destination of the enemy were known—Broken Hand's band of the Mimbrenos, a branch of the Gila People, and now moving west by north for their fortress stronghold in the Pinos Altos Mountains below the Sierra Diablo.

Short Dog struck first, and by pure guess, for Horsehead Crossing, the most used of the horse Indian trails from New Mexico to Texas. They came to the crossing, over one hundred and fifty crow-flight miles of buffalo pasture, with dawn of the third night from Quanah's camp in the Concho River country. There in the pink light of growing day they found Short Dog to be wrong. There were no Apache pony tracks at Horsehead Crossing newer than two weeks.

"We will go up to Toyah Creek," said the squat brave. "If not there, then they crossed at Quito. We can go to sleep on it."

With dusk they turned up the river. Short Dog's second guess was good. The pony prints at Toyah Creek Crossing were fresh, made within three days. Big Bat and Frank Go-deen got down and sorted out the individual horses of the party. Looking at one another, they nodded in agreement, Go-deen turning to Ben.

"Eleven," he said. "That's the right number. With the woman's horse it makes twelve. That's what's here. Eleven Apache prints and a shod horse from Dominguin's stock. How old?" he said to the Comanche, using hand-signs. "Three days, you said? *Eeh!* I can do better than that, and I'm only half Indian."

Short Dog got down and felt the Apache pony tracks very carefully and with his eyes closed, face upturned, as though trying to guess what it was he felt. Then he lay on the ground and smelled the tracks. He moved on, picking up some of the droppings left by the New Mexican ponies. He squeezed them, picked them apart, sniffed of them. He found a place where one of the geldings had spraddled and staled the ground. He dug in the sandy earth, sifting and turning it in his fingers. Finally he looked up at Go-deen, replying to him, as addressed, with hand talk.

"Two days and one-half. It was noon of the third day they stopped here. They made no fire. Only watered and relieved the ponies and themselves. That's the best I can do; can you do better?"

"Thank you," Go-deen signed to him. "I was only having a little fun with you. You read trail better than a Sioux, even an Oglala."

The Comanche grinned, showing canines filed sharp as the fangs of his namesake.

"Come on," he said, "I'll show you where they made their third fire."

"What?" said Go-deen. "It's broad daylight now!"

"Sure. Are you afraid?"

"But it was your idea to travel by night."

"Only in my own country. In the Apache country," he pointed across the Pecos, "I do not know the land well enough to track by moon. I must have sun."

Go-deen gulped, nodded, turned to Ben.

"You catch those signs?" he asked. "He says we've got to travel daytime now. He doesn't know the country well enough from here on to go by night. What do you think?"

Ben shook his head, referred the matter to Big Bat and Lame John. The former grinned and said that it was no time now for thinking. That time was long past. Lame John, who had recovered enough from his beating in the Comanchero camp during the ride out to have said perhaps ten words, now looked at his questioner.

"I have but one thought, Brother Ben," he said. "You know what it is."

Ben knew what it was. Since losing the Johnston woman to the Apaches in Dominguin's camp, the proud Nez Percé had been acting like a man in a trance. He would reply to direct questions monosyllabically and no more than that. He had not spoken a volunteered word since

128

leaping for the Comanchero's throat back on Clear Fork. In his heart and mind was a single resolve: to find Amy Johnston again or die on the trail to that end.

"All right," said Ben, "that's it. Let's go—"

They put their horses into the Pecos, sent them splashing across to the far bank. Over there, there was no more talk. Short Dog led the way; the others followed. They were in the land of the enemy now. Talk would serve no purpose save to disturb the stillness.

In Apacheria that was a poor idea.

They went sixty-five miles across country as desolate as the Great Salt Sink. Not even Frank Go-deen, that tracker and man of the northern wilderness par excellence, could follow the trail of the Mimbrenos over such sandblasted rock and greasewood scrub. Short Dog, on the other hand, seldom hesitated long enough to get off his pony, reading the enemy signs as though he had dipped his *n'deh b'ken*, his soft-tanned Apache boots, in red barn paint.

At the end of the dry going, they struck a mountain chain, the Guadalupes, Short Dog said, and followed the foothills—drier than the approaching desert—north to Guadalupe Pass. Here they found the headwaters of the Delaware Branch of the Pecos and rested two days refreshing their mounts on the excellent streamside grass. Going through the pass they came into arid desolation once more. Beyond Granite Peak, skirting the Cornudas Mountains, striking for the Hueco chain and Hueco Pass, they found the entire way a deathtrap of dehydration in the fierce summer heat. Save for the uncanny memory of Short Dog—the Comanche found water each day where no natural sign of it could possibly have guided a stranger—they would have been dead and sun-dried a dozen times between the Pecos and the Rio Grande del Norte. As it was, they came safely through the Organ Mountains at old Fort Fillmore shortly before dawn of the thirteenth day. Below them spread the fertile valley of the river, the stream itself lying out beyond the silent walls and weed-grown irrigation *acequias* of the historic post where Baylor and Sibley dreamed briefly of adding all the West to the Confederate States of America. In the eerie green light of the last stars, the brick and adobe buildings and the abandoned bottom-land and fields edging the willow-dark channels of the "Great River" took on a ghostly patina effective even upon the stoic Short Dog.

"No good," he sighed uneasily. "Come on; we go quick."

They swung south of the fort, going across the Rio Grande at the old Indian crossing of Santo Tomas. On the west bank they struck a trail without a wheel track or buffalo hoofprint in it, yet wide and deep and rutted with countless ages of horse and foot travel.

"What is it?" Ben asked Short Dog in Spanish.

"*Camino Apache*," grunted the other.

"The Apache Road?"

"*Si hombre;* it runs from here to the Arizona country; to the Big Colorado River even. Also south into the Sierra Madre in old Mexico and north as far as the Sierra Diablo. There are branches, too, leading to all the Apache places. White Mountains, Mescalero, Chiricahua, Gila, all of them. From here there is no tracking; we only follow the road."

"*Por Dios!*" exclaimed Ben. "Isn't that asking for trouble? Using the same trail they use?"

"It's their country," shrugged Short Dog. "They know it better than we do."

"So?"

"So the road goes where the water is; where the road does not go, neither does the water. That's it."

Ben looked at the barrel-chested Comanche.

"So we go where the road goes, or we don't go at all, eh?"

"I said that's it."

Ben sat silently, eyes narrowed to study the brooding stillness ahead. Behind him and Short Dog, the others held their ponies quiet, watching with him. The only sound came from Malachi, serving the little band as pack animal and, according to Ben, as Indian watchdog. Ben swore the old mule could smell a hostile farther than a Sharps big fifty would shoot one. Whether this claim had served him merely as an excuse for bringing the obstinate brute along or was a legitimate talent of Malachi's had yet to be demonstrated. To this point in the trail they had seen neither feather tip nor lance tassle of the retreating Mimbrenos or any other Apache. And now Malachi, lifting his jug head to sample the New Mexican morning air, gave a
130

snort of impatient approval accompanied by a rusty-lunged bray loud enough to awaken the soldier dead four miles away at Fort Fillmore.

Ben looked around at him and nodded a grinning "thank you" in English. Then quickly in Spanish to Short Dog:

"The mule agrees with you. *Vamonos!*"

At fifty miles west of Santo Tomas Crossing the Apache Road led into the dry river bed of the Rio Mimbres. For another forty twisting miles the road followed the course of the waterless stream, turning sharply northward at approximately mile twenty. The second, roughening twenty miles ended at Mimbres Station on the abandoned Overland Mail line to Tucson. Here the channel sands began to moisten, the road abandoning the stream bed and taking to the left, or west, bank. Here, too, Short Dog called a day-long halt. They would rest the present night through, he said, then give the following day to their horses on the strong feed which grew in the damp swales of the Mimbres. They would take cover in the charred timbers and still-standing walls of the burned-out stage station, and as for the stock being seen, they would simply have to pray a little. The ponies had to have the rest and the grass. Also, they were getting too close to the Apache now. They were but two short rides from Sierra Diablo, one long ride from the Pinos Altos foothills where dwelled the people of Mangas Coloradas. As for Broken Hand and the particular band they were trailing, that was getting a little too warm for comfort as well. The pony droppings in the river bed just now were still wet inside. Under a sun such as that they had ridden under since morning, they should be dry to the middle. The answer was that the Mimbrenos who had the white woman had ridden through here, where they now sat their poines, not later than that same day. Short Dog was sorry, he concluded, but he had somehow missed two camps of the Apache. They had fooled him and were now only miles ahead. With this thought-provoking confession, the homely Kwahadi brave turned to Ben and the others.

"*Pues, hombres,*" he said, "*que dicen?* What do you say; you want to push on and run into them or rest here as I have suggested? It's up to you. Quanah ordered me to show you where they took the woman, and I am going to do it one way or the other."

"What do you mean, one way or the other?" said Ben.

"My way or your way."

"What's the difference?"

"I don't know; you haven't said your way yet."

"Listen," said Ben hurriedly, glancing around at the loneliness of the river bed where they sat their hipshot ponies, then upstream at the gaunt skeleton of the old station, "this is your decision, not mine. You do what Cousin Quanah told you—*your* way."

"All right." The Comanche nodded. "We stay here."

"Boys," said Ben to his waiting companions, "Short Dog says we're right on old Broken Hand's tail. Says we'll run up his rump if we're not careful. Wants to lay over here one day. Give them time to move on a little."

Go-deen looked at the blackened stage station, then at Big Bat Pourier.

"You afraid of ghosts, Baptiste?" he asked.

"*Non, mon chère*, only of good women."

"How about you, Lame John?"

The tall Nez Percé shook his head quickly.

"Being close to her makes my heart wild," he answered. "But I have given my word to follow Brother Ben, and I won't break it. We'll stay."

"Good," said Ben. "Let's get on up there and settle in before sundown. We'll eat cold tonight, so we might as well *sleep* comfortable."

He turned to Short Dog, apprising him of the decision.

"*Bien*," grunted the latter, kneeing his pony forward. "You will be safe. You can sleep with both eyes shut. They won't bother you up there." He pointed toward the roofless station, and Ben asked nervously how he could be so certain of this safety.

"You see the line of their pony tracks?" said Short Dog, indicating the low bank where the Apaches had climbed their mounts out of the river bed. "They lead out there in a big circle around the station. Way around. But up above we will find them coming right back to the river again. Do you know why, *señor*?"

"No, *hombre*," said Ben. "Why?"

"A simple thing," shrugged the other. "Once they kill a place, they never come back to it. It's bad luck."

Ben shivered and said nothing.

Somehow he had the feeling that the Apaches were right.

22

Short Dog's Reassurance

THE SUN was swiftly down. A purple twilight lingered with the reluctance of a young lover to be gone. But at last, and then suddenly, it was blotted up by full darkness. They ate in the station, then went outside.

It was a wonderful summer night, that July first in old New Mexico. Ben sat with the others in front of the station wall listening to the sounds of the desert and counting the fat stars which burned so brilliantly that not even the garish light of the filling moon could discourage their cheery winking and blinking. The very stillness, apart and in itself, was superb. And the air—well, the air was equal parts of piñon nut, artemisia sage, espino mesquite, bear grass, hot sand, red rock and juniper berries carbonated with the dry wine of the near mile-high altitude, and just to inhale it cautiously was enough to set a man's ambition soaring out of bounds. It was the kind of night where one just sat and smelled and felt. Unless, of course, he were a heathen Comanche Indian. In which case he talked.

"*Seis años*, six years ago," said Short Dog, breaking the quiet with an unexpected nod to Ben, "the stage was running on this road." He pointed at the windblown iron-tire marks of the long-gone Abbott & Downing coaches of the Overland Mail. "Back that way, one stop, is Mimbres Springs. Did you ever hear of Mimbres Springs, *señor*? There was a massacre there, this also six years ago—just after the stage quit running—you know, *senor*, when you whites began to fight among yourselves. There were seven people caught in the station at Mimbres Springs by these same Mimbrenos we follow. These were the band of Red Sleeves himself; he was alive then, Mangas Coloradas, the greatest white-hater of them all. It was his subchief Lobo, however, who directed the attack. Mangas

134

was pretty old then; I think nearly seventy. He had lost some of his interest in fighting but not in hating.

"Well they got six of those seven people in that station back there. The seventh one was a woman. They took her alive. She was never heard of again. The story goes that she was a spy for the White Father in Washington. She and the six men with her, they were trying to get some important papers out of El Paso ahead of the army of the southern white men. They were taking these papers to Tucson. In one light spring buggy, imagine. Six men and one woman. With all the Apaches out. I never heard of such foolishness, or maybe it was big heart. I know this; no Indian would die for some pieces of paper. What is paper? You can't eat it."

"To the white man," said Ben soberly, "paper can mean many things. Our whole lives are wrapped up in paper."

"I have found but one use for it." Short Dog shrugged. "To start fires."

"We use it to start wars," said Ben and fell silent.

"Well," the Comanche began again, after a thoughtful pause, "now you take the first stop the other way." He pointed west, toward Arizona. "That's called Cow Springs up there. It got burned out, too, just like where we are here. Nobody got hurt but the stock tender. He lived two days with half his hair off and crawled seventeen miles on his hands and knees to bring the warning about the station burnings to Soldier's Farewell—that's the second stop going to Tucson—and when he got there, he had to talk with his finger writing in the sand, because the Mimbrenos had pulled out his tongue with a pair of shoeing tongs from the blacksmith shop at Cow Springs. Some of you whites are pretty strong."

He lapsed into another spell of Indian thinking.

"The other white man, the one who led the party at Mimbres Springs, he was tough, too. He was only a little man, but he lived a day and a night shot through both lungs with a buffalo gun, and he killed five Mimbrenos after he got hit. The woman they took was his woman. He was only a stable hand at El Paso. She was a government lady. But they say they had a great love. Still, you know how it is in a lonely country like this, *señor*. A story gets improved constantly."

135

"What was this fellow's name?" asked Ben. "He must have been a real *Tejano*."

"No, he was just a southern white man, they say. But he believed in the other flag, the first one with the red and white stripes. His name was Sparhawk, I think. The Apache called him Sparrow Hawk after that fight. That was for his small size and great spirit. They thought a lot of him; that's why they took his woman and didn't hurt her."

"I suppose," said Ben, looking around, "that this station has some similar cheerful history."

"Ah sure, you can see that. *Mira*, look about yourself. However, the loss of life here was not so serious. They were all Mexicans here at this station. Eight, I think the story goes. The tender and his wife and six children. Wait, there was a baby, too. Seven children. All beat or stabbed or stoned except the baby, which they just hit against the wall like you do a sick or hurt or female puppy. They never waste bullets on Mexicans or children."

"Por Dios!" said Ben. "And you call that not so serious? Nine human beings murdered in cold blood?"

"Well, certainly!" said Short Dog indignantly. "But did I not just explain to you that they were Mexicans?"

Ben let it go. It was an opinion of the land clearly not subject to dispute. Moreover, racial injustices were not the issue here; not except as they applied to their own relationship to these Mimbreno Apaches who did not believe nine *mejicanos* the equal of one *norteamericano*.

"Short Dog," he said, "why do you remind me of these atrocious happenings at this time? *Que pasa en la cabeza?* Do you enjoy seeing the gringo squirm? Watching the 'white eye' grow pale beneath the ears?"

"No, no," objected the Comanche, "it is not such a poor thing as that at all. It is just that Apache history has a bad habit of happening again. So I give you a little history, no?"

"But why?" persisted Ben, never sure that these simple people were as simple as they seemed—or preferred to be considered. "Why wait till now?"

The thickset brave shrugged.

"Now is the only time which counts, *señor*."

"Si, es verdad," agreed Ben. "Please to go ahead."

"Sure, *seguro, señor;* I merely wanted you to under-

136

stand the Mimbrenos a little better before you get any closer to them. *Comprende?* I want you to be ready for tomorrow."

"Tomorrow?" questioned Ben, small voiced.

"Most certainly no later than that," answered Short Dog. "You see, those Mimbrenos are loafing along now. I can tell by the way the tracks wander. Probably they are only now thinking of a good story to tell Mangas about the woman. That's Young Mangas now, the old man's boy. He doesn't believe it pays to take white prisoners. Like father, like son."

"You think they might kill her at the last minute?" asked Ben, horrified. "My God and us so near again!"

"It's not what I meant, although they are easily capable of it. No, what I am saying is that Broken Hand is slowing up for some reason, and my guess is that he has just now thought of how he is going to keep Mangas from gutting his pretty blue-eyed doe when he brings her into the *ranchería* up in Pinos Altos."

"Jesus," groaned Ben, "I never thought of *that!*"

"What white man would?" asked Short Dog. Then, in a rare gesture of sentiment, he leaned over, patting Ben's knee. "*Mira, amigo*, don't worry. I have told you everything you need to know. So why fret? Go to your blankets. Close your eyes; get a good night's sleep; Short Dog is here."

Ben looked at him, the wry grin breaking dubiously.

"Thank you ever so much, dear Short Dog," he said in English, "for absolutely nothing."

23

The Switchback

SHORT DOG brought them up with the Apaches at eleven
A.M. It was a clear day, bright and hot. The Comanche,
who had ordered them to leave the river trail an hour
earlier, had since been leading them on a parallel route
which threaded the rocks flanking the Mimbres off its east
bank. Now he signaled Ben, next behind him, to get down
off his mount and come forward. The latter did so, joining
him where he crouched in a V of hard red sandstone
looking over the river valley. Far below, on the stream-
bank trail—the west bank now—he could see the crawling
dots. Counting them, he came out with the correct number, thirteen, and Short Dog said sharply:

"How many do you make it with the eye alone?"

Ben told him, and he nodded but turned in the same
motion to signal Frank Go-deen forward with the "glass
eye," the telescope. The breed brought up the instrument.
Short Dog took it from him, studied the Apaches through
it, handed it directly to Ben.

"See if it is the same," he said.

Ben took the glass.

"All right," said Short Dog, "how does it go? You see
twelve braves? You see the woman? You agree these are
the band of Broken Hand and that I have done what
Quanah ordered of me"

Ben put down the glass. It was the Mimbreno party
with Amy Johnston all right.

"Yes, that's the band. I could even see the chief's
shriveled arm."

"Which one was it?"

"The left one."

"That's right. Now you have seen it, no?"

"Yes, now I have seen it."

Short Dog nodded abruptly to this final agreement, got
back up on his pony and made the farewell sign to Ben.

"Hasta luego, señor," he said. Soberly he touched his fingers to his brow. "You're pretty brave for a white man. I hope all goes well with you." He was turning his wiry Spanish mustang before it got through to Ben that he meant, actually, to leave them. He jumped then to his stirrup and put a restraining hand on his naked thigh.

"Un momento, por favor!" he pleaded. "How can you do this to us?"

"Very easy," replied the Comanche, not smiling. "Watch me." With the instruction, he kneed his pony between the mounts of Lame John and Big Bat. The latter gave trail to let him through. He never looked back. And Ben and the others dared not call after him to do so. When he was far enough down along the ridge trail, he put his mustang on the lope and within the time they watched him was gone from sight, south and east, homeward bound.

"My God," said Ben, breaking the long silence "now what do we do?"

"Easy, like he said." Big Bat Pourier grinned. "Now we pray."

"That's fine for you," complained Go-deen, "but how about me? I have no gods."

"Try Wakan Tonka," said Big Bat. "He's good enough for the Oglala, he should be good enough for you."

"Bah!" said Go-deen. "But then what else could one expect from this whole crazy idea? Actually, things have turned out excitingly well, though. Here we are in the middle of the Apaches' land, knowing no trails, no water holes, no way in, no way out, except to go back the way we came on their own road to the Rio Grande. Isn't that wonderful? Didn't I say it was exciting?"

"Even more than you think." Ben nodded. "You forgot a little something. We've got to get the girl and take her with us. But that oughtn't to be too difficult for four mealy brains from Montana."

"Three," corrected Go-deen irritably. "The Nez Percé is from Oregon."

"I wasn't thinking of Lame John," said Ben. "I meant the mule." Old Malachi had come up past the ponies of Big Bat and Lame John to stand near Ben, peering outward and downward through the V-notch in the sandstone at the distant Apaches. "What do you think, old-timer?"

139

Ben now inquired of him, reaching to put a friendly hand on his bristly withers.

Malachi nipped at his hand, shook his long ears, took another look at the Mimbrenos, blew out softly but spookily through his crusted nostrils.

"Just what I thought," nodded Ben. Then to the others, "That was his Indian *whoof*. I know it, believe me. If we don't want to trust our own sight or Frank's spyglass, we can still bet on Malachi's china-blue eyeballs. That's our bunch yonder."

"Somehow, *mon ami*"—grinned Big Bat—"that was not just the question which disturbed my mind."

"No, nor mine either!" agreed Go-deen. "Come on, brothers, let's get the hell out of this place!"

Lame John, who without words had taken the telescope from Ben and focused it on the Mimbrenos, now lowered it.

"Brother Ben," he said, "I took my vow to follow you to the end of the trail. Is this then the end of the trail? Am I free of my word?"

"I told you in the beginning I didn't want your word," replied Ben. "You owed me nothing then; you owe me nothing now."

"You didn't answer my question. Is this the end of the trail for you? Are you turning back with the others?"

Ben looked at Go-deen and Big Bat. The one scowled; the other smiled. Ben nodded and felt very good.

"What others?" he asked. "I don't see nobody turning around."

Lame John studied them all, his dark face clouded.

"You still mean to get the woman?"

"Well, that's the general idea."

Lame John looked at them again; two white men and a half-white Sioux mongrel hundreds of miles deep in Apache territory with very little ammunition, only the water in their canteens, no knowledge of the implacable desert closing them in upon all sides, and yet shrugging and scowling and smiling and telling him they were going on with him in the hopeless, foolish, impossible chance of seizing away from eleven Mimbreno murderers, in the very shadow of their mountain-fortress home, the brooding blond woman captive who didn't even know she was

140

of any blood save Indian and who had glared at them and called them all liars in the camp of Soledad Dominguin.

"I can't believe it," he said at last and slowly. "It is not the way of white men to keep their words like this."

"That's normal white men you're talking about," said Ben. "It ain't nothing to do with us half-witted ones."

"No," agreed Frank Go-deen glumly, "and not even with us half-breed, half-witted ones."

Lame John's gaze went unconsciously to Big Bat who had said nothing. The latter at once raised his hands.

"Don't look at me!" he cried. "You know my motto; *cherez la 'squaw!'* What are we waiting for?"

The Nez Percé's fierce eyes softened with his reply.

"I guess for Brother Ben to lead the way," he said, low voiced; "and for John Lame Elk to have the sense to follow with his true friends."

Ben took a deep breath. He had put himself in the hero's corner again. All he had to do now was sneak himself out of it. Well, God had halter-led him so far; maybe He would hold onto the rope for another seventeen hundred miles. Or at least for another twenty-seven—the distance remaining to the Pinos Altos *ranchería* according to Short Dog's educated guess of last evening.

Ay de mí! as the Mexicans put it. The fixes a fellow got himself into. Ben squared his long jaw, stared down through the sandstone notch, squinting to cut through the high-noon heat shimmer building up over the white sands of the river bed. Suddenly his eyes widened.

"Frank," he said, "reach me that spyglass."

With the telescope he scanned the west-bank trail, moving with extreme care past the place where the last look had pin-pointed the Mimbrenos. The others, watching him, saw the tension go out of his shoulders.

"They've disappeared all right," he said, "but it's good rather than bad would be my guess. There's a high saddle over there—sandstone same as the stuff on this here side—where it looks to me as though the trail switches back to snake over the the top and drop down again. I can't see beyond the saddle, or the switchback, rather, but I can't pick up the trail again on the far side of it either. I'd say we're safe to make a run for that switchback, gambling to get to it before they top out again farther up. Frank, what do you think?"

141

Go-deen took the glass. He studied the broken ridge where the west-bank trail appeared to vanish into blind rock. He lifted the lens beyond it, combing the backing scarps and timbered mesalands which led upward to the Pinos Altos and Sierra Diablo ranges. Like Ben, he had to lower the glass and admit the odds seemed favorable.

In turn, Big Bat and Lame John concurred.

Again the decision came back to Ben.

"You know," he grinned, swinging up on his pony and giving Malachi a friendly swat on the rump, moving him aside so that he could lead the way down the steep trail beyond the V-notch, "some days it don't pay to duck."

Ten minutes later they were down in the river bed galloping for the west-bank trail. In half an hour they had reached the head of the climb on the far ridge and were slowing their mounts for the last, steep scramble up to the switchback. It took them possibly another ten minutes to negotiate this risky going. It was hardly over three-quarters of an hour from Ben's tart grin starting down through the V-notch to his softly breathed, *"Jesus—"* as he led his followers around the blind S of the switchback and to an unbidden halt under the cocked rifles and waiting, wolflike stares of Mano Roto and his ten Mimbreno Apaches.

24

A Prayer of His People

"YOU SURPRISED?" asked Broken Hand in heavily accented English.

The simple question, where a crackle of rifle fire had been anticipated, startled Ben's numbed mind into moving again. He automatically made the greeting sign as he replied uncertainly:

"Well, chief, that's one way of looking at it."

"*Unh,*" said Broken Hand, nodding.

They all sat there. The red men stared at the whites, their broad faces expressionless. The white men returned the compliment but not blankly. Even Frank Go-deen, the half-white, showed unmistakable apprehension by wrinkling the lance scar across his crooked nose in what was intended as an ingratiating smile. Ben and Big Bat were scared sweatless, both candidly admitting the sentiment with the small, prune-lipped smirks which they presented in lieu of the grins they thought they were furnishing. Only Lame John returned the Apache look, stone eye for stone eye.

In the stillness Malachi, belatedly lounging along in the rear of his party, came around the corner of the switchback. Seeing the Indians, he threw up his head and snorted loudly. Ben gave him a glance of pure poison.

"Thanks a hell of a lot," he told him. "We was just setting here a'wondering what these here fellers was. By jingo, we're downright beholden to you. Indians, eh? Well, I'll be damned."

Malachi rolled his blue eyes. He blew out noisily through his nostrils, bobbed his head energetically, put back his ears and brayed. Broken Hand regarded him curiously, looking from him to Ben.

"You talk to the mule?" he said. "He understands you?"

"Oh, sure," answered Ben. "He understands me fine.

143

It's just me has a little trouble understanding him now and again."

"I see," said the Apache chief. "Well, if he hear you so good, maybe you like him answer you Mimbreno question: ask him how you going get away from Mano Roto?" Ben considered the matter, shook his head.

"It's no use, chief. He don't savvy a word about Apaches. He's a Sioux mule."

"*Unh*, that's bad."

"Chief," said Ben, "we ain't no argument whatever."

Behind him, Frank Go-deen muttered resentfully, his half-breed sense of humor failing him.

"Listen, brother," he told Ben, "perhaps I missed something, somewhere, but I don't think these New Mexican cousins are making fun."

"Brother," said Ben tightly, "you think *I* think they are?"

"I don't care what *I* think; or you; it's them I'm watching, and I don't see any smiles over there."

"You got a point," granted Ben, letting his set grin fade out and the silence return tenfold.

Broken Hand permitted the pause to grow. During its tense seconds Ben noted for the first time that Amy Johnston was not among the Apache ranks. The lateness of the discovery was mute tribute to the shock of meeting Mano Roto around a blind corner, but now Ben shot a quick look at Lame John. Catching the Nez Percé's eye, he asked, low voiced:

"John, you see what I see—or don't see?"

"Yes, Brother Ben, I saw it before I saw a one of these desert monkeys." He stared coldly at the small, bandy-legged Mimbrenos, his gaze settling finally on Broken Hand. Making the least gesture with the Winchester in his right hand, he said to him very carefully, "This is the *new* gun, not the old one like yours." Broken Hand and his braves looked at their assortment of single-shot Springfields and Mexican muzzle-loaders, then waited, watching the tall northern Indian. The latter twitched the Winchester again. "I am very fast with it," he said, "and not afraid to die. *What have you done with the yellow-haired woman?*"

The Apache thought it over, understanding the terms of the question. If harm had come to the white captive, this

144

big English-talking Indian was going to take a few of them with him. If not, he was open to further negotiation. It made sense, even to a Mimbreno.

"What do you know about the woman?" asked Broken Hand, genuinely interested. "What do you care about her?"

"She is my woman," said Lame John and moved the hammer of the Winchester to full cock.

"Well, now, I thought she was my woman." The Apache chief nodded. "I just give lots money for her."

"Produce her," said Lame John. *"Or die."*

Broken Hand studied the Winchester carbine enviously.

"That's a wonderful gun," he said. "I think maybe you able do what you say with it. You brave man, too. I do what you ask." He made a sign to his braves, and when they hesitated to obey its order, he snarled, "Bring the woman! Goddam, you want to get shot?"

Apparently they did not, for after another moment's scowling, three of them rode over to a pile of boulders, one dismounting to drag Amy Johnston, bound hands to leg irons and gagged, out into the tiny meadow of the ambush.

The look of glad relief in Lame John's dark face was brief. It flickered and went out like a blown candle. He looked from the dirt-stained, miserable captive to Ben Allison. It was a glance which plainly begged for help or backing in the wild resolve forming in his savage heart. Ben could not speak Nez Percé, but he was a gifted reader of men's faces. He threw Lame John the wait-a-moment sign.

"For God's sake, John," he said, "don't do nothing."

The Nez Percé hesitated just long enough for Broken Hand to push his pony forward, the first move any of the Mimbrenos had made toward the trapped men.

"That's good advice. Your friend is smart." He nodded. "You hold still. Girl all right."

He seemed not unfriendly with the words and Go-deen and Big Bat both spoke quickly to Lame John urging him not to start anything. Ben, seizing the opportunity to take the play away from the single-minded Nez Percé youth, kneed his pony up to Broken Hand's.

"We're glad to see the woman is well," he told him. "We've come a long ways to see her."

145

"Why?" said Broken Hand.

Ben repeated the Amy Johnston story. He did a great job with it, practice having improved his memory of its more dramatic aspects—some of the best of which he now added for the first time. The Apache chief was impressed.

"Hell of good story," he grunted. "You talk fine."

Frank Go-deen, tempted beyond fear, threw up his hands in exasperation.

"Sure, you bet, Cousin Broken Hand! He's the biggest talker north of the Arkansas River. I always said it!"

Broken Hand iced him with a stare.

"Half-breed," he ordered, "close mouth."

"Very much what I had in mind," decided Go-deen, edging his pony behind Ben's and alongside Big Bat's.

The latter gave him a look to equal the Apache's.

"You have *le caractère remarquable, mon ami;* it passes belief," he told him. "You have the absolute talent to say the precise right thing at the exact wrong time. *Zut!* Did you hear the chief? *Gardez-vous le silence!*"

One of the Apaches, a sullen youth, little more than a boy really but carrying a sawed-short double shotgun big enough for any man, now rode up to Broken Hand. He pointed arrogantly at the huge French Canadian and the potbellied Milk River breed, both special privilege and an end to his young warrior's patience showing in his angry manner.

"Too damn much talk!" he declared. "Too many tongues busy. Let's go."

"You're right, Chaco," agreed Broken Hand immediately. "This is no place for talk. We will go up the river a ways."

"I want to go home," said the youth. "Why will you go up the river first?"

"Be patient, boy. There is yet some thinking for Broken Hand to do. You know Mangas. We don't want him to get excited."

"You going to camp upriver then?"

"Yes, one more night. Then ride in."

"It makes no sense."

"We do what I say, boy. We make camp. Then I go on into *ranchería* when moon come up. Talk easy with Mangas. Maybe say he can have woman after me. Maybe before. Whatever necessary."

146

The youth looked at Ben and the others.

"What of these?" he demanded.

"You keep them in camp. Good bait for trade to Mangas. Use to put him in bad position. We bring four prisoners, what can he say to woman?"

"This woman has changed you. You're sick with her."

"It's a lie, but I paid much money for her. She is my woman. I won't have him to kill her."

"Basta!" snarled a hard-faced subchief, driving his scrubby mount out of the Mimbreno line and up to face his chief and the angered youth. "That's enough, you hear, Mano? If you want to camp one more night, all right. No stay here talk all day though. Come on. Goddam!"

"Yes, I agree, Hota." Broken Hand nodded. *"Vamonos."* He pointed to the new prisoners. "Tie feet under pony's belly. Get that big Indian first. You, Chaco, you do it."

The ill-tempered boy rode over to Lame John and put the shotgun into his ribs with a curse.

"Go over there," he said pointing to the other Apaches who were shaking out binding ropes. "Move quick!"

He jabbed his weapon hard into Lame John, wanting only the excuse to close his finger on the first trigger and blow his side out. The Nez Percé accommodated him. Snaking his right hand across his own body, he seized the gun barrels, jerking them back across his flattened stomach. When Chaco's finger shut down, the charge blasted the horn off the saddle but did not touch Lame John. In the next instant Chaco was swept bodily off his scrubby mount and pinned in front of his opponent with a left-arm strangle hold. With his right hand, Lame John jammed the stolen shotgun between his hostage's kidneys.

"Now," he said to Broken Hand, "if you want to shoot, shoot. I am waiting."

Of the Apaches, only the chief moved. And he only enough to raise his twisted arm in mute protest.

"That is my nephew," he said, "the son of my sister and her husband who are dead. He is last of my blood."

"How do you love him?" asked Lame John.

"As a son. What do you want?"

"To get away; only to get away."

Ben, Go-deen and Big Bat exchanged glances. Ben was

147

stunned, but the other two were something less. "He's an Indian," shrugged the one, while the other snapped, "Even worse, an idiot. I always said it."

Ben shook his head numbly. "By God, it ain't so," was all he could manage.

But it was so, and John Lame Elk in the last corner was bargaining for his own life.

"How you expect to get away?" Broken Hand wanted to know. "Where you hide we no find you?"

"I will take the boy." Lame John would not look at Ben or the others. "When I have reached the Great River I will release him unharmed. If you try, meanwhile, to come after me or to get him away from me, I will kill him. You have my word both ways."

"No," said Broken Hand slowly, "I will not let you take him away. Not to the Great River. First I say you kill boy right now."

"How far then?"

"You take him one sun. We no follow. I promise it."

"You mean you will give me a twenty-four hour head start. Then I turn the boy loose without hurt, and I have your word you will not come after me?"

"Yes."

"*No one* will follow me?"

"I have said it."

"All right, I take your word. I'm going now." He motioned with the shotgun. "Bring his pony over here. Be very careful." The pony was brought over by the ugly subchief. Chaco slid onto him, still dazed from the suffocation of the strangle hold. Lame John poked him savagely with the gun. "Ride straight," was all he said.

"God Almighty," breathed Ben to Big Bat as the Apache boy started his pony toward them, "he ain't going to take the word of that red ape! They'll ambush him sure!"

"Say nothing—stand still," warned the Canuck giant.

"Frank," he said, appealing to Go-deen, "we can't let him ride out of here like this, double cross or no double cross. He's rode the river with us. It ain't human!"

"Neither is Broken Hand. Do what Bat says—don't move your eyelids. Your friend is as good as safe across the Rio Grande right now. The chief has guaranteed it."

Ben couldn't accept the assurance or wouldn't. "No, sir,

by God!" he muttered and reached for the .44. It was then he found he could not move his right hand. The reason was Big Bat Pourier's paw closed over his wrist with the grip of a Green River bear trap.

"Petit Ben," he said out of the side of his mouth, "if you move, I will break your bones like a chicken wing. You do not get yourself killed for that dog of a Slit Nose. Pull away and let them past!"

Ben looked at Lame John, now but a pony-length distant. The latter stared through him, kept his rangy Appaloosa moving directly toward him. Ben's pony stepped back, letting Chaco's mount pass, with Lame John's shouldering through behind the Apache boy's scrub. They were gone around the blind turn of the switchback then, with only the brief, flinty ring of their animals' hooves striking back from the bedrock depths of the trail to mark the passage. Then the hoof sounds, too, were gone, and there was only the bake-oven silence of the high desert to answer for the disaffection of John Lame Elk.

After five seconds of listening to this stillness, Ben Allison shook his shaggy head, gathered his slack reins.

"Sonofabitch," he said under his breath.

"What was that? What did you say?" demanded Broken Hand, pushing forward querulously.

"Nothing," answered Ben, "just a prayer of my people; come on, let's go—"

25

Mimbreno Mercy

THE APACHES went up the Mimbres only as far as old Fort Webster. The crumbling post, abandoned in 1861 by its Confederate-sympathizing garrison, had an excellent well in the nearby river bed and was a favored, indeed protected, stopping place of the nomad Mimbrenos.

Here the prisoners were put in the still-intact *"juzgado"* of the moldering ruin and allowed the freedom of their arms and legs. The liberty was no risk. The cell door was of mountain oak four inches thick, the bars of one inch drill steel, the walls of thirty-inch adobe. The temperature inside the eight-foot-square room was comparable to that of an Apache beehive bread oven. They were given no water; the cell room had no window. They breathed, or rather gasped, for air through the eighteen by twenty-four inch opening of the door bars.

"It is not a prison cell," groaned Big Bat; "it is an invention of the Holy Roman *Inquisiteur! Voilà!* I am dying. I am a fish on the river bank!"

Ben and Frank Go-deen echoed his groan but could not add meaningful words to his estimation of their quarters. This was at four P.M. At seven thirty, the sundown and the long purple twilight fading, the cell was opened and the prisoners ordered outside. Big Bat, his enormous bulk more vulnerable to the intense heat, had lost consciousness and had to be dragged forth. It took four of the Apaches, one to each arm and leg, to move him. Go-deen, an older man than either of his companions, was also near the edge. He still had his eyes open, but his senses were not responding properly. The subchief called over Broken Hand, who looked at the two and ordered water given immediately and in regulated small amounts.

"They will not live the night otherwise," he said.

Ben, in better shape, was motioned by the chief to follow him. He led the way to the sutler's store, roofless

150

and doorless and windowless but located centrally in the fort's ground plan, hence the proper place for the chief's fire. Bidding Ben to sit down along the front wall of the empty store, he gave him food—parched corn and sun-dried mule meat—and fresh water from the river well.

"Eat a little first," he advised; "then drink sparingly."

For a time Ben said nothing, too busy obeying the elemental urges of survival. When he had finished, he sat quietly waiting for Broken Hand to lead the talk. After several minutes of smoking his Sonora cigarrillo, the latter tamped the butt carefully out, placed it in his shirt pocket, nodded soberly, to his silent guest.

"For a white man," he said, "I like you."

"I am a quarter-blood Tshaoh," said Ben, "a Kwahadi of Quanah's people. My mother's mother was a Water Horse."

"The Tshaoh?" said Broken Hand. "Hmmm. Much interesting. I was wondering how you got so far into Apache country without we see you. You bring Comanche guide, do I lie?"

"You don't lie; he deserted us this morning."

"When he saw us?"

"Yes, when he saw you."

"Smart Comanche."

"Very smart," agreed Ben.

"Smart Nez Percé, too."

"No," said Ben. "Treacherous. He was a brother on the long trail with us. The Comanche only came because Quanah ordered him."

"You don't understand Indian. Nez Percé no traitor. Just smart."

"Well maybe so. I notice you trusted him."

"Sure. He is Indian."

"And you?"

"We both Indians. No lie to each other. The boy will be all right; you will see."

"I wasn't so much worried about him as about us," admitted Ben. "You're going to kill us, aren't you?"

"No, not me—Mangas."

"You mean when we get to your *rancheria* up yonder?"

"Yes."

"But why? What have we done?"

"You white man."

"Only part," claimed Ben hopefully.

"Most part," grunted the Mimbreno.

Ben nodded, tried another tack.

"How about my friends? One of them is half Sioux."

"Other half white. Half white worse than all white."

"Then you simply kill all the whites you catch, is that it?"

"All but woman. If she young, good face, good body."

"All others, though, eh?"

"No, sometime we save a strong boy-child. You know, one not cry out or act with fear. Make good Indian. All tribe, Apaches, Comanches, Kiowas, have some like that."

"You mean like my cousin Quanah?"

"Quanah half-breed, no good."

Ben gave it up, returned to the original thought.

"Then Mangas will kill us tomorrow?"

"Oh, no. He take longer than that."

"Torture?"

"You ask foolish question. You one-quarter Comanche; know better."

"Yep," said Ben. "I did, I am, and I do."

To his surprise, Broken Hand smiled at the flippant reply. He reached out and patted Ben's arm.

"You good man. Make joke like Indian."

"I know a hundred of them," said Ben. "My grandmother was a great wit among the Comanches."

"Good, good—" The Apached nodded and fell still.

After a time, during which Ben noted that his weathered, simian frown grew deeper-lined by the minute, the tough-looking chief shook his head and held up his shrunken arm.

"You know how I get sick arm?" he asked. He pointed out through the gateless hole in the fort's wall, into the westward night. "White man own trading store—not here, out there, over by place call Apache Well, He say I steal from store. I say I no steal from store. Say no Apache steal from white man." He slid out of its sheath an eight-inch skinning knife and made a dramatic slash through the darkness. "But white man, he say I lie. He have five man hold me, cut me bad with knife, cut arm, all arm, muscle, sinew, very deep. He say to me, 'There, you steal no more.' "

152

His story trailed off, fierce eyes stalking the night out beyond the walls.

"But white man wrong. I steal one more time. I come back to store with many friend. They hold white man. I steal both arm, here—" he demonstrated with the blade—"just below elbow. I take all arm off, bone, everything. Next day soldier patrol find him that way. He no die. Soldier chief Major Mowry good man from this fort here." He stabbed the ground upon which they sat, blading the dry earth deeply. "Major, he say tell Broken Hand, '*Dah-eh-sah*, death to him.' Soldier scout, White Mountain Apache, say yes, he tell. He find me. I say him tell Major Mowry, '*Zas-te!* Kill him.' Scout, he say, '*En-neh*,' he do."

He paused again, pulling his knife free of the earth.

"So long war now. No peace for Apache people till last soldier gone. No peace for soldier till last Apache gone."

This time when he stopped he did not offer to continue, and Ben said presently:

"But I'm not a soldier. Why kill me then?"

"Soldier no go till last white man dead." The chief shrugged. "So kill all white man, then soldier go. Simple."

"Very," agreed Ben.

Broken Hand nodded, his gnarled hand touching his arm again.

"Too bad you white. But no change Apache law. I do you favor though."

"Well, thank you," said Ben, imagining many things at once, the least of which was commutation of sentence to slavery. "My friends, too, eh?"

"No, no can help friend. Only you."

"Thank you, chief, but I take what my friends take. That's a law of my people."

"Law of your people no good. You get Apache law same as friend but not from Mangas." He pointed to the revived Big Bat and Go-deen over by the prison wall. "They get from Mangas; you get from Broken Hand. They wait, you get first thing in morning."

"Get?" said Ben, throat constricting. "Get what?"

"Honorable death. We no cut you. Put you on wall like soldier do Apache. You die quick, many bullet. Honorable."

For a moment Ben said nothing. Then, as steadily as he could, he made known his gratitude.

"Many thanks, chief," he said. "I would purely hate to die dishonorable."

"Dismiss it from your mind," waved the other. "It is nothing—even less than that."

"Broken Hand," said Ben, "you couldn't be righter."

"Thank you. Here"—the Apache reached impulsively inside his shirt, brought forth the stub of a cigarrillo butt—"have a smoke. From Sonora. Very good." He plucked a brand from the fire, lighted the butt for Ben, inquired with concern as the latter drew in the first lungful. "All right? You like fine?"

Ben exhaled lingeringly.

"Honorable," he nodded, "real honorable."

"Good," said Broken Hand, relieved. "Smoke deep. Take time. Enjoy flavor." Then, with a friendly smile and gesture to dispel any remaining tension, *"Last one—"*

26

The Gentling Sound

THE FORT'S OUTER WALLS were of Pinos Altos cedar logs planted vertically and tied together with an inner catwalk of milled lumber. The horse shed against the rear, east wall was also of timber. The quartermaster's depot was an adobe hovel lodged against the jail, which in turn was wedged into the front, northwest corner of the quadrangle. Officers' quarters on the north wall were of adobe and cedar, the approved Santa Fe type of Spanish construction. Enlisted barracks were the cedar-pole-and-adobe-plaster architecture called by the scornful and miserable occupants "Early Apache *Jacal.*" The post sutler's store, heart of any western horse Indian trading area post, military or otherwise, was of notched split logs and raftered roof—long, long gone—and stood just within the yawning gates centrally in the enclosure's forecourt. From it to the jail was perhaps forty feet. The entire compound was no more than thirty paces squared, measured inside the barracks, horse-shed buttresses of the walls.

Listing this plot in the near-stygian gloom preceding moonrise, Ben Allison found little of hope in its offering.

The only practical way out was the open gateway; and across this single avenue the Mimbrenos had thoughtfully strung their picket of highly nervous desert mustangs, the best watchdogs to be found on either the North or South Plains. No one but an Indian could come near that line of spooky, half-wild horses and not be snorted and neighed into an instant announcement of intent of good-bye. Which in Apache country amounted to a guaranteed farewell of shoot first and scalp afterward.

No, a man could just as well quit looking out that damned gate. There had to be some other way.

Ben tried piercing the darkness in the direction of the jail and could not. He then called softly to see if his friends were still all right. He heard Big Bat answer,

155

"Oui," and Go-deen growl something to the effect that he
had never felt better in his life and that to ask an idiot
question was to get an idiot answer. Ben grinned, and as
he did, a Mimbreno moccasin smashed him in the mouth
and knocked him back against the logs of the sutler's
store.

When he got the blood out of his mouth and the stars
out of his eyes, he looked up and saw Hota Du-chuz, the
ape-faced subchief, standing over him.

"No talk," suggested the Apache.

Ben spit some more blood and part of a front tooth.

"Good idea." He nodded.

At once the horse-hide moccasin slammed into his face
again, this time missing the mouth and nearly ripping an
ear away.

"No talk," repeated Hota Du-chuz.

This time Ben gave the nod without the comment. Hota
Du-chuz watched him a moment, then put his foot into
the ribs of Broken Hand, sleeping beside Ben. The chief
awoke with a start and sat up.

"What's the matter?" he asked. "What's happened?"

"Nothing," said Hota Du-chuz. "These big mouth talk
too much. I shut up quick."

"Well, thanks. I must have dozed away. Hmmm—
bad."

"Yes. Good thing you tie Tall One to you."

"I watch him; you watch others. I do my job; you do
your job. Understand?"

"Sure. When you go see Mangas?"

"I already said; when the moon comes."

"Pretty quick now," said Hota Du-chuz, eying the early
stars. "Maybeso fifteen minute, maybeso twenty-five."

"I'll be ready," grumbled Broken Hand. "You go back
and watch others. No, wait—" He held up his hand as the
subchief started off through the darkness. "Better bring
them all over here; put in house with woman." He gestured to the sutler's store behind Ben and himself. "We
watch more easy all one place."

Hota Du-chuz stood a moment as though he might
argue the order, then went off without a word. He was
back in a short time, followed by several braves dragging
Big Bat and Frank Go-deen by their heels through the

156

compound's choking dust. The two were trussed in the same way Ben was, hands to ankles behind the back.

"Put in house," said Broken Hand. "Him, too," he gestured to Ben. "I will sit in the door till the moon comes. You others lie down, rest." His own braves were already asleep, sprawled in the dirt beyond the fire. Hota Du-chuz's followers dumped Ben and the others in the pit blackness of the store building, glad to be rid of the responsibility and to join their brothers on the warm ground of the fireside. The sharp chill of the altitude was getting into the air now, and the fire felt good. Its dying embers purred and spat softly. The spread horse blankets and weary bodies made good company to the lulling sounds. Like good soldiers anywhere, the Apache braves were soundly sleeping within minutes of Broken Hand's order.

In the doorway sat Mano Roto, waiting for the moon. On the wall beyond the doorway sat Hota Du-chuz, waiting for Mano Roto. The chief was too soft with these white eyes. Especially the tall one who talked too much. When Broken Hand was gone up the trail to see Mangas, things would change quickly. Meanwhile, the moon could not be long, and a man who would be chief in Mano Roto's place could well afford the brief patience. There was the woman too. For all her hard looks she had a body soft as a baby foal's nose. Hota Du-chuz had felt it. *En-neh!* No wonder the lecherous old devil in the doorway yonder had paid such a price for her! And another thing. She was no breed as he thought. Hota had seen her body where the clothes protected it from sun and wind. It was white as mare's milk. *Eyeh!* This was meat for a younger man than Mano Roto. And one who stayed awake better.

Hota Du-chuz looked over at his chief. Broken Hand was already nodding again. The grin which lifted the upper lip of his lieutenant was the same grin which bared the canines of the waiting dog wolf when the antelope doe's head began to drop and the spotted fawn to wander from her couched side.

The old fool. Let him sleep. Hota Du-chuz was awake and watching. His time would come and soon, very soon.

Hota Du-chuz was a prophet beyond his knowledge. As the pleasant thought of his ascendancy passed in his mind,

157

a sudden stir of the ponies on the picket line across the gateway caught his acutely sharp ear. He came to his feet, crouched and peering off toward the restless horses. They quieted quickly enough and any other Indian would have let the matter go as a harmless night shadow or vagrant scent of desert predator from the hunting reaches of the Mimbres bottoms. But Hota Du-chuz was not any other Indian.

He went forward through the black velvet well of darkness filling the high-walled enclosure of Fort Webster. Ahead of him the solitary opening of the gate showed a lighter gray from the outer desert, where he could see its faint luminescence through the legs and over the backs of the picketed ponies. Ten feet from the line he paused. Nothing moved save the mustangs themselves. They pricked friendly ears, and two or three uttered the muffled snuffing exhalation with which the prairie horse greets the familiar, welcome smell of its master.

Hota Du-chuz straightened, let the steel go out of his muscles.

"Hoh, shuh," he told the little mustangs, answering them with the old Apache gentling sounds. "Be still now; all is well." With the words, he turned to go back to the pinpoint of coals which marked the fire before the sutler's store. The tiny beacon was the last sight of Hota Du-chuz's life.

As he took the first step out from beneath the front-wall catwalk, a tall shadow dropped from it soundlessly. The drive of the knife was true and deep. Hota Du-chuz went into the silted dust of old Fort Webster as quietly as though lying down to sleep. Bending over him, the tall shadow waited for the time of one long breath, then stood up.

"Hoh, shuh," said John Lame Elk and stepped over the body and went through the noiseless dust toward the Apache fire.

27

The Tongue of Strangers

UNTIL THE MOON came over the palisaded walls, flooding the compound with its dazzle of white light and awakening Broken Hand, there was no attempt at talking to Amy Johnston. The three friends whispered among themselves, discussing their nonexistent chances in English, which the girl could not understand, and trying to decide whether to risk going for Broken Hand's knife—where they could see the silhouette of its belted haft in the doorway—or to simply wait for morning and pray for deliverance from a God none of them had particularly worked at pleasing prior to the present emergency. Human nature being what it is, the vote went rather speedily to going for the knife, and selection of the one who was to inch across the floor like a ripe-corn worm, to try stealing the weapon with his back and bound hands to Broken Hand's back, went at once forward. Go-deen was ruled out for the size of his belly, Big Bat simply for his size. Ben was judged the best sneak, given the farewell whispers, nudged on his way by the breed's plea to see if he could not get only himself killed, in event of failure, and avoid bringing the Apache temper down on the rest of them.

Ben began hunching through the dirt upon his side like some grotesque, wounded reptile. He knew the risk, knew that Frank Go-deen's parting request was valid. To fumble the theft of the knife could bring far more than another moccasin in the mouth. Not from Broken Hand perhaps, but from the hair-trigger Hota Du-chuz, squatting but three or four feet from the former. Should he hear or see Ben behind the chief, he would likely strike to kill and not wait to determine if the captive had freed himself, was armed or another solitary fact. In the dark, sights and sounds were struck at blindly. To react in any other manner was to invite destruction in the unmerciful code of the desert.

But Ben did not reach the knife haft of Mano Roto. As

159

he came up behind the chief and was twisting to get his back and hands presented toward the knife, a long shadow fell athwart the doorway. There was light enough now from the moonrise which was lightening the low skyline of the river hills to distinguish substance and shade. This shade was not cast by the bandy legged Hota Du-chuz. Ben writhed around, watching the doorway. In the instant that he did, the moon broke free of the hills and shot the fort full of day-bright illumination. Mano Roto stirred, and the long shadow froze. The chief rubbed at his eyes, yawned, turned to blink and peer into the lightening gloom of the store's interior. Behind him Ben saw the shadow move again. An arm, substance not shade, appeared from the frame of the door as if grown there by some magic of the moonlight. But the arm ended in a human hand, and the hand held a loose adobe brick shard the weight and size of a small anvil. And the hand raised the shard and brought it into the back of Mano Roto's skull in the precise second that he said to Ben, *"Eh? What are you doing there, boy?"* And Mano Roto slid onto his face in the dust with no more sound than Hota Du-chuz before him.

Lame John stepped over him into the store, and said in guarded, apologetic tone:

"I didn't kill him, Brother Ben, because we exchanged our words, he and I. And I'm sorry, too, I had to lead you to think I would leave you and my friends here. I saw no other way at the moment. Will you forgive me?"

"John" said Ben, no grin and no grit in the answer, "it's us owes you apologies. Let's get out of here."

The Nez Percé put a restraining hand on his shoulder.

"Wait," he said, "I must see the woman; I must talk with her."

"All right," muttered Ben, "but make it quick. She's here, in yonder corner under that old shelf. We ain't tried talking to her. Feared she'd make a fuss. But we heard her stirring around in the dark."

"It's strange she wouldn't speak to you," said Lame John. "She knows Frank can speak Shoshoni."

"There's more queer here than in a circus side tent," rasped Ben. "But the price ain't so reasonable. Here, slice me loose before you mess around with that girl."

Lame John cut him free, and he quickly pulled Broken Hand's body back up into a sitting position in the door-
160

way, while the Nez Percé went over to Amy Johnston. Ben, turning away from propping up the chief, saw Lame John beckoning to him. He cut loose Big Bat and handed him Broken Hand's knife to tend to Go-deen, then went on over to where the Nez Percé stood over Amy Johnston.

"See," he said, "here is why she didn't talk to Frank; they gagged her so she couldn't say anything which might help you. I'm going to cut her free now. Are the others ready?"

"Yes," said Ben, "but wait a minute on the girl. Can we trust her? Suppose she's addled some and yells out the minute you pull the gag? Remember, she wasn't exactly on our side last time we talked."

"I must free her; she has suffered too long now." He bent to slash the rawhide gag, but Ben pinned his arm and twisted him roughly against the rear wall of the store.

"John, you can't do it. You could get us all killed. Think, man, think! Just look at her there! She's glaring at us wilder'n a cornered she-lynx!"

"Brother Ben, don't hold me, I beg of you."

He said it softly, and Ben knew he would never cry out and betray them, but he knew as well that the next moment could bring that knife winging for him if he did not somehow get through to its savage wielder that this woman was as great a danger to their lives as any of the sleeping Apaches—or might be far worse.

Fortunately he got help from a sympathetic quarter and one long wise in the ways of Indians.

"Here, *mon ami*," whispered Big Hat behind him, "give him into my attention." He slid past Ben and had Lame John in his bear's grasp before either Ben or the Nez Percé could guess his intent. His giant strength crushed the breath out of Lame John's lungs and held it out, leaving the tall brave as helpless as a newly whelped kitten. Ben seized his knife in the next moment and handed it to Frank Go-deen, who had just drifted over from the doorway.

"All still quiet outside," he said; "let's work fast in here, brothers."

"*Oui*," said Big Bat. "Petit Ben, you know what to do with the woman. She has *got* to stay quiet. *N'est-ce pas?*"

Ben nodded grimly.

161

"You pull her out and hold her up, Frank," he said.

Go-deen obeyed the order, pinning the woman to his chest, facing Ben. Ben measured her and hit her as hard as he dared. Her head flew back into Go-deen, rebounded, fell forward and hung slackly.

"All right, Frank," Ben said, "now pull the gag."

He went over to Lame John, looking close into his face.

"John," he said, "you know I was right. Will you be yourself if we let you go? I want your word."

For a count of five it appeared as though the proud Nez Percé would give his word only to kill his questioner. Then the wild fire died from his dark eyes, and he nodded his head weakly.

"Ease off him," ordered Ben, and Big Bat let go the rib-cracking pressure and stood back. Lame John would have fallen in the first moment had Ben not caught and steadied him. Directly, he was all right and said remorsefully to Ben:

"Brother, it was wrong of me. I talk like you do, but I still think like an Indian. You had to do it. Let us go quickly now. I will carry her."

Ben shook his head, sliding to the doorway and looking out. He was back in an instant.

"Nobody will carry her, John. We got work to do out yonder first. We don't bring it off out there, ain't nobody going to have to worry about toting Amy Johnston out of here. You savvy?"

Lame John was thinking like a white man again; there was no hesitation now and even a flicker of the old sober smile.

"I savvy, Brother Ben. *Hookahey!*"

They all went to the doorway, four shadows moving as one. Facing the outside, they hesitated.

"I can't see the subchief," whispered Ben. "He's gone."

"That he is, brother," said Lame John. "Forever."

"You got him?"

"Yes, with the knife. Now how will it be with the others, knife or rock?"

"I like the rock," said Ben. "A knife can miss."

"True." It was Big Bat, adding his expert's opinion. "And the pleasant thing is that one can use the rock

162

without knowing what he did with it. With the knife you *know*."

"I don't mind knowing," put in Go-deen. "Killing these monkeys means nothing. It's just that to cave a head in is quieter and quicker. I say the rock also."

"Good," said Ben. "We'll work in pairs; me and Lame John, you and Big Bat. One to rock and one to knife. If the rock fails, the knife can follow it. All right?"

"Sure." Big Bat's white teeth flashed like a snowbank in his black beard. "François and I will start on the ones near the gate."

"No, wait," broke in Lame John. "We had better pair Frank and me for those near the gate. If those ponies get a smell of white man, we're done before we start."

"Nobody knows Indians like Indians—amen," said Ben. "Come on, Bat, you and me will start on them farthest from the horses. And don't be giving off no French Canadian odors on the way."

"Petit Ben," vowed the other, "you have my word; I will keep the buttocks tensed."

"No fear of that," said Ben. "Let's go. Hit true and pray hard."

They set off through the moonlight, two and two, circling the sleeping Apaches. It went well to a point. Seven Mimbrenos were knocked unconscious before the eighth awoke. Go-deen's descending rock missed him, but Lame John's waiting blade did not. He fell, however, backward across the ninth man, who came rolling to his feet, rifle in hand.

He fired at Go-deen, face close, the powder blinding the breed momentarily, but the bullet ricocheting off the wall top and crying harmlessly out into the desert. Big Bat had him from behind then and broke his spine with a grizzly hug whose bone crack made Ben physically sick. The Apache was still moving when Bat dropped him, and Lame John went to one knee beside him and slit his throat. In the paper-white light of the moon the dying man's blood pumped black as squid ink. It made a pool in the dust of Fort Webster's forecourt as wide as a pony's staling spot. Ben saw Lame John dip his fingers in it, touch them to his forehead and then point them in rapid succession to the four winds of the prairie before plunging

163

his knife in the dirt to cleanse it and standing up to join his white and half-white fellows.

Ben suppressed a chill not of the high altitude night. The Nez Percé had told him the truth in the sutler's store. They *talked* the same. And not much else.

It was something to remember.

28

Good-by to Broken Hand

THEY PUT the seven unconscious Mimbreno braves in the stifling pit of the old guardhouse. Through the rusted hasp of the door they wound the heavy chain of the leg irons taken from Amy Johnston. The cuffs of the irons were then linked and locked together. A second set of irons, found on Broken Hand's saddle horn, were placed upon the chief's ankles. The single ancient Spanish key to both sets of chains—a macabre idea of Lame John's—was forced into the mouth and down the gullet of the dead Hota Du-chuz. "Let the secret be his that he may not rest easy," said the taciturn Nez Percé. "He was a bad Indian."

Broken Hand was left outside the prison so that upon return of consciousness he might bring water to his warriors in its fierce crucible. Should he leave them to try crow-hobbling his way for help, he could not be sure to return in time to prevent their deaths from dehydration, a fact of the desert known to the Apaches above any other people. All clothing was stripped from him and from his braves. All weapons and ammunitions of the Indians were dumped down the well in the river bed. The entire action, a charity of Ben's, since both Frank Go-deen and Lame John advised killing the Mimbrenos and hiding their bodies in the dry cistern inside the palisade, took less than thirty minutes. Funeral services—dumping down the cistern—for Hota Du-chuz and his two comrades took another five minutes. Indian saddles, bridles, blankets, moccasins, camp bags, everything of Apache evidence inside Fort Webster, were "buried" with the cistern dead. The horse herd, including Malachi who had been taken along by the hostiles as a curiosity to show the folks at home because of his "white man's eyes," was now brought up by Lame John and Go-deen. Their own mounts were selected and saddled. The Mimbreno ponies were not freed for

165

fear they would make their ways up to the Pinos Altos *ranchería*. Instead, they were roped in threes and made ready to lead along to such a point in the flight as they might be safely abandoned. Malachi was turned loose, his only instruction the terse one from Ben to "keep up and shut up, happen you pine to see Montana again." Inside three-quarters of an hour all was done that could be done, and Amy Johnston was brought out and placed aboard her mount. She was conscious now, and Ben ordered her hands left bound and, indeed, made fast to the saddle horn. Lame John scowled but said nothing. Ben, noting the fact, gave the woman's pony to the Nez Percé to lead, thus putting him on his Indian honor and forestalling any possible move on his part to follow his heart rather than his head.

The moon was by this time an hour high over the stockade wall and the departure from Fort Webster readied in its last detail save one.

Ben, in a final weakness of his "white side," sloshed two buckets of water over Broken Hand, bringing the old chief sputtering and spitting awake. He then explained to him the situation with regard to himself and his men in the prison house, saying nothing of the other details of the abandonment, and concluding with the apologetic statement that it was more than his one-quarter Comanche heart could bear to depart not knowing if Broken Hand were dead or alive, hence risking the lives of his friends in the *juzgado*. He also assured him that his nephew, Chaco, was all right and would be released within the agreed time. To have left without these small courtesies would scarcely have been the act of an honorable enemy, he finally maintained.

Broken Hand, perforce, agreed.

Looking up at Ben and wincing with the pain of his throbbing head, no less than that of his injured reputation, he waved lugubriously to Ben.

"Go on. You good man. I knew it, too. Should have killed you like Hota said. Well, goddam, I don't care. I like you. Go. Run fast. Look out for smoke."

Ben, thinking he meant the smoke of Indian fires, or camping places, nodded gravely.

"Many thanks. We'll be careful." He touched fingertips to brow. "His Comanche brother salutes Mano Roto."

166

"Go to hell," groaned the old chief. "But go quick."

Ben grinned tightly. He reached down, patting the bowed red shoulder.

"*Mucho hombre,* Mano Roto," he said and went quickly back toward the others.

In the utter stillness of the moonlight they mounted and went out the gate. Lame John led the way, the first objective to pick up the captive Chaco where the Nez Percé had left him. This proved to be in the brush of the river bed not a mile north of the fort. Lame John had merely circled the post on the far side of the river and had never been farther from the Apaches the preceding day than the width of the stream. The prisoner reclaimed, they rode on. Chaco was gagged, and they left him that way. Their objective, the sole one which their combined number could suggest, was Fort Craig on the Rio Grande. Big Bat had known of its existence and general location— somewhere between Mesilla and Socorro, a give or take of a hundred miles and more, but northerly rather than southerly. If it *was,* as Big Bat guessed, nearer Socorro, then their best possible line of flight would be due northeast, their shortest possible straight-line distance, seventy to ninety miles. Of water enroute they knew nothing; nor of trails. They had filled all the Apache canteens at the Fort Webster well, and they did know that somewhere north and east the Rio Grande flowed down its wide valley. A direct run for it, due east, had been discussed and voted down. What good was water with the Mimbreno Apaches sharing it with you? No. They would gamble on hitting the river where they could both drink and keep their hair to enjoy the refreshment. That in white man's arithmetic had added up to Fort Craig. None of the comrades said any more of the earlier decision as they now rode onward through the night, with Chaco and the still-silent Amy Johnston staring holes in their tense, already tired backs.

With first light they built a small fire and enjoyed coffee, parched corn and salted Mimbreno mule meat. They offered the fare to Amy Johnston and Chaco, neither of whom would accept it. The Indian boy was now released. Big Bat and Frank Go-deen were very angry over this move, and Ben could not help but be deeply uneasy over it. Yet Lame John would have it no other way. He had given the Apache chief his word. The twenty-four hours had passed. The boy went free, or Lame John would fight.

Ben was absolutely confounded by this display of savage obstinacy in the face of their own extreme peril. But in the end he ruled for Lame John, stipulating only that the boy *not* be given a pony. The Nez Percé was able to accept this condition because his word to Broken Hand had contained no specific reference to the pony. It was a fine point but evidently within the Indian code. While it did not entirely satisfy Big Bat and Go-deen, they had to agree with Ben's grim insistence that they had now to "hang" together or they would all get "strung up" separately.

The boy was cut loose, given the terms of his release.

He said not a word, but turned and started back along the trail. When he had trudged a quarter-mile, he suddenly ducked off the line of pony prints into the brush, laughing, leaping and running with apparent demented abandon.

"Now what the hell?" growled Go-deen.

"Now trouble," said Big Bat Pourier. "I feel it in my guts."

They all came away from the coffee fire, watching nervously. Within a few moments Chaco reappeared on the summit of a low, naked ridge. He was at the exact extreme edge of the carry of either a voice or a rifle bullet. But the New Mexican morning was very still, and the New Mexican air very thin. They heard him acutely well.

"You fools!" shouted the youth. "Keep the pony! I run faster on my feet. All day fast. You see. Watch for smoke. Apache talk with smoke. You watch sky; you fools dead; never reach Big River; never see your people there, anywhere. You see smoke—last thing!"

"Goddam him," said Frank Go-deen. "Talk back to him. I'll get the Sharps. Keep him going."

He started for his old gelding and the big Sharps bull gun, but the metallic shucking sound of a Winchester lever beat him to it.

"No," said Lame John, "don't shoot."

Go-deen stopped, whirled about, went white when he saw the Winchester muzzle held three feet from his face. He looked past the weapon to Ben.

168

"What did I tell you, brother?" he grated. "All the way back in Judith Basin when you first let this Slit Nose come along? Well?"

Ben, having his own misgivings, and bad ones, had no ready reply. Nor did he need one.

"*Mes amis,*" announced Big Bat Pourier, "it has become unimportant. Put up the guns."

Turning, the others looked instinctively to the ridge. Chaco was gone. In a moment they saw him again, briefly, crossing between ridges. He was running evenly and with unbelievable speed. They waited five minutes but saw him no more. Frank Go-deen broke the accumulated quiet.

"*Chaco,*" he said softly, "that's a Spanish word, isn't it, Brother Ben?"

"Yes, it is," admitted Ben uncomfortably.

"Would you mind, I wonder, telling us what it means?"

"Well, I'd rather not."

"But do, please do, eh?"

"I'm not exactly sure."

"Take a guess. Eh?"

"Oh, hell," said Ben with his lemon-twist grin, "it means 'the laugher.' Ain't that something?"

"I don't think so," said Frank Go-deen. "Let's get out of here."

They brushed out the fire spot, got back on their horses. Ben looked around at Big Bat.

"You believe the kid about running fast as a horse?" he asked.

"Sure. Some Sioux can outrun a horse. That is, on an all-the-day race. You understand?"

Ben nodded.

"Might as well cut loose the spare stock then?"

"But of course."

"Frank?"

"Sure, Bat's right. The boy will beat the horses in now. Easy."

They let the Indian ponies go. The animals scattered a little, then regrouped and stood watching the white men. Bat and Frank exchanged looks, the latter nodding.

"It's a good thing all the same that we set the boy afoot, Baptiste. You agree?"

"*Oui* François. No blanket, no smoke, is that what you are thinking?"

"Not thinking—hoping."

"Well, *mon cher,* it won't be easy without the saddle blanket, I would estimate."

"No, not unless these small monkey brothers know some tricks to cut off the smoke that my Oglalas don't. But then, curse it, we don't use the smoke too much. The Cheyenne do some talking that way and the Arapaho a little, too. But the Sioux like the mirror better."

"*Oui*, they learned this from the Army."

"One time I had no use for the soldiers," said Go-deen. "Now I would like to see about six hundred of them riding over that hill up there. Even two hundred. Or two dozen."

"*Mon ami,* I would wish for even *one* dozen!"

"Yes, well, if wishes were war ponies, Mandans would ride," growled the Milk River breed. "*Hookahey.*"

"*Hopo!*" responded Big Bat, with the other Sioux go word, and put his heels in his reclaimed Comanche bay. The little animal leaped forward behind Go-deen's old white. When they had caught up to Ben and the others, they settled into the steady jog trot of the Indian mustang which devoured the miles as no blooded gait before or since bred into the plainly superior horses of the white man.

Behind them, as their mounts dwindled to sun-dancing flecks in the vast roughness ahead, the raw blue sky stretched empty and serene to the last curve of the high country's horizon.

Not even a hawk swung in its endless domain, nor drifted in it a cloud so big as a single-blossomed cotton boll.

The fair weather held. Late that afternoon, in a lovely small meadow of springs and hock-high forage, fringed by small timber and huge, house-sized boulders, they made a happy camp. By the expert reckoning of Go-deen and Big Bat Pourier, they had covered forty miles since daybreak; a total of seventy-odd since leaving Fort Webster the night before. The horses were caked with grime and tired out. But they were sound of wind and limb, and a cool evening on the good feed and water here found would put them

170

back ready to go another sixty or seventy miles if need be. However, if Big Bat's original guessing was even near accurate, there would be no need. They must be within fifteen or twenty miles of the river and quite possibly that close to Fort Craig itself. They could, had there been reason—such as sign of close pursuit—have pushed on that same night after a few hours rest for the stock and made it to the Rio Grande by first light. Lame John, watching the ears and actions of the horses, told Ben that he knew from these things that they were within easy ride of "big water." Since this could mean only the Rio, no other stream of size being anywhere near in that country, Ben had decided against forcing their precious mounts, and all hands devoted themselves to the pleasures of settling down for the rest of their lives that lazy summer night in high New Mexico.

For Ben, while the strange green daylight of the late afternoon and early evening held on, there were duties other than decisions involving Apaches to attend to. One of these was the matter of Amy Geneva Johnston. Calling Go-deen aside, he asked him to come along as interpreter. When the breed asked for details, Ben looked guilty and lowered his voice to match his manner.

"Frank," he said, "I feel awkward as a calf caught nursing the herd bull, but one way or another we got to give this lady a bath."

"Eeh!" cried Go-deen. "Not me, brother! You, maybe, but not Frank Go-deen. Not even for money would I do it, let alone for love. Have you seen the look in her eye? That she-devil would kill us all if she could. My God, that dirty Crow-heart and his murdering boy must have given her a life like a dog among their Shoshoni. *Wagh!"*

"Pipe down " snapped Ben. "Damn it, I didn't ask you for a legal opinion. Just come on along and keep your big mouth shut."

"I won't do it. Shoot me. Go ahead. I'd rather bathe a she-wolf with a litter of blind pups!"

"Goddam it," said Ben, "I'm not asking you to help scrub her back. I ain't going to lay a finger on her myself either. That ain't the point. But I got to talk her into doing it her own self and for her own good."

"What? You lie! You want to see her body."

171

"Lord, I couldn't be less interested in her body, Frank. But I got to be interested in her mind."

"Her mind! Hoh! that's funny! That's very, very funny!"

"To a Milk River mushhead, maybe. To Ben Allison of San Saba, not even a little bit. Come on, Frank, for God's sake give me a hand. We got to do it."

"Oh? Why?"

Ben scowled, chewed his lip, kicked dust, took a whirl at putting it in terms a cousin of Crazy Horse's might comprehend.

"To set off with," he said, "she's a woman. Now right away that makes her different than you and me."

Go-deen looked at him, amazed.

"How many summers did you have when you made this discovery?" he asked. "And why have you kept it a secret from your friends who trust you?"

"Don't give me any of that half-Sioux humor," gritted Ben. "You know what I mean. She *thinks* different than a man. We don't worry nor fret about smelling bad or looking like a piece of wet side meat drug through the dry dirt. But a woman, well, a woman she just naturally has got to care how she looks when there's men around; even galoots as creepy and far off of handsome as me and you."

Go-deen looked at him suspiciously.

"I'm beginning to understand," he nodded. "So you caught her watching you today, too, eh?"

"What the hell you mean? I don't even know what you're talking about!" fumed Ben. But his color didn't go with his declaration of innocence, and Go-deen nodded again.

"You and that double-crossing Slit Nose," he said. "She can't seem to make up her mind which one of you she's going to go for. That's after she kills the rest of us, naturally. But it doesn't matter; we won't argue it."

"You'll help me with her then?"

"Well, that depends. Do I get to peek also?"

Ben colored up again but held his temper.

"Nobody peeks, damn it. I'm just aiming to let her get herself cleaned off and spruced up. I even brung along a bar of soap I been carrying since starting out from Madison Canyon, Montana. She's a woman, by jingo, and

172

a white woman to boot; I don't care that she's been reared Shoshoni or any other blasted Indian way; she'll light up when she sees this here cake of settlement soap. Now you going to come along and talk to her for me or not?"

Go-deen was still studying the logistics of the problem, or rather the moral mechanics. He scratched his bullet head, wrinkled his lance-scarred nose.

"If I don't see her and you don't see her, who sees her?" he asked.

"I said nobody."

"What's to stop her running away?"

"I got that all figured out." Ben held up a length of Apache rope. "I aim to make a surcingle of this," he said. "I'll put it around her belly with the knot in back and the slack leading to me, around that big rock yonder. Far side of the rock's a dandy big pool of spring water. The knot gets wet she can't possibly work it loose, and before you can say, 'Gee, horse fat!' we'll have us a spanking-clean woman and one what'll talk to us and listen to us talk back. We got to try it, for we can't go on lugging her along tied up. It cuts down our speed too much, and watching her all the time tuckers us. You want any more guarantees?"

"She'll chew that rope up and spit it out like kite string," grumped Go-deen, "but I'll go with you anyway. I wouldn't want to miss seeing her running naked across the open into the trees. Bat was right. She's got a body like sixteen summers. *Wagh!*"

"Shut up," said Ben, "and don't say nothing I don't tell you. You give her any dirty half-breed side words, and I'll spread you out on that rock like a green hide."

"Brother," leered Go-deen, unleashing his wall-eyed smile, "I don't understand you. Just to listen to you one would think you don't trust me."

Ben clutched his bar of soap and strand of Mimbreno rope with renewed determination and paling gills.

"Come on," he said, "I'm fading fast."

The girl—or woman—Amy Johnston, sat by the supper fire, blue eyes downcast, blond hair freed from the grit and grease and lodge smoke of a thousand Indian campgrounds, flowing in a dully burnished, golden flood over her shoulders. Her drying clothes clung to her re-

173

vealingly, keeping the eyes of her companions divided between the sinewy, graceful figure and the unexpectedly compelling face. She was not a beautiful woman unless even white teeth, clear, sun-bronzed complexion, a short, straight nose, slender chin, full-lipped mouth and oval, high-cheekboned facial contour meant beauty. But when a man looked at Amy Johnston, as Ben Allison was looking at her now—for the first real time—he wasn't conscious of the individual feature or line of figure, but rather of the whole lovely harmony of a young woman of natural good looks reared and conditioned by a life of strenuous physical advantages and hardships such as no white woman could ever boast. And with the sheer physical vitality there came, also, the fascination of a wild thing being tamed or, more exciting yet, of willingly allowing herself to be approached and gentled.

Ben and his rough companions were presently enjoying this rare male experience. There was more of conquest and exhilaration in it for them than the bedding of a hundred compliant Indian women or sleazy-virtued settlement drudges. Big Bat and Go-deen, as the strange girl warmed and thawed to the open fire of their admiration, strutted and puffed as vainly as two disparate but friendly fighting roosters, vying for her attention and applause—which was indicated by a fluttering raising of the startlingly blue eyes, a dazzling flash of the perfect teeth, or a flooding of dark, pleased color into her sunburned face and never by more than one or two spoken words. In hard fact, she uttered less than a dozen sentences in the swift, happy hour the men spent in questioning and complimenting her. They played it precisely as if they were soft-talking a newly-trapped wild horse, wanting and expecting only to achieve a degree of confidence and calming down, which would allow them to leave her for the night and not find, next morning, that she had dashed her life out against the corral poles.

In all of this Lame John sat aside. He said no word to his woman nor to the whites who attended her with such animation and eagerness to please. The transformation wrought in her by Ben Allison's bar of soap was not as apparent to his savage eyes as to their civilized ones. To him the unexpected wild beauty was not unexpected. He had seen it in the first moment his fierce, proud glance

174

met hers in the silence following the bloody fight with Iron Eyes and the Horse Creek Shoshoni, back in far Montana when, for the twelve sweet hours before the Sioux of Slohan had struck and scattered his little band of Wallowa Nez Percés, he had known the wondrous company of this Wasicun woman who was more Shacun, more Indian, than any red girl he had known through all his twenty-one winters among the Wallowas.

But if the crippled Nez Percé youth could not see the change in his white woman, he could, and very easily, see that in the conduct of his white companions toward her. And, seeing it, his dark heart ached with jealousy; his primitive mind grew clouded with doubt.

He got up and left the fire, walking away from its cheerful company to the side of his grazing Appaloosa. He spoke to the spotted horse, stroking his black muzzle and shining red-bay neck. He glanced at the other mounts, making sure they, too, were at ease and grazing well. Then, before seeking his lonely blanket, and in the invariable custom of the plains and mountain red man to briefly guess the weather upon rising and retiring, he glanced up at the sky. As he did, his thoughts left Amy Johnston and her awkward entertainers as though separated from them by a scalping knife. And the next moment he was leaping for the supper-fire, all taints of jealousy and doubt plunged under by the larger instinct of self-preservation.

The others, seeing him come, were on their feet when he drew up.

"Brothers," said John Lame Elk, "don't look at me; look at the sky."

They did as he said, and the popping of the juniper embers sounded like small artillery in the heavy stillness.

In the opal green and desert purple of the New Mexican twilight, the Apache smoke columns hung as if etched on water crystal—one to the southwest between them and Fort Webster; one to the northeast between them and Fort Craig.

They were cut off, head and tail.

29

Boulder Meadow

THE WAR TALK at Boulder Meadow held a singular difference from the one at the sutler's store in Fort Webster. There they had set out with a forty-eight hour start and a general idea of where they were going. Here they were caught with no idea of where to go and with only the remaining ten hours of moonlight to get there. Even Ben Allison, as given to euphemism as was Frank Go-deen to dire prophecy, could see no hope for the coming sunrise.

"We got two problems," he summed up after an hour of desperate suggestions and counter-suggestions by the four friends. "Water and Apache Indians. Way I see it, if the one don't get us, the other will. We go for the only water we know, the Rio, and we got Indians there waiting for us. We go the only way we ain't sure there's Apaches, and we got no way of finding water." He waved vaguely off to the west. "Looks like we lose no matter what."

"I'd rather fight Indians than no water," said Go-deen. "You die quicker. I say we run for the river, brothers."

Big Bat shook his head quickly.

"*Non,* François, never. Ask yourself what have they done? They have put themselves to the south of us and their friends to the north of us. They know that we are not familiar to the country to the west, but that we have just come from the Rio Grande. *Comme ça,* where will we run? *Certainement,* you have said it, right for the river!"

"Bah!" growled the breed.

"Well," said Bat, "that makes more sense than running for the river; I'll accept it."

"It wasn't an opinion," said Go-deen; "it was an insult. But you Canucks; you're harder to discourage than a whisky drummer. I give up. Go to hell."

"Way I see it—" Ben began again, but Go-deen hadn't finished.

"Be quiet, brother," he said abruptly and turned to the

176

silent Lame John. "Well, Nez Percé, what do you say? I am weary of listening to white men. What do you see out there in the night? Which way do we go?"

Lame John lifted his head. The breeze, just stirring now with moonrise, was off the great sweep of land to the west. He sampled it, sniffing as carefully and warily as a wild horse. He wet a forefinger and held it up. He swung his head from due west to due north, crossing the whole area of the compass in that quarter. Finally he grunted something in his own tongue, then nodded to Go-deen.

"There's no water out there, unless you know where to look. That wind is as dry as the Great Salt Sink. It's a bad choice, Frank, but I make it different than you."

"How so?" said Go-deen, frowning.

"In this way," answered the Nez Percé youth simply, pointing a lean red arm into the northwest. "That is my home up there."

Ben shook his head despairingly.

"I'm sure with you, John," he said. "If we only knew our way out of New Mexico and could get up into Utah—"

"Utah?" queried Big Bat. "You know that country?"

"No, but I've got the best damned map of it you ever saw. Drawn by Joe Meeks. Chilkoot Johnston gave it to me. Made me take it, fact is. Said it would steer me around more trouble than a platoon of Pawnee scouts. Even claimed it would—"

"*Joe* Meeks?" interrupted Big Bat, white teeth gleaming with sudden intensity. "The old mountain man? François, you are right—he talks too much. Give me that map, Petit Ben."

"But it ain't of New Mexico, I told you!"

"You tell me nothing. I know of Meeks. He spent as much time in Taos as he did in the Tetons. The map!"

"Well, hell," said Ben and dug it out.

Among the lanky Texan's sterling qualities infallibility was not one. Joe Meeks's map, brought forth and poured over with brow-drawn squints and held breaths, delineated the entire western one-third of New Mexico, including all of Taos, Rio Arriba, Santa Ana, Bernalillo, Valencia and Socorro counties lying west of the Rio Grande. Only below the Pinos Altos country they had just left, in Grant County, did the detail fade away to sketchiness. For the rest of it, a blind man with a good pony and a fairly large

177

canteen could have ambled right straight up into Utah with not a dry camp nor a grassless one to discomfit him along the way. The back slaps which Frank and Big Bat exchanged were only diminished in their gladness by the looks they paused to insert for Ben's benefit. As for the latter, he only grinned and bore the onus of being the company blockhead as best he could, meanwhile defending himself with a slow-drawled, mightily pleased, "Well, for hell's sake, how was I to know he spelt New Mexico, 'A-p-a-c-h-e C-o-u-n-t-r-y'?" Which, being not altogether an unfair question, his comrades accepted as the apology due them under the circumstances.

It was now agreed they would rest until midnight, forcing on from then until first light. They had remaining to them at least a week of moonlight strong enough to read Joe Meeks's map by. In the seven nights—as the Apaches, unlike the Comanches, did not move by dark— they might with but ordinary luck and no lame ponies make the mountain lion's share of the three hundred and fifty indicated miles to the Utah corner. Since the map showed not only water and grass but also suitability of daytime cover—rocks, timber, canyons, ridges—at the various campsites, their principal concerns were reduced to two: laying a blind trail for the Apaches in getting from camp to camp; not coming into a water hole already occupied by them. Of the two problems, Lame John accepted responsibility for the first, Big Bat for the second. Go-deen generously offered to supervise both performances. Even Amy Johnston, evincing her first genuine excitement when informed they were now turning north-west to strike for her Shoshoni homeland, made a shyly impulsive suggestion that she be permitted to "cook for the warriors on the long journey." Delighted, the comrades agreed.

The blankets were spread, the horses brought in and put on tether, rifles laid to hand. It was nine o'clock.

Ben took the first of three one-hour watches. Lame John was not asked to share guard duty. The Nez Percé said nothing, but he knew.

The camp quieted. Seated on the rock which overhung the fire spot, Ben looked down on his companions and felt a little taller than any of them. He realized how far he was from Montana and quest's end. Yet, having gotten Chil-

178

koot's willowy daughter safely away from the famed Apaches who never surrendered a female captive, even having succeeded in finding her at all after a quarter-century of trail dust blowing over the tracks of time, a man had to admit he had done fairly well so far. It maybe wasn't Christian to take such a secret pride in something he had bossed but hadn't exactly brought off unassisted. But Ben couldn't help it. He felt so entirely good about the whole affair that if he hadn't been sitting smack in the middle of Joe Meeks's "A-p-a-c-h-e C-o-u-n-t-r-y," he just naturally would have reared up on that rock and hurrahed the moon till hell wouldn't put up with it.

So ran the satisfied, uncomplicated mind of Ben Allison. Directly, self-approval became a better sedative than seventy miles of hard riding. Ben's shaggy head nodded, fell forward. He slept through his own watch, Frank Go-deen's and fifty-five minutes of Big Bat Pourier's. At that point he was awakened by a loud rattle of dislodged stones. Rubbing his eyes and peering hard while trying to keep his heart from pounding right out through his wish-bone, he was able to make out some approaching movement in the southerly brush. At once he rasped down a hoarse "All out!" warning to the sleepers below.

Bat, Go-deen and Lame John came off their blankets, rifles sweeping the scrub, bellies knotted tight. There was another rattle of stones and bobbing of juniper tops, then an amazed, happy yell from Ben.

"Hold your fire! It's the God-blessed, blue-eyed, wandering watchdog!"

Which, indeed, it was.

While Big Bat swore in provincial French, Go-deen cursed in Milk River Sioux, Lame John smiled in grave Nez Percé amusement and Ben greeted him with unprintable San Saba sentiments, Malachi Johnston—missing and presumed lost since the latter reaches of the night march from Fort Webster—strolled in out of the New Mexican moonlight, sniffed disdainfully at his detractors, selected Frank Go-deen's blanket and lay down with a vast grunt by the still-warm coals of the supper fire.

Ben jumped down from the rock and confronted his irate fellow campmates, slow drawl rich with Texas sincerity.

"Boys," he said, "I'll hand whip the first one of you even *thinks* a unkind word of this here mule."

30

The Judas Mule

BEN'S PERSONAL PLEASURE over the return of the old mule was short-lived. When camp was broken minutes later, Malachi refused to get up off Frank Go-deen's blanket and join the exodus. The breed would cheerfully have shot him and hauled him off with a saddle-horn towrope, but Ben said no. Let the butt-headed brute have the blanket. He would get up and follow along when, as and if he was of a mind to, and that was that. It was the way, Ben said, that mules were built. And most especially this mule. They left it—and Malachi—there.

Going on through the night they had no cause to regret their decision to gamble on Joe Meeks's map. By its landmarks, easily seen in the glaring moonlight, and by Lame John's Indian skill at picking the places where their tracks could be either entirely lost on bedrock or bewilderingly tangled by combinations of sand, wash gravel, hardpan and heavy grassland, they made both excellent and accurate mileage. The pre-dawn starlight brought them into the first camp, a beautiful spot where a small, clear stream wandered in a narrow, timbered draw with fine feed and a leafy cover of aspen, birch and red willow growing wall to wall in the miniature canyon. On the map it was marked "Sweetwater," and a sweeter place to rest and hide from horseback Indians in a fiercely hot and arid land could never be imagined.

Lame John's probe of its silent beauty proved it to be unoccupied, and they moved in just as the true daylight was coming in the east.

All that day—as near as Ben could come in his crude system of marking fingernail scratches for each day on his saddle fenders, it was July fourth—they lay up in the luxuriant oasis. The time was divided between keeping an arroyo-rim watch of the back trail with Go-deen's brass-

180

bound telescope and in working at the very rewarding task of "civilizing" Amy Johnston.

In this direction the Shoshoni-reared woman both came on and held back with typical Indian ability to confuse the white educator. Go-deen had the best luck with her because of his Shoshoni tongue and experience. Having seen the breed in the camps of her Wind River people, she seemed inclined to give to him where she would not with the others in the matter of communication. When it came to other attitudes, or rather other ways of "talking," she was not so reluctant. None of them missed the manner in which her lovely blue eyes followed the lank figure of Ben Allison about the Sweetwater camp. Least of all did Lame John fail to observe this interest in the tall Texan.

For his part the Nez Percé was still unable to approach the woman who owned his heart and whom he had sworn to follow to the death. He remained as tongue-tied upon the New Mexican map trail of Joe Meeks as he had upon the Montana war trail of the Horse Creek Shoshoni. He, as Ben, could have made reasonable contact with her through the hand-sign language, the lingua franca of all the North Plains tribes, as well as of the northwest mountain peoples of the Oregon and Idaho country. Yet, unlike Ben, he would not try. He would only sit and watch his white woman follow his white friend with her beautiful eyes which said more than all the Shoshoni words or high plains hand signs in the Indian world.

Ben, lost in the sudden discovery of his ward's lively intellect and not a little undone by the long looks she kept giving him, failed to note Lame John's increasing tendency to sit apart. It was, after all, not nearly so interesting as Amy Johnston's new tendency to sit together.

The clear twilight came on. With it there was a momentary alarm when Big Bat, on the telescope watch, passed down the warning word. The next moment, however, he was spurting Gallic curses and threatening to quit and ride back to Fort Cobb on his original business of reporting the Kiowa-Comanche war talk. When Ben could get him calmed sufficiently to detail the strength of the enemy, he spat out another string of French in four letters and bellowed down:

"*Ennemi*, you say! *Quel ennemi? Sacrebleu!* It is the damnable mule again!"

181

It was Malachi. He did not bring Go-deen's blanket with him, and the breed, like Big Bat, made noises and motions as though Ben had better keep a close watch on his long-eared friend if he did not want fricassee of Montana mule for breakfast. Actually, and Ben knew it, both the threateners would have shot a stranger who said a bad word about the gray-nosed beast. His odd sense of loyalty and his downright wrongheaded toughness were qualities much appreciated on the frontier. Malachi, to put it directly, would do to ride the river with. All of them knew this by now, and Chilkoot's china-eyed pack mule was as welcome as the summer dusk which came just behind him.

But the dusk did not come alone.

With the very last of the green daylight, on a skylined, low mesa top overlooking their little canyon from the southeast, a row of sharply-cut silhouettes appeared. They sat their scrubby desert ponies without a sound or movement to announce their appearance or purpose or to describe their intention. The stillness hung on interminably and then, floating down from the mesa to the frozen watchers in the trees below, came a familiar, high-pitched, crazy laughter.

"Jesus Christ," said Ben Allison softly, "it's Chaco."

"Sure," said Frank Go-deen, his words dripping like acid into the frightening quiet. "They never could have followed that trail the Nez Percé laid out for them, but thanks to you they didn't have to."

"What," said Ben, hard-eyed, "the hell are you talking about?"

"The mule," muttered Go-deen hoarsely. "They followed the goddam mule!"

31

White Man's Choice

"THERE IS NO OTHER way," said Lame John, low voiced.

The others nodded and felt their stomachs shrink.

To sit in the shadows of a small canyon somewhere between the San Mateo and Rio Mimbres mountains of a quiet summer's evening agreeing to the idea of night-crawling a camp of wolf-pack Apaches not a long buffalo-rifle shot away was ample prospect to tighten the gut of any white man alive. Or any half-white man.

"It's true," growled Frank Go-deen; "we may as well admit it. It's get them tonight, or they get us tomorrow."

"It's a Hobson's choice," said Ben miserably.

"Eh? A what, *mon cher?*" Big Bat asked.

"A shotgun choice—no choice at all," explained Ben and had the curiosity remaining to wonder as he said it how he should remember such trivia when he couldn't recall his own name. "You see, there was this feller Hobson back a long spell ago—over in England it was—he kept him a stable, livery stable sort of, and when a customer would come in to rent a horse, old Hobson he would—"

Big Bat put his melon-sized hand over his face, shutting off the story of Thomas Hobson of Cambridge.

"Another time, Petit Ben," he said. "Right now let us consider the suggestion of going up to the mesa and murdering eight Apaches."

"Seven," corrected Lame John.

The giant Canuck eyed him.

"I counted eight," he said.

"You counted right; but I want the boy."

"Eh? For what purpose, Jean?"

"A hostage—and this time no one-day limit."

"Damn," said Ben, "sort of a Apache passport."

"Yes, what's wrong with that?"

Frank Go-deen broke in quickly.

"One thing," he said. "You can't depend on using Broken Hand that way again. You ought to know that; you're an Indian."

"What is it you talk of?" scowled the Nez Percé.

"The old chief; he has lost face. We made him look like a fool back there at the fort. He would have been luckier had we caved in his skull. We did him no kindness letting him sit guard over his seven friends in the jail cell. Even the squaws will spit on him from now on."

Lame John nodded thoughtfully.

"I had forgotten," he said. "Forgive me, Frank; you are right. The boy is useless to us now."

"Then it is eight?" asked Big Bat.

"Yes, it is eight. But I still want the boy."

"You can have him. All you must do is be first to him before François or myself. Eh, François?"

"I wish we could talk them to death from down here," complained the fat breed. "They'd be dead already."

Ben, thinking desperately the whole while, now shook his head, held up an objecting hand. He made the no-good sign and talked quickly.

"Listen, it won't work. It's too damn risky for what we stand to gain. We're putting all our chips on the table, at one time and on a blind bet at that. You just can't walk in on eight Apaches like that. We might get some, even most of them, but they would get all of us in the process. That ain't good poker where I come from."

Lame John, surprisingly, agreed.

"It's true, Brother Ben," he murmured. "But it is still the best gamble we have. Sometimes there is no good way out; only the least poor one."

"That's true, too," said Ben, "but in this case let's play it my way—white-man style—according to Hoyle."

"Do not ask him who Hoyle is," said Big Bat hurriedly. "There is not the time to listen. Accept his word, and hear his plan."

"I did not know he even had a plan," said Lame John stiffly.

"I've been working on it." Ben grinned. "It's good poker, providing you're down to your last stack of blues and been dealt nothing but two deuces."

Lame John's frown deepened.

184

"In plain words, brother," he demanded, "what do you talk of?"

"A bluff," answered Ben slowly; "a pure, cold, beautiful, brass-out bluff."

"Go on, *mon cher*," said Big Bat, leaning forward, white teeth gleaming in the moonlight. "You have something exceptional, *une idée par excellence*, I can taste it. *Allons!*"

Once more Ben's sunny grin widened.

"You ought to be able to taste it," he said. "It's your own cooking warmed over."

Chaco slept fitfully. His mind would not let him go deeply to rest. The eagerness to be up in the ghost light of the pre-dawn and belly-creeping that camp of *yanquis* was greater than the weariness of the trail which had brought him to their hidden canyon. Murder was in Chaco's heart, and its pleasant image reflected in the imagination would not allow him to sleep well. He turned upon his saddle blanket, putting his back to the rising of the moon and to the peaceful picket of the Apache ponies staked just back from the canyon's edge on the mesa.

The movement put his hatchet face toward the canyon and the camp of the enemy. He saw the flicker and leap of the firelight rebounding its shadows from the far wall of the gorge and sat bolt upright. What was this? The fools building a fire in the middle of the night? With eight Mimbreno Apaches lying on the lip of the mesa above them? Idiocy! Strangeness! White insanity! But, no, wait—

That was no white man's sound coming from that canyon camp and from that leaping flare of midnight flame.

Chaco crouched, half arisen, listening fearfully.

But there could be no doubt of it:

> "*Iha hyo oya iya iya o iha yaya yoyo.*
> *Aheya aheya yaheyo ya eye heyo eheyo . . .*"

There could be no doubt whatsoever; it was the death song of the Sarsi Kiowas. And being sung with the true words in deep, growling voices. *Wagh!* There was even the high-pitched yipping of a squaw's voice wailing over the heavy ones of the men. *Eeh-heyih!* How, by all the gods, had Kiowas gotten to that canyon down there?

185

Now his braves had left their blankets and come up through the moonlight to crouch with him, rolling their eyes and grunting questions in guttural Apache, both to him and to themselves.

This was a trick of the *yanqui* devils; it had to be. But these were resourceful, hard-fighting white men. They had proved that to Chaco and to all of the seven braves who were with him—the same seven who had been locked in the Fort Webster guardhouse and left to die but for that old woman, Broken Hand, and what water he might bring them from the well in the river bed. So it would be better to go have a look at what they might be up to this time. You couldn't trust crazy men like those. They might even be packing up and leaving in the middle of the night, just as though Chaco and his seven were not up there on the mesa. *Wagh!* Better go look. Don't take a chance wasting all Chaco's hard work in shooting away that rusty leg-iron lock to let them out of the *juzgado*. Nor all their foot running up to the *ranchería* to get fresh horses and guns and warn the main people of the whites' escape. And all their hard pushing ahead of the main band, following that cursed blue-eyed mule. Ah, no, it was still *dah-eh-sah!* death to the white man, no mistake of that.

They rose silently, following Chaco to the canyon's rim. They were followed, in turn, by a strange phenomenon. Though there were but eight of them, they cast nine shadows. The ninth shadow was very tall. Its maker let them look into the canyon long enough to see the figures of Baptiste Pourier, Frank Go-deen and Amy Geneva Johnston moving through the tree leaves against the light of the newly lighted fire and long enough for them to listen to one more chorus of the Kiowa death song—their own chorus.

Then the shadow spoke.

"*Cuidado*—look out!" barked Ben Allison in Spanish and pulled the long-barreled .44.

Chaco wheeled in time to take the first smashing slug through the chest at twenty feet. His body jackknifed backward, off into space. His braves panicked and broke like rabbits, their only thought to get to the pony picket, precisely as Ben had gambled they would.

They fired at him on the way. But on the foot run, in moonlight, the rifle is not the weapon. Not even at twenty

186

feet. But the hand gun, fired from fixed crouch and by an expert in unsighted pistol work from ranges as short as the width of a card table to as long as the span of a cow town's dusty street, *is* the weapon. Ben got three more of them down before the remaining four ran into the sudden, hip-levered blasting of Lame John's Winchester at the pony picket. One of the four, hit but still on his feet, got a mount free and galloped off, hanging on the far side of the animal. Lame John shouldered the carbine and put five shots through the running horse, slamming it to its knees. The Apache rolled desperately to avoid being pinned, but was caught by one leg. Before he could work the member loose, Lame John came up and knocked his brains out with the Winchester's wickedly curved steel butt plate. As he did so, Ben's tall form shadowed up behind him. He straightened, wiping the butt plate on his elkskin leggings.

"You had a good idea, Brother Ben," he said. "Let's go."

32

Six Nights to Four Corners

THEY DUMPED the bodies of the Apaches into the canyon, hiding them there under the trees and in the water of the stream so that decomposition might be delayed and sight denied the omnipresent vultures of the wasteland. This precaution against early discovery of the Mimbreno dead by their alerted fellow tribesmen taken, they packed the camp gear on Malachi, took fresh mounts from the Indian picket, set out once more.

They made good time. Malachi, on a lead rope now, dug in and stayed with the Apache ponies. Go-deen's old white gelding and Lame John's big Appaloosa followed behind him faithfully as sheep dogs. The second camp was made at four that morning at a spot marked "Rock Tank" on Joe Meeks's map. This was past the Sierra Luera, halfway to the Ki-ah Mountains. There was no Indian sign the next day. The following night they stayed in the dry course of the Zuni River, west of the arid Zuni Range. There was a good cover of cottonwoods rooted in subsurface water, and again no Apaches were sighted through the day. The following night, they swung wide of old Fort Wingate and that dawn camped just north of Fort Defiance on the headwaters of the Rio Vara, fringing the Chusca Mountains.

It had been early agreed that they would not contact the military. The war conditions being what they were, the far garrisons had all they could do to defend themselves. Moreover, they were all watched by the hostile Apaches. To have gone into one of them would have been to simply join a surrounded, cut-off detachment of frightened men, with further complications of explaining Amy Johnston. They would certainly have been detained by the post commander until a proper escort could be furnished out of the area, and that could mean anything from thirty days to three months. All the party, including Amy Johnston, preferred the little risk now left in reaching the Utah line.

A sole concession was made to Big Bat's conscience.

The little cavalcade waited in the moonlight a mile from Defiance, while the big Canuck rode in and tossed a note wrapped around a rock over the stockade and aroused the sleepy sentries on the catwalk with a cautiously subdued bellow of *"Allons! mes petits!"* to make sure they understood the message was not from Mangas the Younger or any of his murderous friends.

The note contained what meager information the French Canadian scout had been able to buy from Soledad Dominguin concerning the intentions of the Comanches to join the Kiowas in building a late summer war fire on the South Plains. Added was a terse instruction to put the details on the telegraph to Colonel Adam McNair at Fort Cobb, Indian Territory; the whole, not over six or seven sentences marked with the soft lead of a knife-shaved bullet nose on the flyleaf torn from Lame John's Bible, was signed and sealed with an undecipherably flourished "Baptiste Pourier."

This intelligence would, conceivably, make no least difference in either the personal plans or military preparations of Colonel McNair, but it salved Big Bat's official honor, allowing him to march on north with his friends secure in mind as well as emotion. And, besides, he said, the Army had not paid him his salary in sixteen months and he was thinking of looking for other work regardless.

Beyond Fort Defiance, but one serious situation remained. This was in striking and following down the San Juan River through the Jicarilla country of extreme northwest New Mexico Territory into southeast Utah Territory. They set out on this dangerous passage with earliest dusk of the fifth night, reaching the Rio Pajarito and the camp marked "Little Bird" on Joe Meeks's map shortly before sunrise. They were then still in New Mexico, some twenty-five miles west of the main Jicarilla *ranchería* on Rio Plata. That day they saw three parties of Apaches but did not believe them to be on the search for them, as they had women and children along as well as camp equipage on pack animals. That night, the sixth from Boulder Meadow, they struck for the Utah line. By dawn, driving hard,

189

they had made forty miles and were fifteen miles past the Rio Marcos Fork of the San Juan which on Meeks's map marked the famed "Four Corners" of Arizona, Utah, Colorado and New Mexico.

One month to the day later, they were in Montana.

33

The Return of the Tall Man

THEY HAD COME through Wyoming on the same track Ben and Go-deen had traveled to, and away from, Wind River; this to let Amy see her homeland and to visit the good old chief of the main Shoshoni, Washakie. This latter move, an idea of Go-deen's, was successful in its aim of letting the Indian-reared woman see her people once more and, most importantly, to get from the head of the tribe the advice which Go-deen felt Washakie would provide.

The patriarch of the Wind River Shoshoni did not disappoint the breed's canny expectation. He embraced Amy, treated her rescuers with every dignity and respect, including the provision of an escort of Snake warriors as far as Gallatin Valley and first civilization, the large, newly founded cattle ranch of Nathan Stark at the valley's head. As well, he informed Amy of the death of her Horse Creek husband, Iron Eyes, giving Go-deen a poor moment until it was added that the brave had been found scalped on the trail, dead by an unknown hand. He also told of the recent cleaning out of Crowheart's band by the cavalry from Fort McGraw, down on the Popo Agie, and the long-delayed trial and imprisonment of the renegade Horse Creek chief. So instructed, Amy realized she had no home to return to, and when Washakie gently told her it was her duty as a good Shoshoni to go with the white men to Montana and there find and live with her aged father, thus serving both the cause of peace between red man and white and the blood loyalty a proper daughter owed her sire, she agreed with an alacrity which was no small payment to the adventurers who had ridden and fought two thousand miles to bring her back to her own people.

The only reservation to the glad, good feelings with which the white party started on north were on the part of Lame John. The Nez Percé still pined over Amy Johnston, who had not helped matters when, during the latter stages of the journey from New Mexico, she had begun dividing the "arrows in her glances" between him and Ben Allison. Previously he had been able to nurse a good healthy case of envy and of noble, injured pride. When Amy began to include him in her continually increasing consciousness of her ability to attract male attention, he became confused and did not know what to substitute for the defence formerly provided by his wounded Nez Percé ego. To cap the bewilderment in his Indian mind, she also practised a little admiration for the great bulk, bulging muscles, huge black beard and brilliant white smile of Baptiste Pourier, whose Latin vulnerability to a tender look was frankly admitted in his ribald motto, "*Cherchez la squaw.*" In worrisome fact, the only one he did not have to watch was Frank Go-deen, who, having a woman of his own waiting up on Milk River—not to mention eight children, whom his friends had not learned of until revealed in a fit of melancholy induced by crossing into Montana—required no attention save a generous helping of sympathy.

So the friends, enjoying their various moods of elation, depression, relief and confusion, came through the last mountain pass into the upper valley of the Gallatin River.

Here in long sight of the Stark Ranch their Shoshoni escort said good-by. Westward, through the low passes of the Beaverhead range, lay Madison River and Virginia City, only some thirty miles as the mountain crow flew. From the "ranch of the spotted cattle," which they saw below them along the Gallatin, there was an easy trail that rounded the mountains northerly and came to Alder Gulch and Virginia City on a road that even wagons could travel.

They had but to go to the ranch, the Shoshoni escort leader told them finally, and ask the way to the big settlement "where the gold was ripped from the stones."

With that, and with a shaking of hands all around, Washakie's men turned their ponies and were gone back over the narrow trail to Wyoming and Wind River.

Ben, a strangely mixed feeling of eagerness and foreboding arising within him, led the way down the steep flank of the canyon to the fertile meadows of the river. Somehow it hammered upon the closed door of his memory that he had been here before, had seen this place and

192

knew it and not, either, from too long ago. The lush grasslands, the sweep and sparkle of the sunlit stream, even the red and white and multi-colored specks of the long-horned Texas cattle grazing the deep forage, struck hard at the fetters of his mind. He was still frowning, still trying to let the remembrance free, to force it to come back to him, when his horse, unfamiliar with the wet northern mountains, lost its footing in a spring seep of mossy bedrock running across the trail. The fall was not a fatal one only because a warped cedar, growing from the canyon side, caught man and mount as they went over the edge. Ben recalled trying to get out of the saddle as the little Apache mustang twisted in mid-air, and that was all. He didn't see the contorted cedar or feel the smashing impact with which he and the pony struck and hung on its rough-barked fang, four hundred feet above the rocky bed of the Gallatin.

When Ben regained consciousness, a handsomely blond, big man was bending over him. Ben knew him at once.

"Mr. Stark," he muttered. Then, puzzled, "What the devil happened?"

"Don't you remember, Ben?" said Nathan Stark.

"No. All I remember is me and Nella and the boy starting home to Texas from Virginia City. I was riding lead, and the road just went out from under me."

"You remember the road?"

"Sure I do." Ben sat up, fighting a momentary nausea induced by the fierce ache in his head. "It was the Virginia-Salt Lake stage road over Rotten Rock."

"They never found you," said Stark, "or the money."

"The money!" said Ben. "Good Lord, I was packing ten thousand in a belt, wasn't I?"

Stark nodded. "Your split of the trail-herd profit, Ben. There was a snowslide that night. Took out a quarter-mile of the road and you with it. Nella and the others looked all night for you down below, but all they found was your drowned horse." He paused, shaking his head. "We've all thought you dead these nine months."

"Nella!" said Ben suddenly. "Where's Nella?"

"She's my wife, Ben. We were married when she was convinced you were gone. There's a child now."

193

"Just born?" said Ben.

Again Stark nodded, and Ben bowed his head.

It was all in his mind now, clear as spring water. He and his young brother, Clint, killed by Sioux on the drive, had trail-bossed three thousand head of Texas cattle for Stark, bringing them all the way from Fort Worth to Virginia City and Gallatin Valley. Stark had insisted on giving him his full share of the herd's huge profit when sold off in the beef-hungry mining camps of Alder Gulch. With the ten thousand he had started home to Texas on a bitterly cold December night in 1866, almost a full year ago. Accompanying him had been his two top trail hands, Chickasaw Billings and Waco Fentriss. Also in the party, his promised-to-be, green-eyed Nella Torneau, an adventuress who had come with Stark from Texas, only to fall in love with Ben on the long drive north. Now she was here with Stark again, his wife now and with a baby to seal it. It was a hard way to go that Nathan Stark had just handed Ben, and thinking of it, his lean head moved uncertainly.

"There's more," said Stark quietly and reminded him of the dangerous trail he had just ridden to bring Amy Geneva Johnston back to Montana. "Very plainly," he concluded, "you've bought yourself a new life that will not fit into the old one. You are going to have to begin all over again, the same as myself. I want to wish you luck, Ben, on any trail you take from here."

He paused, smiling, as Ben gingerly fingered his bandaged head. "Your friends brought you in to the ranch early this morning, sacked over the spine of a china-eyed mule. Said your horse had gone over the edge up yonder, and you'd taken a bad spill. You remember any of that now?"

"Yes, sir." Ben grinned painfully. "It's beginning to shape up some. I must have took a hell of a belt. Here I been nine months gone, clean down to Texas and New Mexico, and it don't seem ten minutes since you and me settled up in Virginia City."

Stark nodded wordlessly to this, adding abruptly that his old friends Chickasaw and Waco were still on the ranch payroll and would take him over to Nameless Creek with the Amy Johnston girl when he felt up to the effort. Stark, himself, would have taken him, but he had other

194

and personal business which would not allow him to leave just then. When he came to this latter statement, Ben noted the stiffening of his blunt-chinned face and asked quietly:

"You want I should go now, Mr. Stark? I feel all right."

Stark stared at him, hard-eyed.

"You do what you like, Ben," he said.

"It's Nella, isn't it?" said Ben. "She ain't here, and you want me to move on before she gets back." He looked at the blond Montanan steadily. "I agree, Mr. Stark," he said softly. "I better get along before she shows up."

"No, Ben," said Nathan Stark, "that won't be necessary. Nella's not coming back."

The way he said it warned Ben, and he asked very quietly:

"Where is she, Mr. Stark?"

"In the next room," said Nathan Stark and turned and went out the door, leaving Ben on the edge of the bed where he had been placed when brought in from the canyon trail. After a moment, he stood up. His head swam, and he had to grip the nearest upright of the four-poster. When he could, he walked across the room, following Stark through the door. Two steps into the long-walled living room he stopped short.

Stark stood near the stone fireplace looking down at the coffin placed upon two chairs in front of the hearth. He heard Ben enter and glanced up.

"Do you want to see her?" he said.

Ben shook his head mutely.

"It happened two days ago," said Stark. "It was the baby; she never got over it, never quit bleeding inside, the doctor said. She didn't suffer. Just went weak and slipped away. The boy's fine, normal and strong."

Ben bobbed his head, his feelings too complex for his straightforward mind to separate into meaningful differences or useful facts.

"Well, Mr. Stark," he said gently, "I'm glad you have the baby—your son—to remember his mother by. That's somewhat, I reckon."

"No, Ben," replied the still-faced rancher, "it isn't. I don't have a thing left but my love for her; not even her love for me. She never forgot you, Ben."

"But the baby—" Ben began.

"The baby," said Stark, "is yours, Ben. You have your son to remember his mother by. Nella told me that at the last." He paused, sighed deeply. "I knew it anyway. A man feels a thing like that. But I'm glad she played it fair."

"She always played it fair, Mr. Stark," said Ben, "the same as you."

Nathan Stark raised his eyes, a faint, constrained smile tightening his wide mouth.

"And you, Ben," he answered with acrid softness, "still see roses where ragweed grows alone."

The rest of it went swiftly to its destined end.

Stark would not keep Ben's child, though Ben believed he should. There was a bitterness in the big Montanan, however, which would not down. He could see only that Ben was the boy's natural father. Neither did he appear to want the baby around to remind him of the woman he had loved and lost. That same night Ben and his friends, declining the guidance and company of the cowboys Chickasaw and Waco, left the Stark ranch with the child.

By the wagon road skirting the Beaverhead Forest, they came into Alder Gulch and Virginia City about midday of August 15, 1867.

Amy Johnston created an immediate sensation, and Ben nearly came to the point of gun fighting before he could get her through the brawling, crooked streets of the mining community. Big Bat had physically to restrain Lame John to prevent the fierce Nez Percé from knifing several of the rude and suggestive men from the creeks who crowded in to eye the "white Injun" and to make their leering, raucous comments as to her obvious good looks and lithe figure. The travelers halted only long enough for Ben to purchase a decent outfit of settlement clothes for Amy, then pushed on rapidly out the Salt Lake stage road, away from the Gulch and its crude citizens. The experience, however, had shaken up the Shoshoni-reared woman, and she rode now stirrup to stirrup with Lame John, as though unconsciously seeking the Indian's clean company in this unfamiliar, frightening and disgusting world of the white man.

At the foot of the Nameless Creek trail, Ben ordered a halt while he instructed Amy—from behind a screen of dead-fall timber—in the secrets of getting into a white woman's clothing. The instinct of the female for adornment being what it is, his help was largely wasted. Amy reappeared moments later to the applause of a company gasp and an unabashed round of whistling stares which had her blushing to the roots of her long blond hair. Even Malachi, following along in the rear with young Ben tied securely in an Indian cradleboard atop his pack load, gave her a good look and brayed three times; his equivalent of canonization or, as Ben grinningly put it, "Anyways, getting elected to Congress."

The old mule's bray served, also, to bring Chilkoot from his cabin and stumbling down the rough bank of the creek to meet them.

"By God!" he cried, seeing Ben round the last turn into the cabin clearing. "I knowed it was you, boy; I could call the voice of that Madison Canyon canary just as far as you could hear a cannon shot on Appomattox Day. Malachi! You moth-eaten old sonofabi—" He had started toward the prodigal pack mule, arms spread to embrace his scrawny neck, when his dimming eyesight discovered Amy. He halted as though struck in the face. He turtled his neck, squinted, put his hand to his eyes to shade them. Then he stepped back, lips moving but no words issuing from them. He turned helplessly to Ben, and Ben nodded simply.

"It's her, old-timer."

After that, it was rough for a while. Chilkoot broke down and cried for half an hour. Amy couldn't, or wouldn't, take to the idea that he was her father. Go-deen got mad and quit translating. Ben nearly wore out his hands trying the sign talk, but it was no use. Finally, it was Lame John who stepped forward and asked her soberly, by hand sign, if this were the way a good Indian woman greeted her white father who loved her and who had sent Brother Ben to bring her to see him before he should die, never knowing that she lived or lay dead herself in some far, unfriendly place. At this, Amy hung her head, said something in Shoshoni, shyly reached out and touched Chilkoot on the face and smiled. That did it.

For the rest; it went as happily as such a thing should. The old man had just shot a deer two days before, and Go-deen now prepared a roast of venison banquet which

197

lasted until nine o'clock that night. In the waiting upon and the eating of the feast many things were settled which had seemed to Ben insoluble.

The baby would stay with Amy Johnston, and Amy Johnston—all long looks at Ben Allison aside—would stay with John Lame Elk. In the last choice she was what Frank Go-deen had first said she was those long months gone on Wind River. In Lame John, a Christian Indian who knew he must take the white man's road, and who had vowed to take it before ever he met Amy Johnston, she had found the perfect mate for a woman who must meet and overcome the handicaps of her savage upbringing, as she sought to live and to rear her own children in a white world. With the grave and thoughtful Nez Percé youth she could bridge the difficult chasm between settlement and reservation, and Ben, feeling that this was so and seeing, too, the shining light in the dark eyes of John Lame Elk, knew a depth of contentment which was to ride with him along many a lonely trail.

The agreement was that Lame John and Amy would take Chilkoot with them to Lapwai and the Oregon-Idaho homeland of the Wallowa Nez Percés. The old man could stay and find work on the reservation, where he would have white company. Lame John and his blue-eyed woman would return to the people of Joseph, in the Valley of the Winding Water, Oregon's lovely Wallowa Basin, there to resume the horse ranching which was Lame John's life work. The ten thousand dollars, which was now legally Ben's, would be taken half in trust for young Ben by Lame John and Amy and half to be invested in the horse ranch by way of what the lanky Texan called "a quarter-blood wedding present from your Comanche cousin." There were arguments, of course, but to no gain. Ben wouldn't have it any other way, he said, and his head was harder than any Indian's who ever lived.

Lame John conceded the point, and they shook hands for the last time.

"I promised to follow you to the end of the trail, Brother Ben," said the dark-faced youth. "This is the last turning then. Do you agree?"

"I agree, John," said Ben, and their hands held hard and long before they let them fall away.

Big Bat and Frank Go-deen had decided to travel together as far as Cow Island in the Missouri River. There Big Bat would turn west, taking the first Army packet upstream to Fort Benton and his long overdue appointment to explain how he had used nine months for a thirty-day scout. The breed would go on over the Mini Sosi, the Mud Water, following its Cow Creek tributary up through the Bear Paws into the Milk River buffalo range and, he hoped fervently, the welcoming arms of his two hundred and fifty pound squaw. They, too, shook hands with Ben and said some little speeches which he took along, like the memory of Lame John's shining eyes, to warm himself with on cold days in far and friendless camps.

In the end, all were asleep, and there were only Ben and Chilkoot and Malachi to share the slowing pop and crackle of the coals. Finally the old man, too, got up and stood awkwardly. He looked at Ben a long time, and Ben saw the glitter of the tears running down his seamed cheeks. He pawed at them, embarrassed; and coughed and cursed to make out that it was the smoke of the venison fat burning in the fire which bothered him. Then he quieted down and said huskily, and just before going into the candlelit dimness of the cabin:

"You done it, boy—God cain't possibly bless you no more nor you deserve, nor than you've rightly earnt."

Ben said softly, "Sleep easy, Chilkoot; she's all downhill from here on."

He waited only for the candle to gō out and for the old man to quit moving around. Then he got up and went soundlessly to the picket line where their ponies drowsed hipshot. Selecting the Comanche bay which Big Bat had ridden from Quanah's camp, he saddled him and led him down to the creek trail. Malachi, grazing free in the streamside pasture, raised his head, snorted, wig-wagged his ragged ears. Ben went up to him. He ran his hand down the welted, rough-furred neck; patted the thin, high-boned withers.

"Hoh, shuh," he said softly. "Don't say no more."

The old mule looked after him as he swung up on the Indian pony. He was still looking after him when man and mount had turned the bend in the trail and were gone. Then he blew out through his graying nostrils and went back to the rich feed of Chilkoot Johnston's clearing on

199

Nameless Creek, Montana. In this quiet way began the legend of Ben Allison—the Tall Man who returned from death to ride out his life in the service of his brothers, red and white, whosoever and wheresoever they might be, who had not his strength to serve themselves.

Henry Wilson Allen wrote under both the **Clay Fisher** and **Will Henry** bylines and was a five-time winner of the Golden Spur Award from the Western Writers of America. Under both bylines he is well known for the historical aspects of his Western fiction. He was born in Kansas City, Missouri. His early work was in short subject departments with various Hollywood studios and he was working at MGM when his first Western novel, *No Survivors* (1950), was published. While numerous Western authors before Allen provided sympathetic and intelligent portraits of Indian characters, Allen from the start set out to characterize Indians in such a way as to make their viewpoints an integral part of his stories. *Red Blizzard* (1951) was his first Western novel under the Clay Fisher byline and remains one of his best. Some of Allen's images of Indians are of the romantic variety, to be sure, but his theme often is the failure of the American frontier experience and the romance is used to treat his tragic themes with sympathy and humanity. On the whole, the Will Henry novels tend to be based more deeply in actual historical events, whereas in the Clay Fisher titles he was more intent on a story filled with action that moves rapidly. However, this dichotomy can be misleading, since *MacKenna's Gold* (1963), a Will Henry Western about gold seekers, reads much as one of the finest Clay Fisher titles, *The Tall Men* (1954). Both of these novels also served as the basis for memorable Western motion pictures. Allen was always experimental and *The Day Fort Larking Fell* (1968) is an excellent example of a comedic Western, a tradition as old as Mark Twain and as recent as some of the novels by P.A. Bechko. At his best, he was a gripping teller of stories peopled with interesting characters true to the time and to the land.